A Witch Hunt in Whitby

Helen Cox is a Yorkshire-born novelist and poet. After completing her MA in creative writing at the York St John University, Helen wrote for a range of publications, edited her own independent film magazine and penned three non-fiction books. Helen currently lives by the sea in Sunderland, where she writes poetry, romance novellas, the Kitt Hartley Yorkshire Mystery Series and hosts The Poetrygram podcast.

Helen's *Mastermind* specialism would be *Grease 2* and to this day she adheres to the Pink Lady pledge. More information about Helen can be found on her website: helencoxbooks.com, or on Twitter: @Helenography.

Also by Helen Cox

Murder by the Minster
A Body in the Bookshop
Murder on the Moorland
Death Awaits in Durham

HELEN COX

A Witch Hunt in Whitby

Quercus

First published in Great Britain in 2021 by Quercus Books
This paperback edition published in 2021 by

Quercus Editions Ltd
Carmelite House
50 Victoria Embankment
London EC4Y 0DZ

An Hachette UK company

A CIP catalogue record for this book is available
from the British Library

PB ISBN 978 1 52941 038 9
EB ISBN 978 1 52941 039 6

10 9 8 7 6 5 4 3 2 1

Typeset by CC Book Production
Printed and bound in Great Britain by Clays Ltd, Elcograf S.p.A.

MIX
Paper from
responsible sources
FSC® C104740

Papers used by Quercus are from well-managed forests and other responsible sources.

A Witch Hunt in Whitby

ONE

Kitt Hartley's stomach churned as she stared at the large purple 'V'. Dusk was falling on what had started out a bright April day, and in the gathering gloom the mysterious marking only seemed more ominous. Her stomach tightened a notch further as the now-familiar sense of dread settled into her bones. Even after the numerous murder cases she'd worked in the past, she still wasn't used to it. Perhaps she never would be. Perhaps, when it came down to it, that was a good thing.

The symbol had been painted on the front door of 33 Foss Side Avenue in the quaint village of Orpington, five miles outside York city centre. The door, and indeed the house behind said door, belonged to Kitt's friend, Ruby Barnett. The word 'friend' was, perhaps, not quite accurate to describe a person who routinely sought you out at your place of work to deliver their latest unsolicited 'psychic' predictions. Still, Kitt had grown rather fond of the old woman. There was no denying their affinity had deepened considerably over the last few years, even if she didn't have much truck with Ruby's 'new-age nonsense'.

Kitt's affections for her somewhat eccentric friend made the marking on the door even more unnerving. It was the unmistakable calling card of the so-called Vampire Killer: a serial murderer who had thus far struck three times over the last three months: once in Middlesbrough, once in Scarborough and once in Malton. The killer had earned the moniker because the victims were always found with two red marks on their necks. Jam jars filled with the victims' blood were also found at the crime scenes and now, it seemed, this killer had set their sights on good old Ruby.

'Told yer,' Ruby said, watching on as DI Malcolm Halloran and DS Charlotte Banks briefed their team on where to focus their search for forensic evidence, both outside and inside the house.

Kitt frowned and looked sidelong at Ruby, trying to acclimatize to her latest home-rinse hair colour: neon green. 'What do you mean, "told yer"?'

'I told yer two weeks ago this would happen.'

'No, you didn't.'

'Don't be daft,' said Ruby. 'I told you straight. Dark doings were brewing.'

Kitt stifled a sigh. 'I don't mean to insult you at a difficult time, dear Ruby, but that's not exactly specific. If I had a pound for every time you told me "dark doings were brewing", I'd be able to solve the funding crisis for every public library across Great Britain.'

'Still, you can't deny it,' said Kitt's assistant, Grace Edwards, who had thus far been preoccupied with photographing the symbol painted on Ruby's door. With a police search of the premises in full swing, a zoom lens was the only way to get a close-up snap of the marking. 'She were right. Dark doings *are* brewing.'

'Oh, good grief,' Kitt said, shaking her head. Ruby and Grace were enough of a handful on an individual basis. Managing both of their somewhat distracting influences at the same time was nigh on impossible.

'Arrrggghhh!' A man's deep bellow sounded from inside the house.

Kitt, Grace and Ruby started and turned at once towards the sound. Halloran, Banks and several other officers dashed into Ruby's cottage.

Holding her breath, Kitt braced for the worst until Halloran emerged a short while after with a pale-faced DS Redmond in tow. Given his appearance Kitt assumed the ear-splitting bellow had come from him, which was a bit of a surprise. Detective Sergeant Miles Redmond wasn't known for his tact, and he was the only one who ever laughed at his own jokes but, in the few dealings she'd had with him, Kitt had never seen him rattled or afraid. For the first time since the police had arrived on the scene twenty minutes ago, Halloran marched over to where the trio were standing.

3

From Mal's expression Kitt deduced that whatever had just happened in the house wasn't too serious, despite Redmond's reaction. When she and Halloran became an item, it had taken Kitt a good long while to be able to read his expressions. After almost two years together, however, she believed she had mastered it. He wasn't wearing his most severe frown which meant, as far as she was concerned, that he was fair game. Perhaps this wasn't the best time to tease him, but he had a complicated past when it came to the matter of serial killers so any opportunity to lighten the mood would, she reasoned, prove a welcome distraction. And besides, she had to do *something* to take her mind off what that mark on the door might mean for her friend.

'Found something unusual?' Kitt said with a small smile.

'Around every bloody corner,' Mal replied, folding his arms over his chest and fixing his stare on Ruby. 'I'm assuming, Ms Barnett, you're aware of the fact that your spare room is home to an assortment of insects.'

'Oh aye,' said Ruby, 'them's me pets. Is that what all that racket were about? A couple of butterflies?'

'And millipedes, and stick insects and woodlice and, from what we can see, the odd cockroach. If they're pets why haven't you got them in cages?'

'I can't cage them up. It's inhumane, that. They're living beings.'

Kitt squeezed her lips together in an attempt not to chuckle. Halloran, Grace, and indeed all of her other friends,

4

thought she was often too short with Ruby. Perhaps if they found themselves on the receiving end of her somewhat unique patter for a change, they might understand why Kitt had to set such firm boundaries.

'Suddenly feeling grateful that we're not the ones searching the house,' said Grace with a little shudder. 'Can't stand creepy-crawlies, me.'

'I take it you haven't found anything that helps to identify the killer?' said Kitt, establishing a more serious tone. 'Or the person who painted the mark on the door – assuming they're not one and the same.'

'You know I can't talk about it,' said Halloran.

'It's all right, you don't need to, I can tell by the look on your face,' said Kitt, before turning to the old woman. 'I'm sure Halloran will do everything he can, though, Ruby, don't you worry.'

'I'm not worried,' said Ruby. 'The second I saw that mark on me door, I knew just what to do about it. I've nowt to fear.'

'I'm glad you're not rattled by this,' said Halloran. 'But I'm afraid we can't dismiss the danger you could be in so easily. This bloke has already claimed three victims in as many months.'

'Oh, I know all that,' said Ruby. 'But I've got all me bases covered.'

'Really,' said Halloran, the lines on his face hardening. Kitt knew from experience that if there was one thing Halloran hated more than murderers, it was people being blasé about the topic. 'Easy as that, is it? Sounds like we should have had you on the case from the beginning, eh?'

'Mal,' Kitt said, as gently as she could, while under-standing that Ruby was the queen of testing a person's patience. Well, maybe more like the duchess. Grace being the queen and Kitt's best friend, Evie being the princess. 'Come on now, I'm sure Ruby didn't mean it that way.'

'I didn't,' said Ruby. 'I just meant I'm gonna have the best people working on the case.'

'Oh,' Halloran said, his voice softening. 'Well, thanks, Ruby, it's not often the public—'

'I didn't mean you,' said Ruby. 'I meant Kitt and Grace.'

Kitt's cheeks burned. Ruby was not one for subtlety – that was an understatement. But to suggest to a police officer, of many years' service, that her sleuthing skills were superior to his investigative chops, well that was nothing short of rude.

'Ruby . . .' Kitt warned.

'Well, what I mean is I wasn't *just* talkin' about you, DI 'Alloran. But you know I can't afford to 'ang around on this one. The Vampire Killer always strikes within eleven days of that mark showing up on a person's door. Which means my days are quite literally numbered. Can't be putting all me eggs in one basket. No. No. No. I've hired Hartley and Edwards Investigations to work the case, as well as hoping the police get to the bottom of it before my number's up.'

Halloran turned his hard stare on Kitt. 'I thought Ruby just called you first because you two are friends. You haven't really agreed to work this case, have you?'

'We couldn't pass up a job like this,' Grace cut in before Kitt had a chance to offer a diplomatic answer. Seemingly she had missed the grave note in Halloran's voice. 'A serial killer who targets victims involved with the occult, that's a once-in-a-lifetime kind of investigation, that is.'

'If you're not careful, it'll be the last investigation of your lifetime. This bloke doesn't take any prisoners, you know? No, no, you can forget it,' Halloran said to Ruby. 'She's not doing it.'

'Excuse me? "She"?' said Kitt.

'Oh-oh . . .' Grace said, her eyes widening before she muttered to Halloran through a fake cough, just loud enough for Kitt to make out the words, 'Undo it, undo it while you still can.'

When Halloran made no move to correct his statement, Kitt crinkled her nose. 'DI Halloran. A quick word alone, please.'

Kitt took a good few paces away from her friends. As she turned her back on them, she heard Grace cheekily whisper to Ruby, 'Oooh, she last-named him, now he's in for it.' Kitt bristled but had bigger issues to work through just then than dealing with her assistant's sassy streak.

Kitt raised her eyebrows and waited. She looked into Halloran's deep blue eyes, trying to make a connection. The last thing she wanted right now was an argument with Mal. On the whole, it was rare for them to argue, save one major blow-out about the best recipe for gravy. But when they did argue, Kitt was always left feeling a bit . . . lost and hollow. She could do without that feeling on a day when her friend had been targeted by a serial killer. If he'd just apologize and calm himself down, they could make up and move on.

'I've as much right to be cross as you, so don't look at me like that,' said Halloran. 'This case is a huge deal. The chief is desperate for results. I can't be doing with any added distractions.'

Kitt lowered her eyes for a moment. A month never went by when Chief Constable Parnaby wasn't putting the pressure on about something and that kind of workplace tension only ever made Mal more dogged and determined than usual. Didn't look like that apology was coming any time soon, then.

'Mal, I really don't think it's fair to say my past contributions to such cases have been nothing more than distractions,' Kitt said, looking up at him again and keeping her voice gentle as Halloran so often did with her when she was being stubborn. 'And regardless of what you think of my professional choices, you don't speak for me.'

At this, Halloran at least had the decency to look shame-faced but it was obvious he wasn't just going to let this issue lie. 'I didn't mean it how it sounded. You know I didn't. But I've got to keep everyone safe, including you.'

'You're not really trying to pretend that reaction back there was purely professional, are you?' said Kitt.

A small smile crept over Halloran's lips. 'If I've not made it clear over the time we've been together that my interest in your welfare is more than professional, something's gone wrong.'

Kitt, conscious of the others watching on, rubbed his arm. 'You can't wrap me in cotton wool, Mal.'

'Oh, I'm well aware of that. You've made it more than clear on several occasions that you don't need me.'

Kitt part smiled, part sighed at him. How many relationships had been ruined by outdated gender politics? she wondered. As chief librarian for the Women's Studies section at the Vale of York University, she'd spent a great deal of time explaining that such disciplines weren't just for the benefit of women alone. If women were afforded more agency, perhaps men wouldn't be left believing they were only valuable if they could provide and protect. She thought she had done a pretty good job of making it clear to her own boyfriend that his worth to her didn't depend on that. Clearly there was still work to do. 'Isn't wanting you better than needing you? Wouldn't you prefer that I was with you because I desire to be rather than because you fulfil a need?'

Kitt's question gave Halloran pause but didn't prevent him from continuing his protests. 'Kitt, I don't have time for a philosophical debate on this. Whoever this suspect is, they know what they're doing to a worrying degree. Every detail is meticulously planned. The force has got nothing on the killer – three bodies and not one shred of forensic evidence. I once made the mistake of underestimating a killer like this and it changed my life for ever. I can't take any risks. I can't lose you.'

'Oh, Mal, I know cases like these are difficult for you but I thought we'd put all that behind us.'

'We have, pet. We have. But the past doesn't just disappear. Besides, we've got a responsibility to learn the lessons and not repeat mistakes. The last victim was under police protection and this killer still managed to strike.'

'I know, I did wonder at the time how they pulled that off when I read about it. I suppose you'll get some big briefing on the case to date, so you'll be able to make sure the same thing doesn't happen to Ruby?'

'Yes, now that a victim has been targeted in this area we'll be privy to any compartmentalized information. Not that compartmentalizing has been easy for the other stations working this case, with the neighbours of the last victim running to the press about the mark on the door.'

'Look, I'm with you on not repeating past mistakes,' said Kitt, 'but even if we could afford to turn down the business, which I can't right now – I'm struggling to keep the lights on at the agency – we can't base choices on fear or live in denial. Otherwise, people like this killer win by keeping us cowering away.'

'I'd rather pay to keep the lights on at the agency myself than have you working this case.'

'Ooh, that's not the point I was trying to make, and you know it,' Kitt said, putting her hands on her hips.

Halloran shook his head. His eyes were filled with unspoken suffering. She loved him so much that his pain felt like her own, but she couldn't compromise here. There was too much at stake.

'You're right that I can't stop you,' he said at last. 'You're right to say that it's wrong of me to try, but I don't have to be happy about it. If you work this case, don't expect any help from me.'

'Sir,' Banks called from Ruby's front doorstep. Halloran took the opportunity to exit the conversation without even a 'see you at home'.

So, he was going to sulk about it? The infuriating flipside to the dark broodiness of him that she couldn't help but admit was part of his appeal. Well, she'd have to let him sulk. Five years ago, maybe she could have left something like this to the state-appointed professionals. But not now. She'd seen too much. She'd come too far. These days, finding justice felt like just as much her duty as it did Mal's.

Looking back across at Ruby, Kitt noticed, perhaps for the first time, how short the old woman was. How small, and fragile she looked. Those weren't usually words she'd associate with Ruby but, for some reason, that's how she looked to her now. Though she didn't appreciate Mal trying to speak for her on a professional matter, he was right about this killer being savvier than most. The police had tried to protect the latest victim and failed. Kitt conceded that she might fail too, but she had to try. If she didn't try to solve this case then it was beyond reasonable doubt that in eleven days poor Ruby would be dead.

TWO

Sitting at her desk at Hartley and Edwards Detective Agency, which comprised a rented office space just beyond Walmgate Bar, Kitt rubbed her eyes and scanned the bookshelves that lined the walls.

When she and Grace had moved into this space at the end of last year, Mal had teased her that he had never seen a detective agency look so much like a library. He had made the same joke about her cottage too, before he had eventually moved in with her there. Kitt had, naturally enough, argued that the books at the office were essential reference materials on profiling criminals, investigative technique and historical case studies but, in truth, a lot of the information was available online or in podcast form. After making a second home for herself at the Vale of York University Library over the last decade, however, Kitt simply found books comforting. In books you could find escape, solace and often much-needed answers. A heartening thought when a friend's life hung in the bal-ance.

Sadly, there was no time to delve into those comforting tomes just at this moment. Their investigative research had started, as it always did, by collating the most recent infor-mation and working backwards, which meant printing off the latest news reports and combing them for connections.

'Is that the lot of them?' Kitt said, glancing at the small pile of papers Grace had printed out.

'That's everything from what I'd call reputable sources,' said Grace. 'A worrying number of them are more about the impact on local tourism than they are about the tragic loss of the victims. I know having a serial killer on the loose has hardly been good for Yorkshire tourism but it's still a bit sad.'

Kitt pursed her lips. 'I know, I've seen quite a few articles like that while the case has been going on. I don't know quite when it happened, when people started caring more about money made than lives saved, but it's not a particu-larly attractive colour on us. That said, running the agency business has been no picnic and it's just a side hustle. Anyone losing money from their livelihood over this must be pretty scared right now.'

'I know. Whoever made the rule that we need money to live?' said Grace.

Kitt was about to answer by offering some recommenda-tions for books on the history of capitalism but, it seemed, Grace had seen her coming.

'Not a genuine question! It's too late for a mini-lecture on the unjust financial structure of our society. Come on, we'd better get logged onto Zoom.'

Kitt glanced at the clock. It was just after midnight. She and Grace had been trawling news coverage pertaining to the Vampire Killer for almost five hours. There had been an intimidating amount of information to work through and in their initial scan they had made very few connections. Their focus had been on organizing the information for further scrutiny in order to formulate a list of possible motives and suspects. Ordinarily, after all this research and given the late hour, Kitt would have wanted nothing more than to climb into bed and wrap her arms around Halloran. When she returned home, however, she had no idea what kind of reception would be waiting for her. A late-night Zoom call with her twin sister Rebecca was as good an excuse as any for delaying the inevitable sequel to their earlier argument.

Rebecca was a doctor at a hospital up in Northumberland and had agreed to chat with Kitt during her break on the night shift. Unlike the police, Kitt didn't have immediate access to a pathologist. Her sister was the closest approximation and Kitt was hoping she might be able to shed some light on what was causing the strange red marks on the victims' necks. Perhaps if they could determine the weapon the killer favoured, it would provide a link to his – or her – true identity.

As prompted by Grace, Kitt logged into Zoom, then said to her, 'You don't have to stay for this, you know. You probably didn't have any grand Thursday night plans but you've got the drive back to Leeds yet. No point in you hanging around to the early hours. I can catch you up on what Becca says tomorrow.'

'I don't mind,' Grace said, though she stifled a yawn as she did so. 'I am a bit tired but even when I do climb into bed, I'm unlikely to sleep much after today's events. Anyroad, I could do with a bit of a distraction in general, to be honest.'

'Patrick took the girl from the coffee shop out on a second date then?'

'You guessed it. You win tonight's star prize,' said Grace.

Last autumn, Kitt and Grace had solved the case surrounding the disappearance of Patrick's fiancée, Jodie. During this time, Grace had developed quite the ill-advised crush on him. Though she was doing her best to keep things light it was obvious she was cut up that, after everything she'd seen him through, he'd decided to go out with someone else.

'I wouldn't take something like that personally,' said Kitt. 'The likelihood is that being around you just reminds him of everything he went through with Jodie.'

'Yeah, I know,' said Grace. 'I thought about that. Suppose I can't blame him for wanting to put as much distance between himself and bad memories of the past as he can.'

'The past is a difficult thing to let go of sometimes,' said

Kitt, thinking again about Halloran's obstinate reactions back at the crime scene. When they had met, she had been a full-time librarian. Though she had ended up helping out with the case Halloran had been working on, there had been no hints back then that she was going to become a professional private investigator. Now, she still worked part-time at the library on a Friday and Saturday, but for the rest of the week she was concerned with building her PI business. Because of this, she had undoubtedly increased her chances of brushing up against people and situations that might remind Halloran of his difficult history. Had she unwittingly put her relationship with him in jeopardy?

Fortunately, there wasn't time for Kitt to formulate an opinion on that as Rebecca's name flashed up on the computer screen, prompting Kitt to focus once again on more pressing matters. She admitted her sister to the meeting and waited for the audio and video function to kick in.

'Hi, Becca,' Kitt said as she and Grace huddled a bit closer around the computer.

'Are you sure you two are twins?' said Grace, looking between Kitt and the computer screen. 'Identical twins, like?'

Rebecca at once started chuckling. She and Kitt got this almost every time they introduced each other to friends. Rebecca, with her pixie-cropped hair, dyed baby-pink, no less, and tattoos peeking out from the ends of her sleeves, probably didn't look like a relation of Kitt's to most casual observers. But those who took the time to properly assess the pair would notice the same ice blue eyes. The same freckles around the nose. The same sharp tapering of their faces near the chin. The differences between them were purely cosmetic.

'No, we're not identical twins,' Kitt said, her tone arid. 'I just go around telling people I have an identical twin for fun.'

Grace frowned for a moment and then, on catching Kitt's raised eyebrows, processed the mockery.

'You've just got very different styles, that's all,' said Grace.

'And you're the very first person to ever point that out,' said Rebecca.

'I see you've got identical sarcasm,' said Grace. 'Now I see the resemblance.'

Rebecca laughed at Grace's cheek, probably because she didn't have to endure it day in, day out, while Kitt shook her head at her assistant.

'So,' Grace said, taking Kitt's response as a cue to move the conversation on. 'Thanks for Zooming mid-shift about this. We really appreciate any insight you can offer.'

'You're all right,' said Rebecca. 'I'm sorry to hear about your friend. She must be feeling pretty vulnerable right now, all things considered. Will she have police protection or something?'

'When I last spoke to Ruby, she said Mal had arranged for her to go to a safe house. Though how safe the safe house will be with Ruby in it is up for debate,' said Kitt.

'From the sound of things, she's a bit of a character,' said Rebecca.

'That's an understatement,' said Kitt, wondering how DS Redmond and DC Wilkinson, who were taking shifts at the safe house, were faring. Kitt wagered that they'd be more pleased than Ruby when the eleven days were up. 'But her own house is a crime scene at present and even if it wasn't, we were all in agreement that staying at her own property would basically make her a sitting duck.'

'I'm glad they've got somewhere for her to stay, sounds like the more she can fly under the radar the better,' said Rebecca.

'Flying under the radar isn't exactly Ruby's strong suit, but the police will do all they can for her while the investigation is under way. Something that helps from the outset is getting a sense of what kind of weapon or method the killer uses. The police have tried to compartmentalize as much information as they can but quite a bit has leaked out through friends and neighbours of the victims talking to the press. The cause of death in those targeted so far has been suffocation but they are also left with these strange red marks on their neck. A jar of the victims' blood has been found at each crime scene, so the police are pretty confident that the marks come from draining the victims' blood.'

'All right, let's not dwell too long on that bit,' Grace said.

'Yes, all right, I share that sentiment,' said Kitt. 'It's also been reported that the victims have all had traces of the drug Xylazine in their system. I've looked it up and apparently it's a sedative most commonly used on animals.'

'That's right,' said Rebecca. 'If I had to guess, I'd say the killer is likely using it to sedate his victims while he draws their blood, before then suffocating them.'

'Do you have any idea what implement might have been used for that?' said Kitt.

'Without seeing close-up photographs of the wound it's difficult to draw any sound conclusions, but my first guess would be some kind of needle. Something akin to those used when blood is donated.'

'So, this could be the work of somebody who has access to medical supplies?' said Grace.

'Is the use of needles alone enough to suggest that?' asked Kitt.

'No,' Rebecca conceded. 'But like any of these cases, if you scour the Internet enough you find gory details the average person doesn't want to read about. I had a go at that before the call to see what I could find out and the red marks weren't on any random place across the neck. They were carefully placed on the jugular vein.'

'Is that bad, like?' asked Grace. 'I must admit it doesn't sound good but then nothing that involves the word vein ever sounds good don't you think—'

'Grace . . .'

'Sorry, didn't mean to interrupt. Tired.'

Rebecca smiled. Kitt wagered Grace's antics were welcome

comic relief next to whatever she was dealing with on the night shift. Though Grace could be trying at times, Kitt wouldn't switch places with her sister. The second-hand stories were more than enough all by themselves.

'It's good for the killer and bad for the victim,' said Rebecca. 'Jugular veins are the major veins in the neck. If the killer doesn't have a medical background then he's done his research. He's looked up exactly where to draw the blood from. It's not just a random act. That said, the marks suggest either that the killer is not a professional and has made a real mess of things when drawing the blood or, in the worst-case scenario, that they did know what they were doing but purposefully made those marks on the victim.'

'Given the symbol left on the victims' doors, there's a good chance it could be the latter,' said Kitt. 'He seems to want to leave clear signs that it's the same perpetrator in every case. So, that's a helpful starting point, thank you.'

'It's just a theory,' said Rebecca.

'At this stage of an investigation, with so little evidence, everything is a theory,' said Kitt. 'Can you think of anything else that might have made those kind of marks?'

'Well, there are variations on the needle theme,' Rebecca explained. 'From the way the wound is described in the media coverage it sounds as though the weapon used is long and thin. So something like those long, tough needles people use to sew leather, or maybe even an acupuncture needle.'

'Aren't acupuncture needles too thin to leave a mark?' said Kitt.

Rebecca shook her head. 'If the person isn't trying to leave a mark, and knows what they are doing, there wouldn't be a mark. But acupuncture needles are still sharp and penetrating. If you wanted to do visible damage with one you could.'

'But it wouldn't be the easiest way to make those marks?' said Grace.

'Probably not,' Rebecca conceded. 'Perhaps more likely it would be some kind of workshop tool that was long and thin – or something like an ice pick or even a kebab skewer – though if they used something like that, rather than the proper medical equipment, the crime scene would be more gruesome than the finale to *Reservoir Dogs*.'

'I'm not sure exactly what the crime scenes looked like,' said Kitt.

'But surely it's easier to come by something like a leatherwork needle or an ice pick than a medical needle without anyone catching on to what you're up to?' said Grace.

'It all depends on if the killer has a medical background or access to medical supplies,' said Rebecca.

'This is a real help, thanks, Becca,' said Kitt, making a list of all the things Rebecca had mentioned. She added a bookbinding awl to the list as her own contribution. She doubted this would have been considered a likely weapon by the other two participants in the conversation but it was long, thin and sharp so, as far as Kitt was concerned, shouldn't be discounted.

'Not a problem. But, bit of advice? Don't tell our mam you're working this case, eh? She worries enough about you already and given that the first killing took place in Boro, not five miles from their doorstep, this one's close to home as it is.'

'Noted,' said Kitt. 'I sympathise with their reaction. With the second murder taking place in Scarborough and the third in Malton, everyone in York has been looking over their shoulder too. Silly really, given how the marks on the door serve as a warning to the victims. It's unlikely, now that we know what those marks mean, that anyone will be taken by surprise. I'll make sure I wait until I've successfully brought the killer down before telling Mam anything about it.'

'Modest, as always,' Rebecca said with a smile, but then it faded. 'One of my Facebook friends knew the first victim. Boro is hardly a safe haven but I've never known anything like this to happen.'

'I know,' said Kitt, picking up one of the news reports they'd printed off. 'Anna Hayes, she was only thirty-seven. She ran a local coven – that was her link to the occult. The other two victims had links to the occult too, of course, which is part of the killer's MO. From what I understand, the police didn't even realize Anna's door had been marked until after the second murder had been committed because she'd cleaned the mark off.'

'She will have just thought it was a local kid with a spray can,' said Rebecca. 'That's what I would've thought, anyway. I wouldn't have thought it was a sign that a serial killer had singled me out, and the police don't have the resources to investigate vandalism now, even if you did report it as suspicious activity.'

Grace shook her head. 'Horrible to think it, isn't it? That being house proud could have cost you your life, or someone else's theirs? If the mark had still been on the door when the first victim was killed, the police would have been able to release the information to the public and when the mark was made on the second door the second victim would have known it was important to contact the authorities.'

'The killer has been lucky up until now,' said Kitt. 'But I'm hoping to put an end to that.'

'Well, your track record is strong,' said Rebecca. 'But watch yer back, eh? This killer, whoever they are, is creepy as hell in their methods, and I'd imagine in person too.'

'Don't worry,' said Kitt. 'I'll tread carefully.'

With that, Kitt and Rebecca said their goodbyes and Kitt ended the meeting before looking at Grace.

'I think that's enough for tonight. I've made a list of all the long, thin objects I can think of—'

Kitt was interrupted by Grace's sniggering.

'For goodness sake, has Evie sent her spirit out on you or something?' Kitt's best friend Evie wasn't one to let even a single innuendo pass unacknowledged. Grace had spent an increasing amount of time in her company over the last couple of years and there were clear signs that Evie's unsavoury influence was rubbing off on her. 'Get your mind out of the gutter, will you?'

'It's less fun than when it's in the gutter, but OK.'

'We'll do our best to add any other ideas to the list tomorrow. We need to keep our minds open about what might have made those puncture marks on the victims' necks. Then we can draw up a list of suspects, people who are likely to have access to those objects and . . .'

'What? What is it?' Grace said, following Kitt's gaze down to the pile of newspaper clippings sitting on the desk.

Kitt put her hands on one particular article, which led with a large photograph of a cordoned off crime scene in one of the backstreets in Scarborough. 'That man, there. In the black T-shirt, holding a phone. I've seen him somewhere else. Have you got any clippings from the Malton and Middlesbrough crime scenes?'

Grace rifled through the pile of cuttings, picking out relevant articles. Kitt examined each clipping in turn. 'Yes, see, here he is again,' she said, handing over a clipping from the Middlesbrough crime scene. 'And here. This bloke's been at all three crime scenes taking photos – or maybe even video footage.'

'Couldn't he just be a journalist for a local paper?' said Grace.

'No, I don't think so,' said Kitt. 'Photographs on your

phone aren't usually high res enough for the local paper – even if they're only being posted online,' said Kitt. 'Maybe they'd post a photo from a person's phone who happened to be at the scene when they weren't, but I'd expect a legitimate journalist making a special trip to report from the crime scene to have better kit than that.'

'I don't know so much with the budget cuts at most newspapers and magazines, but I suppose there's a chance you're right and, just now, we can't afford to turn down any lead,' said Grace. 'If he isn't a journalist, then it is a bit suspicious. It's unlikely a casual bystander would just happen to be passing all three crime scenes given the distance between them.'

'Highly unlikely,' said Kitt, staring harder at the man in the photograph. He was taller than most other people in the crowd and had long, mousey brown hair tucked behind his ears. 'If you ask me, we've just found our first suspect.'

THREE

Meet me at our bridge. Let me know when you're en route.

That's what the text message from Halloran had said. Kitt had only noticed it when she'd checked her phone just before leaving the agency and had at once set off in the direction of Skeldergate Bridge.

That was their bridge.

It had been designed by Thomas Page, who had also designed Westminster Bridge, and with its gothic arches, and its proximity to the library in which she worked, it held a special place in her heart. Her admiration for the bridge had only become more profound after Halloran had pressed her against its sturdy stonework and kissed her for the first time. Next to that bridge, she had realized that Halloran was a man she could easily fall in love with, if only she'd let herself. A possibility that, at the time, she had long since dismissed.

27

When she'd first read the message, she hadn't been sure whether Halloran's request to meet somewhere other than the cottage they now shared on Ouse View Avenue was a good sign or a bad sign. As Kitt descended the last few steps down to the river path, however, and noticed Halloran waiting for her with a small smile part hidden behind his beard, she knew.

Her breath deepened as she approached him. He had that glint in his eyes that she knew so well. The glint that meant it wouldn't be long before his lips were on hers.

When she was just a pace away he slowly backed her against the stonework of the bridge, just as he had the first time they had kissed.

'I'm sorry for overreacting, pet,' Halloran said, brushing a strand of Kitt's red hair out of her face. 'The last thing I want is for you to feel reined in.'

He pulled his face an inch back from hers. Just far enough to see her knowingly raising her eyebrows.

'Well, you know, not in that way.'

Kitt put her hand to the side of his head and ran it through his hair. It had come later than she had hoped it would but he had apologized. His willingness to say sorry always humbled her. It seemed to be a dying quality these days – everyone was always so adamant they were right all the time. But when you loved a person, as Kitt and Halloran loved each other, being right seemed less important. Certainly, less important than being together.

'I understand why you reacted the way you did,' she said,

enjoying the way the warmth of his breath was warding off the late night chill. 'But I didn't take the case to hurt you or make you worry. I need to work this one. This is Ruby's life we're talking about.'

'I know,' Halloran said. 'I've had time to think and the loyalty you show to your friends is one of the things I love most about you. Besides, I can't pretend I'd do any different in your shoes.'

'I'm glad you understand,' said Kitt. 'And, who knows? I may uncover some clues that are helpful to your investigation along the way.'

'The official line, as always, is that the police do not work with private investigators but, if I'm honest, we're going to need all the help we can get if we're going to bring this person to justice. This isn't about sides. People like this, sometimes they commit a few murders and then go underground for years before killing again, only to disappear for a second time before the authorities catch up with them. As well as saving Ruby's life, we need to look at this as an operation to save all the future lives the murderer might take if they continue to elude us. There's never been so much pressure from the top.'

'I suppose it's not surprising that they're pretty desperate to see the killer locked away given the general note of terror they're striking across the county.'

'No, but sadly I think it's more about pressures from local councils than it is about stopping the bloodshed.'

'Because of the impact it's having on local businesses?'

'Aye. We're into the Easter holiday season which, among other regional events, includes a vintage fair at Scarborough and the Whitby goth weekend. Only, people aren't visiting the area, at least not in anywhere near the usual numbers. The coastal councils are complaining that local tourism is significantly down because this killer's still at large after three months.'

'It's a bit strange, isn't it? When the killer, so far as we know, only targets pre-selected victims. Everyone's still so wary.'

'Not everyone thinks of a killer in terms of their MO. You and me are trained to but to most folk living around here, they just think about the fact that there's someone out there with the capacity to kill, and that's enough to scare them off. Can't say I blame them either.'

'Does this mean that your lot are actually going to throw a decent amount of police resources at solving this case?'

'As far as they can, but you know how it is right now. Cuts are worse than ever. We have a few more people than usual working on it across the areas that have been targeted but extra help never goes amiss when you're dealing with an individual like this.'

'So, are you saying that the help of your girlfriend sleuth would actually be appreciated on this case?'

Halloran tried to stop himself from grinning and Kitt was pleased when he failed. 'I'm saying that we should keep communicating about the case. That way, I can help you stay safe and we can collectively pursue more avenues to try and bring the investigation to the best possible conclusion. But we'll have to be discreet. You know what happens if Ricci finds out what I've shared with you over the years on the handful of cases you've helped me with.'

'How could I forget? You remind me every time,' Kitt said with mock scorn.

'I know, it's almost as if holding on to my badge is important to me, eh?'

Kitt chuckled, but understood Halloran's concern. Chief Superintendent Sofia Ricci had turned a blind eye here and there over the time she'd been leading the police force in York but there were some breaches she wouldn't be able to ignore if she ever found out about them. 'I shouldn't worry, DI Halloran, I came across a very important piece of information just before leaving the office and will no doubt have the entire case all wrapped up before tomorrow teatime. You'll hardly have to lift a finger.'

'Oh really? Don't bet on it. I also came across some very important information before I left the nick – information that could be crucial to closing the case.'

Kitt eyed Halloran for a moment. 'Want to trade?'

'I don't know . . .' Halloran feigned a conspiratorial look over both of his shoulders, as though anyone would be walking around Skeldergate at one o'clock on a weekday morning.

'Give over, you daft thing,' Kitt said, tapping him on the chest.

'All right, ladies first.'

'Grace and I have been examining news coverage of the crime scenes at Middlesbrough, Scarborough and Malton. Compiling names, locations, times and dates, standard stuff. But as we were searching through them, we found some clippings that show the same bloke hanging around in the background at all three locations. I think he's filming the investigation.'

'Not a journalist?'

'Not by the look of his equipment.'

'Interesting. We'll definitely need to check that out. It's quite common for serial killers of this kind to revisit the crime scene. They like the idea that they're clever enough to be that bold but stay under the radar.'

'From what I understand, they also get a sick pleasure out of witnessing the grief and chaos they've caused.' Kitt suppressed a shiver. Wasn't it bad enough that people felt entitled to take the life of another in such a callous manner without openly revelling in it?

'Aye, that too,' Halloran said with a nod. 'If you send me the pictures I might be able to help track him down. If not, we can put out a call to the public for information. We'll be interested to know what business he's got at all three crime scenes if he isn't a member of the press.'

'Yes, coming to the case this far in might actually give us

a better chance of solving it. If the killer is starting to get bold or arrogant, they're likely to slip up.'

'Agreed, here's hoping they're feeling a bit too pleased with themselves just now. That's often what happens after the third murder mark. It's what moves them into serial status, really – they're no longer a double murderer. When it gets to this stage it's clear they've got intentions to keep going until they're stopped.'

'And I intend to be the one who stops them, or at least part of the team. On that note, what crucial piece of information did you find?'

'An inordinate number of Ruby's neighbours have home CCTV systems installed.'

'Bloody busybodies,' said Kitt.

'I think it might have more to do with living close to someone as eccentric as Ruby, to be honest. Not everyone sees her as harmless, you know; some people still think witchcraft is about devil worship.'

'Then remind me to recommend several important texts on the subject to Ruby's neighbours next time we're passing.'

'Like you'd ever need a reminder to do that,' Halloran said, and continued before Kitt could interject any further. Likely because he knew she'd happily steer the conversation onto books given even the slightest opportunity. 'One of the cameras is positioned almost opposite Ruby's front door.'

'Mal!' Kitt said, her eyes sparkling with excitement. 'Did

you catch the killer on camera? That could be a real break-through. There hasn't been any footage before.'

'That's because the killer tends to pick residential back-streets where there aren't usually any cameras. But yes, we did manage to find some footage of, judging by how broad they were, a man, just before dusk this evening, painting the V on the door.'

'How come none of the neighbours saw him?'

'It took him less than five seconds to do it. He used a can of spray paint and a V is hardly an intricate design. As soon as the mark was in place, he was off like a shot.'

'Tell me you got his face on camera? If you did, we could compare it to the man Grace and I found.'

'Not his face, I'm afraid. He was wearing a thick black hoodie.'

'Hm,' said Kitt. 'We're still not sure what the V mark even means, are we? I know the media have jumped on the idea that it stands for vampire because of the marks on the victims' necks, but we don't really know why the killer has chosen that particular marking.'

'The teams we've got working on the case are all still speculating on that,' said Halloran. 'There's not much else that the letter V points to. Victory is the most likely idea we've come up with, assuming that the killer sees his acts as some kind of war on people associated with the occult. If it's not that or the vampire angle, the odds are the V relates to something personal. A first or last initial perhaps?'

'Perhaps,' said Kitt. 'I've done a bit of research into it as a symbol this afternoon and like you say, there's not much to it, especially when it comes to links with mysticism and the occult. Apparently, the V shape, or a downward pointing chevron, can symbolise the planet, and goddess, Venus, but I'm not sure if that's really a likely interpretation. Your theory about the V relating to something personal is probably a surer bet. Were there no other distinguishing features of the person you caught on video?'

'The hoodie he was wearing had a white pentagram printed on the back but that was the only distinguishing mark.'

'Hmm. Was the top of the star pointing up or down?'

'Um . . . down, I think. Why? Is that important?'

'Not necessarily historically but in a modern context, a pentagram pointed up is more likely to suggest pagan beliefs. A pentagram pointed down is more associated with satanism.'

'So, if I've remembered right, our killer could be part of some kind of satanic cult or organization?'

'It's possible but not certain. Such people are known for practising their belief system alone. But some of them do join organizations and it would be a break if they were part of something like that. It might make it easier to track them down, so with little else to go on at this stage it's definitely worth drawing up a list of organizations and reaching out to them, at the very least.'

'We'll make that a priority tomorrow. Given the fact the victims have all had some link with the occult, we assumed the killer was more likely to disapprove of that kind of practice. But maybe we were wrong, maybe there is a rogue member of one of these organizations out there and they've taken their beliefs to a very dark place.'

'It's certainly a possibility. We'll make our own list and make sure we share it with you in case we've missed any between us. You're sure there were no other distinguishing features of the vandal?'

'No, he was just dressed in black. Clearly trying to stay inconspicuous. And, of course, we don't know for sure that whoever was caught on video is the person committing the killings. Given the MO and how it compares with similar cases, we've been working on the principle that the killer is male, but he might get a stooge to paint the symbols, in case they get caught. Or there is a possibility that it's not the real killer at all, but a copycat.'

'With so little time, we can't afford to entertain that possibility, can we?'

'We need to treat it like it's for real in terms of the investigation, but we must also remain open to other pieces of evidence that might come from other sources. Such as your man in the photographs. Perhaps he is the real killer, and not the man who spray painted a V on Ruby's door. Or perhaps they're working together. We won't know until we do more digging.'

'Well, I look forward to taking a look at the footage you uncovered from Ruby's neighbours for myself and seeing if I can glean anything from it.'

'What? I never said you could—'

'I'm handing over my evidence to you, it's only fair, and remember you said we needed to do all we can to try and catch this guy.'

'I knew it was only a matter of time before those words came back to haunt me,' Halloran said, pushing his forehead against hers.

'I missed you, Mal.' She knew it was a silly thing to say when they'd only been apart a few hours but whenever they had disagreements she felt much further away from him somehow. It was always such a relief to hold him close again. 'And for what it's worth, I both want and need you.'

'I know,' he said, interlocking her fingers with his and slowly lifting them above her head, pinning them against the bridge. 'I missed you too.'

Her breath quickened as he leaned in and kissed his way down the side of her cheek, down beyond her chin to her neck.

'Mal . . .' she whispered up to the sky as his beard tickled against her skin and he worked his way upwards again until their mouths, at last, met. He tasted of bitter late-night coffee but, as his well-practised tongue circled her own, she didn't care. No matter how many kisses they shared, he would always find some new way of stirring her. This time, it was the way his hands gently cupped her curves, squeezing in just the right places to remind her of all he was capable of behind closed doors.

'Take me home, Mal,' she whispered.

She didn't have to ask him twice.

FOUR

As Kitt was working the late shift at the library the next day and it was simply too bright and sunny to be cooped up in an office, she arranged a morning meeting with Grace at Museum Gardens. There, the daffodils were in full bloom, the scent of freshly cut grass hung on the air and the river Ouse twinkled on the periphery. It was a soothing place. Perfect for setting out all the facts of the case. Though ordinarily Kitt would insist on making the most of the office space they rented, there wasn't a great deal of natural light there and this case was darker than any they had dealt with before. Thus, she welcomed anything that took the edge off the alarming details they would need to discuss. Moreover, the fresh air would surely keep them sharp and alert while devising their preliminary theories about the killer, their motives and their movements.

Evie had also invited herself along to the meeting as she didn't have any clients to massage at the salon until later in the afternoon. Even though Kitt had warned her that the agenda was purely shop talk, she had insisted on coming along since they hadn't had a chance to catch up all the week before and, in truth, it was rare for the pair to ever be apart for too long.

'Morning, both, glorious day, weather-wise, isn't it?' said Kitt, her smile considerably wider than one might expect given the mammoth task ahead. She breezed past Grace and Evie who had beaten her down to the meeting place and were sitting on a bench. She then unrolled a large tartan blanket from her satchel and began spreading it out on the grass near the weathered ruins of St Mary's Abbey. The opportunity to lounge out on the grass surrounded by what arches and columns remained of a Benedictine place of worship on a sunny day was just one of the reasons Kitt loved living in York so much. There were so few cities where you could get quite so close to history. Once she was satisfied the rug was lump- and crease-free, she waved her companions over.

'You're in high spirits this morning,' said Grace, as she made herself comfortable on the blanket. 'I'm guessing you made up with Halloran, then.'

'And I bet I know how,' Evie said with a sly smile.

'Give over, you two, will you? This is not an episode of *Sex and the City*. We've got serious matters to attend to.'

'All right, all right,' said Evie. 'All work and no play and all that.'

'We haven't done any work yet,' said Kitt.

'Speak for yourself,' said Grace. 'Alongside catching Evie up on what we discussed with Rebecca last night, I've been compiling every possible shot of our mystery man who's appeared at all three crime scenes to see if there's anything we can use to identify him.'

'You must have been up with the larks!' said Kitt. 'Fantastic work. Any joy?'

'Nothing yet, he wears pretty generic clothing. Nothing with a symbol or logo. I've zoomed in on quite a few pictures of him and as yet there aren't any identifiable details.'

'Well, Halloran is also aware of the individual. I directed him to the news coverage where we'd spotted the amateur photographer and they're going to pull up CCTV footage from the days the reports were made. See if they can catch him getting into a car or using a cash machine so they can track the registration or the card number. If that doesn't yield any results, I think they'll then put a call out to the public for information. See if anyone who knows him comes forward, or indeed if the guy steps forward of his own accord if he's innocent.'

'That'll be a big help,' said Grace.

'Mal also thinks that if he is the man we've been looking for, the call-out for information might make him panic and do something to incriminate himself.'

'Here's hoping,' said Grace. 'Ten days seems so much less time than eleven days did yesterday, it's weird.'

'I know,' said Kitt, wishing, yet again, that she had been able to rearrange her library shifts until after the investigation was over. It had been a while since she'd asked for some leave on short notice but her boss Michelle had been adamant that there was nobody to fill in for this week. Mind you, Michelle was the kind who would have insisted that was the case even if Kitt had had all her limbs in plaster casts. It didn't help the case with her boss that Kitt was only at the library two days a week these days. As far as Michelle was concerned, Kitt should be able to complete any PI work without it interfering with her minimal shift pattern. Ordinarily, this would have been a reasonable ask but with just eleven days to solve the case, every minute counted.

Still, Grace would be able to continue her research in the meantime, and she had managed to wangle the following week off when, if they hadn't already cracked the case, time would truly be running out for them. 'I think we're going to feel that way with each day that passes but we have to stay focused. Worrying isn't going to get us anywhere. And actually, one of Ruby's neighbours did catch the killer – or his accomplice – on a home security camera. Not his face, mind you, but he was wearing a black hoodie with an inverted pentacle printed on the back.'

'Is that going to help us narrow it down?' asked Grace.

'Not on its own,' said Kitt. 'I did a quick web search while eating my cereal this morning. There are so many shops, online and offline, that stock hoodies like that. And of course from online shops you can get stuff shipped from anywhere in the world. But we thought the symbol might be a clue. We'll want to draw up a list of satanic organizations, starting with those based in Yorkshire, to see if they have noticed any unusual behaviour from their members.'

'Are there a lot of satanic organizations in Yorkshire, like?' said Evie.

'I've no idea, but at a guess I would imagine the list to be quite short,' said Kitt.

'That's one lead to follow anyway,' said Grace.

'Indeed,' said Kitt. 'But having spoken to Rebecca about the murder weapon and trawled the press for all the information we can find on the case, we now need to draw up a timeline and look into each victim in turn, their backgrounds, their movements, to help us draw up a list of possible suspects. That way, we can systematically work from most to least likely.'

'All right,' Grace said, taking her laptop out of her rucksack and switching it on. 'Let's start with the timeline and any evidence uncovered.'

'Well, so far there have been three killings, one per month since January. No forensic evidence has been left behind and, up until now, no CCTV footage of the perpetrator,' said Kitt. 'Still, there are some common links. All of the murders have taken place within the county of Yorkshire, which might indicate that the murderer is from this region too.'

At this statement, Kitt noticed Evie looking warily over her shoulder, and, though to others it might seem ridiculously paranoid, she couldn't blame her for it. The scars on Evie's face told the sad story of how she had suffered last time there had been a serial killer at large on her home turf.

'All of the victims had some association with the occult,' Grace added.

'And,' Kitt said, 'the nature of the murders reflects this. The ritualistic markings on the doors. The eleven days between warning and murder – eleven being quite an important esoteric number.'

'Is it?' said Evie.

'Yes, we don't really have time to go into the whys and wherefores just now but I do have some excellent volumes on gematria and master numbers if you'd like a lend?'

'I'm . . . all right, thanks,' said Evie. 'Sounds a bit heavy. I'll take your word for it.'

'There's the fact the police believe the killings all happened around midnight too,' said Grace. 'According to the research we've pulled up it's an important time of day in some occult belief systems.'

'Not forgetting the way in which the killer drains blood from their victims – and the vampiric marks on the victims' necks. If the killer isn't involved in the occult directly, it's safe to say they are in some way obsessed with it.'

'Well, so long as the killer sticks to their pattern that rules me out,' said Evie. 'If they change their target to people who love vintage teapots though, I'll definitely be watching my back.'

'Not much chance of that, I don't think,' said Kitt.

'Poor Ruby though,' said Evie. 'She must be terrified.'

'If that's what you think, you don't know Ruby as well as I do. Wouldn't surprise me if she somehow manages to take this bloke out single-handedly.'

'I know what you mean,' said Evie. 'She's a hardy lass. But I think deep down she must be scared even if she's trying to put a brave face on it. You say "bloke" – you think the killer is male then?'

'We can't rule anything out at the moment,' said Kitt. 'But Halloran suspects the perpetrator is male based on the fact that they've physically overpowered three victims in order to drug them. Plus, sadly, statistically this kind of killer is much more likely to be male.'

'Besides the occult thing, is there anything else that links the victims?' said Evie.

'Not that we know of,' said Grace. 'They all come from slightly different locations. Middlesbrough, Scarborough, Malton. Not a world away from each other but far enough apart that there are no obvious links between them – although we don't have access to their phone and financial records like the police, so I'm just going on what I've managed to pull up online. There are no connections on social media, there's no correlation in terms of sex, ethnicity or age, or professional employment either.'

'That's right,' said Kitt. 'The first killing took place on the seventeenth of January, at midnight. I assume, Evie, that Grace brought you up to speed on that when she talked you through the Zoom call we had with Becca.'

'Yeah, the first victim led some kind of coven, right? And she cleaned the killer's mark off her door thinking it was vandals?'

'That's right. The police found traces of the paint after the fact and, based on the eleven-day pattern of the other killings, it's assumed the mark was painted onto her door on the sixth of January, so that seems like the most prudent place to start our timeline. When we're asking for alibis, it's as important to find out where the suspects were the days the doors were marked as it is the killings themselves. Mal suggested that the killer might use an accomplice, in case they are caught, and certainly we need to be open to the possibility.'

'And if you catch the accomplice, they will lead you to the killer,' said Evie.

'That's the hope,' said Kitt.

'Whether they're working with an accomplice or not, the killer seems pretty determined to avoid any obvious pattern in his victims,' said Grace. 'Anna Hayes was white, and her day job was at the local council. This is a very different profile to the second victim, Roger Fairclough. He was also Caucasian but that's where the similarities end. He was a man in his eighties, a retired police officer who lived in

Scarborough. He ran an online forum about the occult as a hobby. He was killed on the sixteenth of February.'

'Which I suppose means the door was painted on ...' Evie paused to do some counting on her fingers. 'The fifth of February.'

'That's right,' said Grace, making a note of it on her laptop.

'The third victim was Alix Yang,' said Kitt. 'She was a woman in her forties who lived in Malton and had Asian heritage. She self-published spell books online.'

'Was that her main profession?' said Evie.

'No, she was a journalist,' said Kitt. 'From what the papers said about her, the spell books were just a side-hustle.'

'She was murdered on . . . the eighteenth of March,' Grace said, double-checking the date on an article she'd pulled up on her phone. 'So the mark on the door was likely painted on the seventh.'

'And now Ruby has been targeted – a solitary witch.'

'What I can't get over is that the third victim was under police protection when she was murdered. How did that happen? I know Charley attended a big briefing about the case last night after that mark was found on Ruby's door, but unlike Halloran, she isn't a soft touch. I can never get anything out of her about a case she's working on. No matter what methods I try,' said Evie, referring to her partner, DS Banks.

Kitt chuckled. Poor Banks was always so despairing of

Halloran's inability to cut Kitt out of his cases. She couldn't very well argue against the fact that Mal was a soft touch. She liked that he couldn't help himself when it came to letting her in on what was going on. As well as a sign of devotion, it made solving murder cases a lot more straightforward than it would be otherwise. Though Kitt conceded that whenever she was in the middle of solving one, it never felt that way.

'From what I understand, that tragic episode was all very Castle Inverness,' said Kitt.

'What? There were no murders in Inverness ... were there?' said Grace.

'Fairly sure that's a *Macbeth* reference,' said Evie. 'And you'd best move the conversation on sharpish before we get five more.'

'Oh, right, should have known,' Grace half-groaned. 'So what does that mean to us lay-people who don't navigate the world via the works of Shakespeare?'

'It means the officers on guard from the local nick in Malton, one at the front of the property and one at the back, were drugged,' said Kitt, wincing as she remembered the tale Halloran had relayed to her before she left the cottage that morning. During the briefing at York police station last night the officers from Malton had explained their encounter with this devious killer in nightmarish detail. 'According to Mal, the killer injected the officer watching over the victim's property with Xylazine, the same drug that has been found in the victims' systems.'

'Grace said that it was a drug used on animals?' asked Evie.

'Yes, Mal reckons it's most commonly used by farmers,' said Kitt. 'And it's quite difficult to get your hands on it. A vet would have to prescribe it. The police in each area where the killer has struck have been going through a list of vets in their region, asking them to provide details of any Xylazine prescriptions they've dished out in the last six months.'

'It gives me a bit of hope that the police have got something that concrete,' said Evie. 'That's a paper trail and hopefully they'll reach the end of it before anything untoward happens to Ruby.'

'I agree,' said Kitt. 'The police are best placed to locate and interview anyone who's had a Xylazine prescription. We'll focus on the areas they have less time to pursue.'

'God, poor Alix Yang though,' said Grace. 'She would have thought she was safe under police protection. But once the officers on watch had been knocked out there wouldn't have been anything they could do to stop the killer.'

'It's worse than that, I'm afraid,' said Kitt. 'In the quantities the killer used on the officers, the Xylazine doesn't knock you out. Instead it causes a kind of paralysis; an inability to move properly or think straight. From what I've read, they call it the zombie drug. The officers may have had some sense of what was happening but couldn't get to the victim or raise the alarm because of the effect the drugs were having on them. The killer was so swift in their actions neither officer even had a chance to hit the emergency button on their radios.'

'Crikey. I'm not sure Charley would ever forgive herself for that if it happened to her,' said Evie. 'I've never known anyone as dedicated to public safety as she is.'

'Almost every officer I've ever come into contact with is extremely devoted to keeping us all safe,' said Kitt. 'But the boldness of turning up at the victim's property while it's under police protection tells you the kind of person we're dealing with here. And that's why, though Ruby's been moved to a safe house at a location Mal won't even disclose to me, we cannot count on that alone to save her.'

FIVE

Kitt's somewhat unsettling statement gave all three women pause. They fell silent as they considered the task in front of them. Was it possible to get the better of someone as dedicated to their mission as this killer appeared to be? At that thought, it seemed to Kitt that the warmth of the April sun was no longer reaching her. In response, she wrapped her purple cardigan tighter around her body though it did little to stave off the sudden chill.

'Well, no matter how prepared this bloke thinks he is, we can't just sit idle,' said Grace. 'Ruby's hired us to do a job, and we're going to do it. Just like we always do.'

'We'll throw all we've got at it,' Kitt said with a nod, hoping the others couldn't hear the lingering doubt in her tone.

'At least the police have got that lead on the Xylazine ... and there's the occult angle binding the victims together,' said Evie.

'Yes ... although even that element has its variations. Each victim has slightly different associations with occult practices,' said Kitt. 'Still, I suppose if we're assuming the occult element has some significance to the killer, we should presume the same thing about the Yorkshire locale.'

'You mean other than convenience, if he lives here?' said Grace.

'Although the killings have all taken place in Yorkshire, that's a big if.'

'How come?' said Evie.

'Think about it. The most famous serial murder cases have historically happened in America. There's a reason for this. America is huge with numerous states, all with slightly different legal systems that don't quite connect.'

'So, a serial killer can move from one state to another, committing the same acts and reducing the likelihood of getting caught because the police have to start almost at square one each time?' said Grace.

'I'm sure interstate communications are better than they once were, but if you travel across the country, you can probably do quite a bit of damage before the police realize it's the same offender. Especially if the killer makes some slight alterations to their MO and they have no idea what they look like.'

'And you think that's what's happening here?' said Grace. 'The killer doesn't really live in Yorkshire at all, he's making trips here especially to kill people to divert attention from his true location.'

'Crumbs. Lots of people make trips north, south, east and west every day,' said Evie. 'Family visits, remote working, you name it. Picking someone out of a haystack like that would make it even more difficult if the killer doesn't live nearby.'

'I know,' said Kitt, taking a deep breath. 'We can only hope, for Ruby's sake, that he's not as smart as he thinks he is. You both know what Mal's like about cases like this, but this one has got him really rattled.'

'If the Yorkshire angle doesn't help us much, perhaps the question that's most likely to lead us in the right direction is: why target people with links to the occult in the first place?' said Grace. 'I know serial killers are sort of known for being more ritualistic than most, but that still doesn't explain why the killer is choosing these people in particular.'

'Yeah,' said Evie. 'That is a bit of a rum thing to do. Don't killers like this usually pick people they think are easy targets, like the elderly or young women?'

'Yes, that's true, but there's no hard and fast rule,' said Kitt. 'The main takeaway is that the victims serial killers choose often tell you more about them than any other detail of the case. Most serial killers are not opportunists, they're selective. They have criteria, and that criteria often reveals something important about them.'

'So, for some reason, the occult is a proper sore point for this chap?' said Evie.

'You could say that, yes,' said Kitt, deciding not to pass comment on the sheer magnitude of Evie's understatement. 'The most obvious motive is probably extreme religious views, either esoteric or evangelical. For example, Mal was just saying last night that the occult has unsavoury reputations amongst some. If the killer believes the people they are killing are in league with the devil, or some other dark force, they may be operating under the delusion that they're doing God's work, or at the very least cleansing society of a malevolent presence.'

'But as far as I can see, the victims weren't hurting anyone. Do people really still think that way about new-age stuff?' said Evie. 'Especially post-Harry Potter.'

'Not everyone tars the occult with the same brush, but then not everyone is a serial killer. We're talking about a very specific and likely warped mind-set here; someone who believes anyone aligned with the occult is aligned with the devil,' said Kitt. 'Certainly, we could look closer at some of the more evangelical organizations in the area. See if any members have been particularly vocal about the killings.'

'It makes sense to investigate the most radical candidates in both directions – the holy and the unholy,' said Evie. 'Whichever way you cut it this killer is an extremist of some kind. Even the limited descriptions of the crime scenes I've read about online are enough to make your skin crawl. It's obsessive behaviour and no mistake.'

'We covered deep-rooted obsessions like this as part of

my psychology degree,' said Grace. 'Obsessions are usually a sign of a deficit somewhere else in that person's life. For example, an unhealthy obsession with books might betray a deficit in that person's social life.'

'Watch yourself,' said Kitt, while Evie giggled at Grace's jibe.

Grace laughed along with Evie for a moment but quickly recovered herself. 'What I'm saying is, this person has time to obsess over those involved with the occult and their practices. He is likely to be quite a lonely, isolated person.'

'He also has time to meticulously plan these murders,' said Kitt. 'And if you haven't got any friends you don't have to worry about anyone finding the plans you've made or equipment you might have secured to carry out the job.'

'Which might rule out the idea of him being a card-carrying member of a satanist or evangelical group,' said Evie. 'If he's a loner, signing up to a collective or organization might not have been job one.'

'True, although the killer must meet the victims somehow,' said Kitt. 'It's easy enough to think he might be able to find the leader of an online forum, or even an author who self-publishes their books, but someone like Ruby, and the first victim Anna Hayes, they're more difficult to come into contact with organically if you don't have some place to pluck them from. Perhaps the killer looked up the victims on a membership list for one of these organizations.

Or perhaps there's a deeper pattern here that we don't yet understand.'

'But if the victims were all part of the same organization, wouldn't the police in other areas have already looked into that?' said Grace.

'Probably, but the killer might be targeting more than one organization to ensure there's no obvious pattern,' said Kitt. 'Just as he has with the locations, the profile of the victims and their links to the occult.'

'If the serial killer is himself a satanist or into occult practice and is one cheese cracker short of the tin,' said Evie, 'then perhaps he views his victims as ritual sacrifices.'

'Another theory to add to the list,' said Kitt.

'I'll make a note,' said Grace.

'Well, there's not much to go on but these things are a starting point, anyway. I— Oh, hang on,' said Kitt, 'that's my phone. Mal?' she said, once she'd answered the call.

'Thought you'd want to know, pet, we've identified the mystery man from your photographs. Caught him getting into a vehicle on CCTV and tracked his registration.'

'That was quick.'

'Time is of the essence, and as it happens the guy has a record. Once we had his registration details we were able to find his details on file. His name's Peter Tremble and he lives in York.'

'What's he got a record for?'

'Nothing that would indicate a likely serial killing spree.

A B&E and a couple of car thefts in his teens. He seems to have cleaned up his act in the last fifteen years or so but, given a piece of intel that's just landed on my desk, that could be an act.'

'Why do you say that?'

'We've just discovered that our friend Peter happens to run a podcast.'

'What kind of podcast?'

'A podcast dedicated to all things occult,' Halloran replied.

SIX

It was the following day before Kitt was able to arrange a meeting with occult podcaster Peter Tremble. He had been taken in for police questioning before that, of course. And Kitt had tried every trick she could think of to get Halloran to let her watch his interview with the suspect from behind the false mirror in the interrogation room at York Police Station the night before. Despite her attempts at persuasion, however, even she had to concede that if Chief Superintendent Ricci caught Kitt in there that would probably be it for Mal's career. It's doubtful that Banks would have approved either. She'd done a pretty good job of covering up Mal's breaches of police procedure in the past but Kitt wasn't convinced there would be any coming back from that.

Still, who needed to sit in on a police interview when you could conduct an interview of your own? Mal had given Kitt the suspect's name, after all, and given that he hosted a podcast, ominously titled *The Cloven Cast*, it hadn't taken Grace long to track the guy down online. The fact that Peter had been released from police questioning within the hour didn't give Kitt much hope that he would be of help in cracking the case. But even if he wasn't suspect number one, she reasoned that he was still an occult expert and might be able to move the investigation forward in other ways. Certainly, it was worth using her lunch break from her shift at the library to find out if there was any useful information he hadn't shared with the police.

'I've been following this case since it started,' Peter said, tearing open a little carton of cream and pouring it into his coffee before giving it a quick stir. When Grace had contacted him about a meeting, she'd claimed that she and Kitt were bloggers and fans of the podcast, who wanted to get his take on the case of the Vampire Killer. In return they had offered him a cuppa and a slice of cake at a café not far from his house in Fulford, alongside a number of shameless platitudes about his work. Peter had taken his time responding to the email but ultimately he had, as Kitt predicted he might, succumbed to the flattery.

As the café was outside the town centre, it wasn't much like the quaint establishments Kitt was used to, nothing more than a roadside greasy spoon, really. Still, it was the best place that served hot beverages within walking distance of both Peter's home address and the library. She could put up with the smell of bacon fat hanging in the air for half an hour or so if it brought them closer to catching their killer.

'I'm sure this case has sparked the interest of many people who have an interest in the occult,' said Kitt.

'Yes, you've got it in one, thank you,' Tremble said, rapping his knuckles on the metal table. When he relaxed his hands again Kitt couldn't help but notice that the nails on his thumbs were longer than they were on the other fingers and were filed to a point. 'That's a normal person's reaction to noticing an occult podcaster taking pictures at crime scenes like these. I was just there to report on what had happened. But of course that's not how the police saw it when they dragged me in for questioning yesterday. The copper who questioned me made it seem like it was case closed when I walked in there, like he'd already decided I was the one going around draining people's blood. Ruddy bearded oaf.'

Tremble's voice had become louder as he remembered the accusatory nature of the police's questions, and at the mention of draining blood, a couple on a nearby table quickly dabbed their mouths with serviettes and got up to leave.

Kitt noticed Grace doing all she could not to smirk at Tremble's description of her boyfriend. From what little Halloran had been willing to tell her about the interview before they went to sleep last night, he hadn't thought much of Tremble's entitled attitude. She could tell from Tremble's tone just how much he would have rubbed Mal up the wrong way and conceded that if he kept talking about the man she loved like that, staying polite with this interviewee was going to be a challenge. 'I'm sure it wasn't personal, though I don't doubt it felt that way,' Kitt soothed. 'The police have so little time between the warning and the murder that they're probably keen to put the pressure on and get to the bottom of any line of enquiry sooner rather than later.'

'Keen to bark up the wrong tree entirely, is more like it. How about doin' some of your homework, mate?' said Tremble, digging his fork into the slice of chocolate cake they'd bought for him and at the same time digging himself deeper under Kitt's skin. It was clear he wasn't going to stop critiquing Mal's methods and, considering Halloran wasn't the only one with a protective streak, Kitt thought it best to move the conversation forward as quickly as possible before Tremble said something she couldn't let lie.

'Thankfully, in instances like these, you can just provide the police with your alibi and that should be the end of the matter, eh?'

'Ever tried providing an alibi for midnight on three separate evenings a month apart?' Tremble sneered. He was thin in the face and his features became very mean-looking as he did so. 'And they wanted to know where I was on all the dates the marks got left on the doors. What do I look like, a walking calendar?'

'You've a good point there, like,' said Grace. 'Providing

alibis for the days the marks got put on the door is probably easy enough if you keep a diary or online calendar. But when it comes to the killings, I suppose it might be difficult to provide alibis for that time of day if you live alone.'

'I live with my parents, but they're always long asleep by midnight. Get up about five in the morning, you know how folks can get later in life when they're up at crack of dawn for no reason. How do you prove you were in your room reading if nobody else can vouch for it?'

'So, you weren't able to provide the police with alibis?' said Grace, a casual note in her voice. 'I bet that went down like a lead balloon.'

'I did manage to provide them with enough for them to let me go but it was a right old job. And when I hesitated and had a think about it they were straight on my case. Even though it was obvious I was only there because it's something the podcast listeners would be interested in. Thankfully, after looking up some details on my phone, I was able to give alibis for the days the markings were painted on the victims' doors. And I could provide alibis for two of the murders. I happened to be interviewing someone over Zoom for the podcast during the first murder. The guy I was interviewing was based in the US and half eleven GMT was the only time he could do so he can vouch that we talked for more than an hour at the time the first murder took place.'

'Well, that's something,' said Kitt. 'Definitely puts a dent in any argument the police might make that you were involved with this terrible business.'

'Yeah, and during the third murder I was out with some mates having a few drinks. Can't prove where I was during the middle murder, though, not that I should have to. They won't find any evidence pointing to me, I can tell you that.'

'Glad to hear it,' said Kitt, though as she said this she did wonder just for a moment if Tremble believed the police wouldn't find any evidence because there wasn't any to find, or because he believed he'd covered his tracks so well the police would never get onto him. He may have had alibis for two of the murders but that wasn't enough to outright get him off the hook. The murders were intricate enough for the killer to have an accomplice. And who knew how twisted Tremble's obsession with the occult really was when it came down to it? To spend time recording and editing a monthly podcast about it, his interest certainly had to be more than passing.

'Have any of your listeners got in touch about the case?' said Grace. 'With it being so tangled up with the occult, we wondered if perhaps they've come up with some theories that we haven't thought of.'

Tremble scratched the side of his head, ruffling his greasy mop of brown hair at the same time. 'Oh aye, quite a few people have been writing in about the Vampire Killer. I'm not sure anything in them would help catch the guy who's behind it, it is more just people expressing how morbidly fascinated they are by the whole case, while at the same time being scared to death they'll come home to find a V marked on their door. Most of the people who listen to the show are connected to the occult in some way. I must admit I did think about taking the show off the air until they catch the killer, you know, in case hosting it made me a target. But then, I thought, why should I give up doing something I really enjoy because some looney is going around killing people? Intimidation, that's what it is. Whoever's doing this they're in it to generate fear in people like me. People who are a bit different.'

'Hmm, yes. You're likely right about that. The killer must thrive on the idea of generating fear to a certain extent. Otherwise they probably wouldn't bother with the markings. It's arguably more torturous to contemplate your own death for eleven days than eleven minutes,' said Kitt. 'As for you putting the podcast on hiatus, to be honest, for all we know, even if you did stop recording, an individual as twisted as the one we're dealing with might come after you just because you have broadcast on that subject in the past.'

'I hadn't thought of that,' Tremble said, losing a bit of the colour in his face.

'What about you?' said Grace. 'If you had to theorize about who the killer was and why they were doing this, what would be your go-to theory? You must have read a lot on the subject.'

'You're right about that, I have. I spend a lot of time in

my room alone, reading, and there's a couple of things that strike me about this case.'

Spends a lot of time in his room alone? Wasn't that exactly how Grace had profiled their killer yesterday morning? That said, if spending time alone in your room so you could read put you on the suspect list, then Kitt would have been suspect number one for every crime going.

'What things?' asked Grace, when Tremble didn't immediately continue.

It struck Kitt that there was something a little odd about Tremble's conversational skills. He seemed to be waiting deliberately for further prompting before speaking. Was this because he wasn't a natural at conversation? Or because he was carefully calculating his next sentences for darker reasons?

'Having visited all three crime scenes, I would say there's a strong chance this bloke has been planning these murders for some time, maybe even a few years.'

'Years?' said Kitt. 'I agree with you that the killer is well-prepared – otherwise some forensic evidence might have turned up – but what makes you think it's taken years for him to act?'

'It's the intricacy of the murders more than anything else. Look at the way he works. Draining a person's blood isn't a two-second job. Of course, we're relying on information journalists have picked up from friends and neighbours since the police have kept the finer details to themselves so we don't know his exact methods, but he drugs his victims. Takes his time. He's confident he's not going to be interrupted.'

'That is true,' said Grace. 'The killings are quite intricate and sort of . . . laborious.'

Kitt thought for a moment. After Rebecca's comment about the amount of blood at the crime scene betraying the perpetrator's level of medical expertise, she had asked Mal how gruesome the scenes were. His unwillingness to be drawn on the specifics left Kitt in no doubt that she was better off not knowing. The only concrete information he would offer, on the off chance that it became significant, was that the blood drawn had been left in jars that originally contained Kellington's jam. Given this particular brand's popularity, Kitt wasn't convinced this would in any way narrow down the search for the killer. She did, however, decide there and then that she'd never be able to buy another jar of Kellington's herself.

'The killer doesn't let any obstacle stop him either,' Tremble continued, snapping Kitt out of her thoughts. 'He even found a way around police protection. That's not easy by anyone's standards.'

'I suppose not,' said Kitt. 'But from that alone you think the killer has been plotting this for years?'

'I just get an overall picture that he has a contingency for every possible hiccup. No forensic evidence. No CCTV footage, and getting past not one but two police officers. If he hasn't been planning it for some time, then there's only one other explanation I can think of.'

'What's that?' asked Grace, for yet again Tremble had paused where one might have expected him to naturally continue.

'Well, there's one sure way of avoiding being caught in the future and that's to see it before it happens. You're asking me my opinion and based on all that's happened I'd have to say that we're dealing with a clairvoyant killer.'

Kitt resisted the urge to sigh, but only just. Perhaps she shouldn't have expected a serious theory from somebody who ran a podcast called *The Cloven Cast* but she had hoped, given the urgency of the matter, he might have offered a more credible theory than that. She could have got that kind of suggestion out of Ruby, if she'd wanted it. But then, on thinking about Ruby, Kitt's stomach tightened. If she didn't catch this killer, and quickly, she wouldn't be hearing any more of Ruby's wild theories and, for all her protestations, she knew that she would miss them, and the bewilderingly eccentric woman who delivered them.

'Oooh,' said Grace. 'That would make the killer impossible to catch. They'd always know the risks of everything, how they might get caught.'

Kitt glared at Grace for encouraging Tremble.

'What about if they weren't clairvoyant?' said Kitt, keeping her tone of voice as level as she could. 'Are there any other theories you'd care to venture?'

'There is one thing I wondered about. To do with the marks on the victims' necks. There are a few different vampire cults across the UK.'

'Vampire cults? What does that entail?' Grace said warily.

'There are people out there who think they're real vampires and they form these kind of exclusive clubs. People pay a fortune to be part of them.'

'Please don't tell me they drink blood?' said Grace, grabbing her throat and making the most outlandish of expressions.

'The rumours are that they do but all the groups that I've heard of say it's all animal sacrifice, not human. Otherwise the police would be onto them like a shot,' Tremble said, clicking his fingers. 'They use rabbits, apparently.'

'Poor bunnies,' Grace said, her eyes widening.

'Haven't I seen you eat rabbit once or twice, when it's on the menu?' said Kitt.

'Er, well yes, but that's different,' said Grace. 'Oh all right, maybe it isn't. Now I've got a sudden hankering to go vegetarian.'

Kitt, though in agreement with Grace's sentiments, didn't want to be sidetracked and thus turned her attention back to Tremble. 'So, you think one of these cults might be behind the killings? Wouldn't the police in other districts have looked into such organizations?'

'For all I know, they already have and found nothing,' said Tremble, 'which is why they have to come around taking pot-shots at me.'

'Thinking about it though,' Kitt said, while making a mental note to ask Halloran if anyone had spoken to any groups of that nature, 'it's a bit obvious, isn't it? I mean, given the profile of groups like that and the nature of the murders, wouldn't the finger point straight at them? Seems like a pretty quick way to incriminate yourself.'

'I'm not sure if it's a member of the group themselves,' Tremble clarified. 'It could just be a disgruntled wannabe who doesn't have the money to get into the club.'

'If that was the case,' said Kitt, 'they might want to commit crimes that incriminated a cult like that. Make it seem like they were responsible for the crimes as payback for their rejection. Do you know of any cults like that in the Yorkshire region?'

'There is one I can think of,' said Tremble. 'One of our listeners noted that the locations that have been targeted so far, they all sort of revolve around Whitby.'

'Whitby,' said Kitt. 'They think the killer might use it as a base to work from while committing the murders in other places to avoid immediate suspicion?'

'One of my listeners floated that idea on the forum early this morning after the news broke about a possible fourth victim in York. Quite a few people thought it was an interesting idea. Middlesbrough was hit first, if you remember. Then Scarborough. Doesn't seem to be any geographical link between those two except for the fact they're both in Yorkshire, but then Malton was hit and now someone in our city has been threatened. If you draw a line between all these places Whitby is the major settlement in the middle of it all.'

'And there's one of these vampire cults in the Whitby area?' said Kitt. 'I suppose that might be the case given the town's link with the most famous vampire of all – Dracula.'

'Exactly, and actually, the group I'm thinking of call themselves the Creed of Count Dracula. I know, how's that for subtlety?'

A small shiver ran down Kitt's back at the sound of that name. Tremble was right about the locations now that she thought about it. You couldn't quite draw a perfect circle and put Whitby at the middle because on one side of the town, there was nothing but the North Sea. On land however, it was a different matter. As Kitt pictured the map in her mind, she noted that there was a bit of a gap in the circle to the north-west between York and Middlesbrough – forty miles or so – but all of the towns between those two places were quite small. Places such as Thirsk, Northallerton and Yarm. Towns like that were more tight-knit. Residents there were probably more likely to notify the Neighbourhood Watch scheme of suspicious behaviour. With that in mind, perhaps the killer had thought such a target too big a risk, at least at first. Perhaps they planned to fill in that gap once they were done with Ruby.

If one considered only the larger towns however, the major settlement at the heart of all the locations targeted was Whitby. And with a group like the Creed of Count Dracula operating there, doing who-knows-what after sunset, this seemed like a nugget of information that shouldn't be ignored.

SEVEN

'Kitt, come on, this is nothing more than a hunch at best,' said Halloran, sitting on their bed watching Kitt pack the last few things into her suitcase.

'Oh, and you've never acted on a hunch, I suppose? I doubt you and I would be here together right now if you didn't,' said Kitt, struggling with the zip on her suitcase, which, due to the fact she'd had this luggage as long as she could remember and always packed more books than she could ever possibly read while she was away somewhere, was on the brink of breaking from the strain. 'We've mere days left before this killer strikes again, Mal, I can't afford to dither about.'

'I'm well aware of how little time we've got. But that's all the more reason not to squander that time on dead ends. Not one line of enquiry we've explored has pointed to Whitby,' said Halloran. 'Only one of the victims had been anywhere near Whitby in the months preceding her death and that's because she lived in Middlesbrough and had had a daytrip to the coast. The police in Boro have already interviewed the guy who heads up the Creed of Count Dracula – Stoke Bramley—'

'A name changed by deed poll if ever there was one,' Kitt interjected, shaking her head.

'And DS Johnson at the station in Boro said that, other than being one of the smarmiest guys they'd ever crossed paths with, they couldn't find anything incriminating about Bramley,' Halloran cut back in. 'Apparently, he debunked the idea that they engaged in animal slaughter right out the gate. I asked for a list of their members anyway – they're quite selective so even after five years in operation there are only thirty people from across the UK on that list – and none of them are engaging in any kind of suspicious activity according to the local stations where they live. They've all got alibis for at least two of the murders, to boot.'

'Stoke Bramley and his members might not be involved though. This might just be the work of someone in the Whitby area who wants to harm them or discredit them. See them shut down. I can't think that many of the local residents are at ease with the idea of a group of people like that living on their doorstep. I think it warrants further investigation,' said Kitt.

'I respectfully disagree,' said Halloran. 'The list of pre-scriptions for Xylazine are a much surer bet.'

'But you haven't had even one suspect come out of that

list yet,' said Kitt. 'All lines of enquiry are leading nowhere. Grace was researching from dawn until dusk yesterday and we spent the evening after my library shift visiting evangelical institutions. Not exactly my preferred Saturday night activity as it stands but to add insult to injury not one of those visits brought us any closer to finding the killer.'

'Like any investigation, it's a process of elimination, you know that.'

'Yes, I do. But I could have done without that visit to the Priestesses of the Virgin Mary. Grace, the little imp, filled out an application form to become a member on my behalf. I only just caught it before she slipped it into the letter box.'

Halloran chuckled. 'Maybe she thought it was a good undercover opportunity.'

'You might not think it's so funny – they make you take a vow of celibacy, you know?'

'I never would have let you take your undercover work that far,' Halloran said with a smile before kissing her hand.

Kitt gave him a grudging smile in return but then, in a flash, her thoughts were back on the case. 'I know you think it's a long shot, but we've got to start thinking outside the box on this one. I thought for sure we'd get something out of the list of satanist organizations but even that was a dead end.'

'Have you considered the reason we haven't had any more breaks is because Tremble is involved in these killings, and we just haven't found any proof yet?'

'I thought you'd already been through his phone and financial records?'

'We have, but just because we didn't find anything doesn't mean he isn't involved with it. We don't have sufficient evidence to search his property so who knows what's going on behind closed doors. He couldn't prove where he was during the second murder either, which means he could be an accomplice.'

'I have to admit I did find him a little bit odd.'

'Maybe you were picking up on something deeper; maybe your instincts were kicking in because you knew that something wasn't right about him. We are still keeping track of his movements through his phone. We haven't totally ruled him out yet.'

'So you think, what? That he's sending me off to Whitby on a wild goose chase to throw us off the track?'

'It's possible.'

'It's also possible, given the locations involved, that the killer is based in the Whitby area. When you think about it, it makes total sense.'

'How exactly does it make total sense?'

'Well, the killings are vampire-esque in nature and—'

'Don't.'

'What?'

'Don't argue that because *Dracula* is set in Whitby, it's a clue to catching a serial killer.'

'It's not just that,' Kitt said, though she privately admitted that that was going to be the main thrust of her argument before Mal had so quickly dismissed it. 'Think about it in a broader context. Whitby is the home of all things occult. The spring goth weekender is just a week away. The place has become something of a Mecca for all things weird and esoteric. It's not unthinkable that someone as obsessed with the occult as this killer might base themselves there.'

'I suppose that's true,' Halloran said, rubbing his beard. 'But with the goth weekend so close how have you even managed to secure accommodation in Whitby at such short notice?'

'It turns out the pressure the councils are putting on your chief constable isn't totally unfounded. When we went to book online there was plenty of availability. There's no doubt a serial killer on the loose is keeping people away, particularly from the goth weekend. Granted, not every person of the gothic persuasion has occult leanings, but quite a few do.' Kitt tutted then as her phone started buzzing. 'It's Ruby,' she said, with a note of concern in her voice.

'What? She's not supposed to be making any bloody phone calls. If she talks to anyone and lets slip where she is, the safe house is not going to be safe for long,' said Halloran. 'Put it on speaker, will you?'

Kitt swiped the phone and hit the speaker phone button. 'Ruby?'

''Ello, love,' came a familiar voice down the line.

'Ruby,' said Halloran. 'Is DS Redmond there?'

'Aye.'

'Put him on for a minute, will you?'

There was a shuffling sound and then Redmond's voice sounded over the speaker. 'Sir?'

'Mind telling me what happened to the "no phone calls" policy?'

'This is the only phone call I've let her make, honest, sir. I weren't going to. I've been telling her that it's against protocol, like. But then she started giving me this look, like she were secretly putting a hex on me and was going to turn me into a frog or something. Put me right on edge, it did. After what I found in her spare room, I couldn't take any chances. So, on balance, I thought it was safer to let her call. Didn't think you'd mind since it was Kitt.'

'A word of advice, Redmond,' said Halloran. 'Hexes are not real. Serial killers are. Make sure there are no phone calls to anyone else.'

'Yes, sir. Of course, sir.'

There was a moment's pause while Ruby grabbed hold of the phone again.

''Ello?'

'I'm just about to set off for the coast, Ruby,' said Kitt. 'So I'll need to make this quick.'

'Aye, I know, not a minute to waste. But DS Redmond told me you were planning to go to Whitby and I just thought I'd better let you know about a few things that have come out of my meditations and visions over the last few days.'

'Ruby, I don't think—'

But it was too late, Ruby had already worked herself up which, Kitt knew from past experience, meant there was absolutely no stopping her.

'We mustn't ignore the signs, love, never ignore the signs. They're always trying to point the way, guide you to where you're meant to be. To our ultimate destiny and—'

'Ruby!'

'Yes, love. Sorry, love, you know how I get about my signs.'

'Well, right now all omens are pointing to a vampire cult based in the Whitby area. Some people think it's just a hunch, but I think it's an important sign.' Kitt gave Mal a pointed look, enjoying the look of bemusement on his face as he shook his head at her.

'No, no, no,' said Ruby. 'That's nowt but balderdash. Based on what I've been seeing, I don't think you're looking for a vampire.'

'You don't,' Kitt said, narrowing her eyes. Ruby was usually the first in line to float implausible theories.

'No, I think you're looking for a witch, like me.'

'What makes you say that? The fact that the killer is targeting other people associated with the occult?' said Kitt.

'No – each of the killings has taken place on a full moon. That's a very witchy thing to take notice of. Vampires aren't so bothered about it. I suppose now that I think about it, you could be looking for a werewolf or similar shapeshifter but on balance I'd have to say it's most likely the work of a witch.'

Kitt opened her mouth to respond to Ruby, but wasn't quite sure what to say. Did she think Kitt believed she was looking for a real vampire rather than a man who had watched one too many Hammer Horror films? Or that she thought werewolves really roamed the moors on a full moon?

'Can that be right?' said Halloran. 'That all the killings have taken place on a full moon?'

'I wouldn't know, my moon diary is in my other handbag,' Kitt said with a smirk.

'It's right all right, I know because I keep track of the moon's movements, just like the other witches out there. Just like the one who I think you're looking for. Eeee. I wonder if it's a descendent of the Yorkshire Witch who's behind all this.'

'If that's the case, Whitby's going to be a dead end. Mary Bateman hailed from Thirsk,' said Kitt, wondering why she was even bothering to debate this with Ruby. Her wild theories never panned out.

'Oh aye, I suppose you're right. Ooh, maybe it's a descendent of Jeannie.'

'Who?' Kitt said, knowing at once she would regret asking.

'Jeannie were a witch who lived in a cave in Mulgrave Woods near Sandsend. She tormented local farmers, or so they say – any loss of livestock was blamed on her. She was probably just a scapegoat but that doesn't mean that her great-great-great-great-grandchild isn't taking revenge on the uncaring society that excluded their ancestor. I recommend going straight to Hob's cave if you want answers about this case.'

'But Ruby, if a witch is behind this, why the red marks, like a vampire, on the victims' necks?'

'Well that's just the perfect disguise now, isn't it?'

Kitt shook her head at Halloran and rolled her eyes. Though the fact that the murders were all committed on a night where there was a full moon might be significant to the killer, and there was a chance the killer practised witchcraft, she doubted they were looking for a descendent of someone who – for all Kitt knew – was a fictional character in a folktale. More likely they were looking for somebody obsessed with witches and witchcraft. Yes, there was a chance as she had discussed with Grace and Evie in the park that the killer did engage in occult practices and was viewing the victims as a sacrifice, but surely those that had been targeted so far were people that a witch would consider associates, or at the very least like-minded.

'There's another thing too,' Ruby said, just as Kitt thought she'd had her designated quota of weird for the day. 'I saw a butterfly tattoo in my vision last night. It was the main image. I think the murderer has a butterfly tattoo. So look out for that and beware, beware!'

'OK,' said Kitt, doing all she could to keep her tone polite as Ruby continued to get herself far too overexcited. 'I'll definitely make a note of that, Ruby. I don't want you to worry, OK? We're doing everything we can to get to the bottom of this.'

'I know, lass, I don't want you to worry either. I know you'll do your best to catch the killer but if you don't, I don't want you to blame yourself for whatever happens to me. I'm not afraid of dying.'

At Ruby's words Kitt suddenly felt very close to tears. 'You may not be afraid of dying but I'm not about to just stand aside and let that happen.'

'I know, love, but there are some things that are just beyond our control. When it's our time, it's our time. Look, I'll be in touch again if I have any more insights. If they won't let me phone, I'll use telepathy.'

'Or you could just ask Redmond to pass a message on through Mal.'

'Telepathy is my preferred method but admittedly the message doesn't always get through.'

Kitt, at last losing patience with Ruby's shtick and getting concerned that she might miss her bus to Whitby, reassured the old woman as best she could and ended the call. As she did so her black cat Iago leapt onto the bed, sat facing Halloran and fixed his yellow-eyed stare on him.

'You will remember to feed Iago while I'm gone, won't you?' she said. Iago and Halloran had never really warmed to each other. Both believed they should take prized place in Kitt's heart. For a long time Iago hadn't had any rivals for Kitt's affections and when she took up with Halloran he didn't take well to the possibility of being usurped.

Halloran looked at the cat but managed to keep his expression just about on the right side of disdain. 'I'll feed him. If things busy up at this end or for any reason I have to come out and join you in Whitby, I'll ask next door to make sure he's fed.'

'You know,' Kitt said, thinking, 'I don't like to encourage Ruby so I didn't say anything on the phone but it's funny she should bring up the subject of tattoos. Becca said that the holes in the victims' neck could have been caused by a needle and tattooists use needles.'

'That's an avenue we've been exploring too,' said Halloran. 'We've been canvassing at tattoo parlours and acupuncture clinics in all the locations there have been murders. So far we've turned up nothing. But we'll keep looking. Something is leaving those marks on the victims' necks and we intend to find out what.'

'I think that's where I'll start when we get to Whitby,' said Kitt. 'Any tattoo parlours or acupuncture clinics.'

'Not the Whitby Bookshop?'

'Sadly, due to how little time there is left between now and when the murder is due to take place, all shopping will have to be saved until after I've brought the killer to justice. Although . . .'

'Yes?'

'I was reading online about an occult bookshop in Whitby that might be worth stopping off at first.'

'Why am I not surprised that you managed to find a bookshop that links with the case?'

'It's not a pleasure trip, thank you very much. I may find some volumes that serve as useful research, and who knows? Maybe the owner has the inside track on the Creed of Count Dracula?'

'A pretty flimsy excuse for prioritizing a bookshop visit but I'd expect nothing less,' Halloran teased, but Kitt wasn't laughing. Instead, she nudged Iago out of his spot – and received a startled hiss in reply – so she could sit next to Halloran on the bed.

'What Ruby said, about not being afraid to die. Are you able to say the same?'

'I'm not sure,' said Halloran. 'I think it's closer to say that, because of the job I do, I accept the fact that I might die at some unexpected point, sooner than expected, but I don't see a great deal of point on dwelling on it. It's going to happen to all of us and we don't really get a say in when that is.'

'Very philosophical,' Kitt said with an admiring note in her voice. 'I don't think I'm there yet. To accept the truth that there'll be a time when me and all the people I love just aren't here any more. You'd think by my age I'd have processed that. Especially given how many times I've worked on murder cases. But then again, maybe that's part of why

I fight so hard to find the truth about those who we have lost too soon.'

'I think it's a difficult thing for anyone to process,' said Halloran.

'Even though we all have our time to go, nobody should have to go at the hands of cruelty. Like Ruby will if we don't find a way forward. We need to solve this one, Mal,' she said. 'Ruby's a lot to handle sometimes but when it comes down to it, she spends so much time seeking me out because she hasn't really got anyone else. We're the only ones she can turn to right now.'

'We'll solve this, we will,' he replied, wrapping his arms around her.

She smiled at his reassurance but deep down the feeling of dread that had been making her stomach churn for the last four days seemed to grow stronger.

When it came to investigations, Kitt knew what she was doing, to a certain extent. She'd worked several murder cases now and had always been more help than hindrance, just about. But there was something about the meticulous planning of these murders that made her wonder if she really had what it took to catch the killer out before the eleven days were up. It was a doubt planted by a little voice that she didn't much want to listen to. A voice that was telling her that she was in way over her head.

EIGHT

Broomsticks, Black Cats and Books was possibly the quirkiest little bookshop Kitt had ever seen, and she'd been in her fair share over the years. Its signage boasted swirling typography in dark purple. The window was packed with boxes of tarot cards and thick hardback books on every esoteric subject Kitt could think of. Even the shop's geographic position had dramatic flair. It stood at the base of the 199 steps which led to the East Cliff in Whitby. Hundreds of tourists climbed up there every day to visit St Mary's church and the windswept ruins of the abbey. From there, they could look over this idyllic harbour town that graced the front of many a postcard. Kitt looked up the winding stone steps for a moment, towards the brooding sky. The weather had turned gusty and cloudy since she and Grace had arrived at the coast the previous afternoon which made it a bit easier to turn down sightseeing opportunities in favour of official case business.

Yesterday afternoon had, for the most part, been taken up with the bus ride between York and Whitby. Grace, who didn't travel so well up and down dale, had spent the vast majority of the journey pushing her head up to the narrow bus windows trying to get some fresh air into her lungs in much the same way a dog might hang its head out of a car window. What little remained of the day after they had arrived was spent settling into the Elysium Guest House over on the West Cliff and doing as much online research as they could about the Creed of Count Dracula. The leader of the cult, Stoke Bramley, seemed to have said enough to appease the police. Moreover, Halloran had confirmed that all thirty of the current members had alibis for a significant number of the murders, and the days on which the marks were painted on the victims' doors. Still, Kitt couldn't shake the feeling – given the nature of the murders – that the killer had some connection to their 'organization'. Alongside Tremble, Bramley and his followers remained on the suspect list at least until Kitt had had a chance to speak to the cult leader for herself.

'Wouldn't it be better if we spoke to the people who have access to long, sharp objects first?' said Grace. 'The acupuncture clinic is just down the road.'

'Before we do any specific digging it's going to be useful to get some background information,' said Kitt. 'And in my experience bookshop owners are extremely knowledgeable people. The killer is targeting people associated with the occult, this bookshop specializes in the occult. The investigation starts here.'

Grace sighed as Kitt pushed open the door of the bookshop. Clearly she wasn't any more convinced by her rationale than Halloran was. And, admittedly, Kitt did have her eye on one of the small, black cat toys that adorned the window dressing and looked the spit of Iago – even though the ruthless beast would no doubt tear the thing to pieces within seconds of her getting it home – but other than that this was to be strictly business. With only six days left before the killer was due to strike again there was no time to lose.

As soon as she was over the threshold, Kitt began admiring the bookshop. It was small but the owner had made the most of the space with floor-to-ceiling bookshelves on two of the walls and a central aisle packed with all kinds of occult paraphernalia. A couple of people were browsing the shelves but as it was still early on a Monday morning, the shop assistant behind the desk was the only other person in there.

Kitt meant to go straight up to the assistant and start firing questions, truly she did. But even between the door and the desk she spotted several volumes she wouldn't mind having on her bookshelf back at home. She resolved to come back after the case was over for a thorough inspection, but for now she picked up a biography of Bram Stoker and one of the plush black cats she'd seen in the window. The Stoker biography might be of help as they took their investigation into the Creed of Count Dracula further, Kitt told herself. As for the cat toy, well, that couldn't exactly be explained away as an investigative essential, but the shop assistant was surely more likely to offer up information if Kitt and Grace ingratiated themselves by making a considerable purchase.

As they approached the counter, Kitt studied the man sitting behind it. He was huddled up in a thick navy cardigan and had shortly trimmed grey hair that covered only the sides of his head. A pair of delicate spectacles rested on his nose and he raised a warm smile as Kitt and Grace drew near.

'Just these for you, lass?' he asked.

'For now,' said Kitt with sincere regret. 'We're on a bit of a time limit today but I will be back for a proper browse at a later date.'

'You'll be very welcome when you return,' said the man, before accepting Kitt's money, counting back her change and wrapping the book and cat toy in a black paper bag.

'Are you the owner of this wonderful bookshop?' Kitt asked.

'Arnold Sykes,' he said with a nod. 'But everyone calls me Arnie, and you can too.'

'I'm Kitt Hartley,' said Kitt. 'And this is my associate Grace Edwards.'

'Pleasure to meet you. 'Ere, you're not wanting to buy the place, are you? People are always asking but I'm not looking to sell, I'm afraid. I know it's a prime location but I love this place far too much to let her go.'

'Oh no, it's nothing like that,' said Kitt, choosing her words carefully. She had already discussed with Grace that they couldn't let on to anybody they interviewed that they were connected to Ruby. If the killer did live in Whitby, their interviewees might know him. In some cases, they might be acquainted with the murderer and not even realize it. If they told such a person that there were people in town who had direct access to their next victim, who knew what that could mean for Ruby? Let alone Kitt and Grace themselves. 'Actually, we're conducting a civilian investigation into the Vampire Killer murders,' said Kitt. 'We heard that a new victim had been targeted and although the police are doing a very good job, I'm sure, bringing such an individual to justice is no small task. We run our own private investigation agency so decided to have a go at solving it ourselves. See if we can save a life or two.'

'It's good of you to step forward and help like that,' Arnie said with a frown. 'It's a terrible business. I daren't turn on't news a lot of the time. I'm scared stiff he's coming for me next. Our shop is quite high profile within the occult community, you know? Most of the time that's a blessing. A bookshop can never have too many loyal customers. But right now, I must admit, I wish we flew a bit more under the radar. It just seems so random. I'm praying the police catch him so I can rest a bit easier, and of course so he doesn't get his hands on his latest target.'

'We're going to see what we can do about that,' said Kitt. 'We thought, given its status in the occult community, your shop might be a good place start asking some background questions.'

'I'd happily be of help but I'm not sure how much use I'd be to you.'

'Maybe more than you realize. We believe that the killer might be operating out of the Whitby area,' said Grace.

Arnie's face turned white in an instant. 'W-what makes you think that? Oh, God, you don't think he's one of me customers, do you? That hadn't even crossed my mind. Folk round 'ere are so friendly, you know?'

'Given the nature of the crimes, there is a chance that you could have served him in this shop if he was doing research into the occult and is based in the area,' said Kitt. 'But that's just a theory, of course, supposition, and you shouldn't let it worry you too much. As far as we know there haven't been any related opportunistic killings. There's always an eleven-day warning.'

'If I saw the killer's mark on the front door of the shop, the bloke probably wouldn't have to come and kill me 'imself. I'm fairly sure that just seeing that symbol would be enough to stop my heart on the spot.'

'You and me both,' said Grace.

'Hopefully we'll catch him before it comes to that,' said

Kitt. 'To that end, I wondered if you'd had any dealings with the Creed of Count Dracula?'

'Oh, you don't think they're involved, do you?'

'We don't have any evidence that they are,' said Kitt. 'We're really just making enquiries because of their link with vampire culture. Do you know any of the members?'

'From what I understand there are a few core members who live at their Whitby address beyond the west side of town. The rest just visit as and when they have residential events. One or two of their members come in here on a regular basis. Mostly on winter evenings when it's dark before the shop closes. You don't see them around much during the day but you can spot them because they wear a silver pin somewhere on their clothing. It's shaped into a letter D in old-style script,' said Arnie.

'Hm,' said Grace. 'A letter to signify membership. Just like the letter V to mark out the victims.'

'I hadn't thought of that,' said Arnie. 'Although, to be fair, we don't know that symbol is a letter V. I was thinking, like, it could be a Roman numeral.'

'Oh,' said Kitt. 'Yes, it could. I'm usually quite good at spotting alternative interpretations but you beat me to that one, Arnie.'

Arnie's cheeks rouged at Kitt's praise. 'I could be wrong, it just struck me t'other week that it's not something anyone's mentioned in any of the coverage. We've assumed V for vampire because of the marks on the victims' necks. But perhaps there's another explanation. Or maybe the numeral is a clue to finding the killer.'

'I'm going to make a note of that, thank you,' said Kitt.

'Have you ever had any trouble with members of the Creed of Count Dracula?' said Grace. 'Or do you know if they've got into trouble in the local community?'

'As far as I know, they keep themselves to themselves. You see them out and about during the goth weekends, of course, but I must admit I haven't heard any complaints directly. They all seem quite mellow folk. Although . . .'

'What?' said Kitt.

'I don't think there's particularly owt untoward about the core members of the group but they do attract a lot of wannabes to the area. They're quite an exclusive club, not everyone can pay the entry fee, if you know what I mean. Maybe someone out there is trying to emulate their behaviour but they've taken it to a dark place.'

'Is there someone in particular that you're thinking of?' said Grace.

'No,' said Arnie, 'I can't say that there is but there are quite a few exclusive covens and groups within the occult community and to me, though the people who set them up seem to always have the best of intentions, any group with a set of criteria to join it spells trouble. Some people don't take rejection well and I know Stoke Bramley has turned a lot of people away. If you ask me, it was only a matter of time before there'd be consequences to that.'

NINE

Kitt paused for a moment, considering Arnie's line of reasoning. Mal had said the group had been in operation for five years, and in that time they had acquired just thirty members from across the UK. She didn't know how many people might apply to be part of an organization like the Creed of Count Dracula on an annual basis but she imagined it to be a lot more than six. Besides anything else, groups like those tended to thrive on their exclusivity. The way human psychology worked, only accepting a handful of people every year was bound to make those places more desirable. Kitt would be interested to know more about what criteria the collective used to select their members and what might make them turn somebody away. As Arnie suggested, exclusion from a group like that would likely cut deep with those who didn't make it through the selection process, but would someone really start a killing spree over something like that? Might they not simply spread some vicious rumours or in extremis commit arson on their premises? At this stage, Kitt couldn't quite convince herself that this alone would be motive for the kind of murders that were playing out.

'What about anyone else in the local community?' said Grace. 'Has there been any unusual behaviour from any of your customers, or have you heard any rumours from visitors to the shop?'

'Good grief,' Arnie said with a light chuckle, 'you've got to remember, this is Yorkshire. Unusual behaviour sort of comes with the territory.'

Grace started to laugh and Kitt joined in, knowing exactly what Arnie meant. When Kitt described the behaviour of most of her acquaintances to people outside the region, they so often wouldn't believe what went on.

Arnie eyed the other customers who were still browsing the shelves and then lowered his voice. 'Truth be told, there are a couple of people that you might want to have a word with. I don't for a second think they've got owt to do with this, mind, but they are people who you would definitely describe as odd. If you're looking for folk exhibiting what you might call strange behaviour, then you probably want to speak to them.'

'And they have links with the occult?' said Kitt.

'In a manner of speaking,' said Arnie. 'There's a bloke in a care home over in Sandsend. It's a sad story, mind. His name's Cyril. Think 'is last name is Armitage. He seems like a lovely little chap.'

'But he's been acting strange lately?' said Grace.

'He's been in a few times over the last few months and bought a series of books about witch hunts and witch hunting.'

'Lots of people are interested in that topic,' said Kitt. 'I've read a few books on the subject myself over the years.'

'What 'aven't you read about?' said Grace, shaking her head.

'Oh aye, but not everyone interested in that subject believes themselves to be the reincarnated spirit of James I himself.'

'He . . . really believes that?' said Kitt.

Arnie nodded.

Kitt frowned. 'Hmmm. Mr Dick.'

Arnie cleared his throat and Grace looked at Kitt sidelong. Once she noticed their reactions, Kitt clarified: 'From *David Copperfield*. Charles Dickens? Mr Dick thinks he has some sort of strange psychic link with King Charles I.'

'Oh, oh, I see,' said Arnie. 'Well, yes, it might be something like that. But I'm afraid the cause isn't anything to do with psychic energy. Poor bloke has early onset dementia, Alzheimer's, from what I understand. I think the doctors have put him on a small buffet of tablets to manage it as best they can. If you ask me, though, just from what I've seen, like, the dosage is a bit too high. He doesn't seem very lucid.'

'The poor man,' Kitt said, shaking her head. Her maternal

grandfather had suffered from Alzheimer's before he'd passed about a decade ago. She had never quite recovered from the abrupt changes in his behaviour and how difficult it had sometimes been for him to recognize those who loved him. Heartbreaking didn't even begin to cover it. 'The medicines to manage such symptoms only provide temporary relief and there are usually side-effects.'

'Aye, well, he has a carer with him when he comes into the shop because he's perfectly lucid one minute and the next he's talking about cleansing the earth of witchcraft,' said Arnie. 'Apparently, a few years back now, just before the dementia set in, he did some am-dram and played James I in one of their productions. What was the name of the play? Oh, yes, that's right. *The Curse of James I, A Musical.*'

'Sounds . . . interesting,' Kitt said, keeping her tone as polite as possible.

'I didn't see it myself but at the time it did quite well for reviews in the local press; well, you know, for amateur theatre. It was written and directed by a local too. Stella Hemsworth. She had a bit of an acting career once over – mostly regional TV and adverts – and now she runs the amateur dramatics company in Whitby. That play was her directorial debut, if I recall.'

'And performing in this play has had some effect on Cyril's state of mind?' said Kitt.

'There were a few gory scenes in it from what I heard but I'm not sure if it's quite right to say the play had an effect on him. His carer thinks he's got himself muddled and relives the play in his head sometimes.'

'Yes, sadly that can happen with people managing dementia,' said Kitt. 'And, of course, there's so little support now for those with mental health issues that anything like that can be a real challenge, especially when it first happens. But the man you describe sounds more confused than anything else. I'm not convinced he's a viable suspect even if he does spend some of his time believing himself to be James I.'

'I'm not big on my history but I'm guessing James I didn't like witches much,' said Grace.

'I think it's fair to say he was somewhat obsessed with them,' said Kitt. 'There were hundreds of witch hunts and witch trials during his reign.'

'So this bloke believes he's the reincarnated spirit of a guy who made it his mission to wipe out witches?' said Grace. 'Since every victim has had some link with the occult, isn't that a motive? Or, at least, a sort of imagined motive?'

Arnie shook his head. 'I felt obliged to mention him because of his delusions but Cyril is quite a frail man in his early sixties, and besides the fact that he seems completely harmless, I don't think he'd have the physical or mental capacity to pull off these murders. The killer has been meticulous. Cyril, well, sometimes he's with it and sometimes he's not.'

'We certainly can't jump to conclusions just because of

his mental health status,' said Kitt. 'It's a strange obsession for a person to have but from what you've said, it doesn't sound like he's our man.'

'And that leads me on to my second suggestion. I know the police releases about the killer have all said it's most likely to be a man, but what if the person you're looking for isn't a man at all?' said Arnie.

'How do you mean?' said Kitt.

'There's a tattoo shop in the old town called Squid Ink, it's run by a lass called Ayleen Demir.'

At the mention of a tattooist, Kitt's senses stirred. Tattooists were on their list of businesses to interview after what Rebecca had told them about the needles. Of course, Ruby had also asserted that tattoos were involved but Kitt, having seen so many of the old woman's visions come to nothing, was less convinced by that.

'And there's something unusual about this woman?' said Grace.

'She's very open about the fact she's a white witch – probably goes down well with her customer base, to be honest,' said Arnie. 'But she let slip once to someone in the town that her parents died when she was young. You know what town gossips can be like, and I don't know all the ins and outs, but apparently they died in a fire and the fire service couldn't get to the bottom of how the fire started. It was suspected arson, I think.'

'And this happened in Whitby itself?' said Kitt, making

a mental note to see what records they could pull up about the incident.

'No . . . she didn't grow up in Whitby, moved here a few years back. From what I've heard, just from town talk, she grew up in the Dales somewhere. Wensleydale maybe? Or Sandersdale? At any rate, it's one of them two. The people I come into contact with are perhaps more superstitious than average but there are folk about who think she might have had something to do with her parents' deaths.'

'They think she started the fire on purpose?' said Kitt. 'That she meant for her parents to die?'

'I'm not saying it's true,' said Arnie, raising his hands in the air, 'but there are folks who think she might have started the fire through supernatural means. Whether there's owt to that or not, if a person did somehow manage to get away with a crime like that at a young age, it might make them believe they could get away with anything.'

TEN

After leaving Arnie's shop, Kitt and Grace spent the next half hour walking up and down the cobbled streets of Whitby's old town, keeping a close eye on Squid Ink Tattoo Parlour. They had passed the window several times over before they saw an opportunity to speak to Ayleen Demir alone.

Usually, walking the quaint streets of old Whitby would have been no hardship but Kitt was already feeling the weight of this case taking its toll. In particular, her eyes stung after getting so little sleep the past few nights. It had been some months since she had lain awake, unblinking and wracked with worry. The sense of time slipping so quickly through the hourglass dulled the usually vibrant pleasure of walking those cobbled backstreets. Grace had managed to rouse some enthusiasm for the windows packed with chunks of handmade fudge, jewellery set with Whitby Jet and the famous Lucky Ducks that very few visitors to the town could resist taking away with them as a memento of their time in this quaint little corner of the coast. Kitt, however, had felt vacant and zombie-like as she trudged along, unable to appreciate the little things that would on any other day have raised her spirits.

'Courage, girl. Strength, metal,' she muttered to herself as she opened the door of Squid Ink Tattoos. And on repeating that well-loved family phrase that her parents had said to her on so many desolate occasions, Kitt stood a little taller and did what she could to pull herself together. Some people seemed to go out of their way to ruin things for others. But, Kitt decided, she drew the line at someone ruining Whitby. Even if they were a serial killer. If she failed, she would never again be able to wander through the whale bones on the West Cliff, buy a sausage roll at Botham's, or watch the fisher folk grapple with live lobsters in the harbour without thinking of her lost friend. Her only choice, as she understood the situation, was to bring this murderer down so that she could forever associate the town with her triumph.

On entering the shop, which she noted was still empty – even Ayleen wasn't to be seen at present – Kitt was struck by the dramatic nature of the decor. She and Grace had caught glimpses from the outside as they had sauntered past, but each time they had been focused on just one detail: was Ayleen in the shop alone? It was hard to ascertain that and take in the environment without making it obvious they were looking in. Thus, several salient details had passed Kitt by. Every wall in the place was painted black. It was clear from the wicker pentagrams, tall black candles, triple moon symbol ornaments and goddess figurines arranged on a shelf behind the counter that Ayleen was in no way trying to hide the fact that she was a witch from her customers.

The most striking details, however, were to be found on the remaining walls which had designs stencilled onto them. One of the designs was of a giant squid, which given the name of the shop wasn't surprising. At the other end of the shop, though, a vampire had been traced onto the wall. A vampire that stood so tall he almost stretched from floor to ceiling. Both of the stencils had been filled in with purple paint.

Purple paint? Kitt's breath caught in her throat.

'Are you all right? Clear your throat if everything's OK, sneeze if it isn't,' Grace hissed over the earpiece Kitt had hooked up before turning onto Sandgate, the street on which Ayleen's shop stood. It had been decided that Kitt would interview any suspects alone so that Grace could take a second undercover pass at them if required. Grace was stationed just round the corner at the swing bridge, which connected Whitby's old town with the new. Far enough away that the pair wouldn't be connected if Ayleen got suspicious about the sheer number of questions Kitt wanted to ask her but near enough that she could come running if Kitt had cause to use their code word.

Grace must have heard her reaction to the paint and

become concerned. As instructed, Kitt cleared her throat to offer her assistant peace of mind that she was in no immediate danger and then looked closer at the designs on the wall, trying to gauge if it was the same colour as the mark she had seen on Ruby's door. It seemed like a very close match indeed.

'Hello there,' a voice said, giving Kitt a start. She turned to see Ayleen standing behind the counter. She must have appeared from one of the back rooms when she heard the bell on the door tinkle. Kitt and Grace had checked the shop's website for a photo of her beforehand to ensure they made a positive ID.

'Oh, hello,' said Kitt, 'I was just admiring your wonderful decorations.'

'They're great, aren't they? I can't claim credit, I'm afraid, it's the work of a local artist.'

'Oh, I must have their name, these are fantastic,' said Kitt. In truth, an artist being in possession of paint was not exactly what you might call incriminating evidence. If someone was running around Whitby with a pot of paint that was an exact match to the paint favoured by the killer, however, Kitt wanted to know who they were.

'Joel Mendoza, he's got a website. Should be easy enough to find with a quick search.' As she spoke, Ayleen scraped her long purple hair out of her face. On seeing her in person, Kitt couldn't help but notice that, just like the graphics on the walls, it was almost the same shade of purple as the paint used to mark the doors of the Vampire Killer's victims. Purple was something of a theme in this place, it seemed.

'I'll be sure to look him up, thank you,' said Kitt.

'Not a problem. So, is there something I can help you with today?'

'Arnie wasn't sure whether Ayleen grew up in Wensleydale or Sandersdale,' Grace said. *'Try and drop them both into the conversation and see how she reacts. If there's anything to these rumours about her offing her own parents, she might give herself away without realizing it.'*

'I'm feeling a bit impulsive today, and I wondered if I could look through some designs you have for a modest-sized tattoo,' said Kitt, while trying to figure out the best way to drop the two areas into the conversation.

A dent formed in Ayleen's bronzed forehead as she frowned. Kitt wondered for a moment if she wasn't the most convincing punter in a tattoo shop and whether she should have found a way of dressing up for this part. Now that she thought about it, they'd passed several shops that sold gothic or new-age clothing. Even if she'd just bought a black jacket and a pair of sturdy boots that probably would have been more convincing than the jeans and woolly pink cardigan she had thrown on that morning.

'We've got several books for you to browse through,' Ayleen said, losing the frown and fixing a smile on her face before handing Kitt a thick black folder. 'Here, start with this one. Those are our smallest designs.'

'Probably best to start small with it being my first tattoo,' said Kitt, opening the binder.

'You're wiser than most of my first-time clients,' Ayleen said, widening her smile. Unlike many people, she had a smile that reached her eyes, making them twinkle. In fact, on first impressions alone, even despite the similarity in her hair colour to the marks on the victims' doors, and her dubious choice of decor, Kitt found the woman most approachable. In her red corseted peplum top and black leggings, she was dressed in a way that would undoubtedly appeal to anyone of the gothic persuasion. But the look wasn't so exaggerated that it was off-putting or intimidating. This probably made customers feel more at ease when taking the leap of permanently marking their bodies. But it struck Kitt that it might also make anyone feel safe with her, say a potential victim, should she wish to deceive anyone.

'My sister has quite a few tattoos,' said Kitt. 'And after she gets one it's all she can talk about for about two weeks, so I've got indirect experience.'

Mal also had a tattoo, of course, and she'd always found it a rather fetching feature on him. But that was a complicated subject to bring up, given the tattoo was of his ex-wife's name and that ex-wife had died at the hands of a serial killer.

'Do you have any ideas about what kind of design you're looking for?'

'I was thinking of maybe getting a butterfly,' said Kitt, seeing an opportunity to test Ruby's improbable theory. If Ayleen had a butterfly tattoo, she might show Kitt as a means of making a sale. Kitt hadn't been under the other-worldly spell of Whitby quite long enough to interpret such a coincidence as hard evidence but by the law of probability one of Ruby's suggestions had to pan out at some point.

'I think a giant skull on your left arm would be much more you,' said Grace, giggling over the radio channel.

Kitt was no longer surprised by her assistant's giddiness, even in situations as serious as these, and did all she could to ignore the interruption.

'One of our most popular designs, that,' said Ayleen.

Inwardly, Kitt vowed not to let anyone know that she had, even for a split second, given one of Ruby's theories any consideration. If a butterfly was one of their most popular designs it was hardly narrowing their field of suspects. That level of ambiguity was peak Ruby.

'I can imagine. I met a lady recently on a trip to Wensleydale who had the most beautiful butterfly tattoo. I should have taken a picture,' Kitt said, keeping a close eye on Ayleen to see if the mention of Wensleydale in any way sparked a reaction.

But no, nothing. No change in expression. No flutter of the eyes. No tensing of the body. If town talk here was in any way reliable, Ayleen must hail from Sandersdale.

'I have a few pictures of tattoos I've done on my phone,

you know, for Instagram purposes, but I don't think I've taken any butterfly shots recently,' Ayleen said, picking her phone up off the counter and scrolling through her pictures. 'Nope, sorry about that.'

'Oh, not to worry. I'm not sure I'll make my mind up today,' said Kitt. She had no intention of leaving this shop with a tattoo, even in the spirit of undercover work, so it seemed best to sow the seeds sooner rather than later that no money would be changing hands here. 'But I live over in Sandersdale, so it's only a few hours' drive, easy to drop back another day. And a scenic drive it is too.'

At the mention of Sandersdale Ayleen's smile faded and her eyes became sorrowful, watery almost. 'Whereabouts in Sandersdale are you?'

'Just settled in Ravensgarth about a year ago,' said Kitt, deciding if she was going to lie, it was probably best to lie about somewhere she knew well. Lying wasn't her strong suit, which of course was a commendable quality in a person. Unless you were trying to catch out a serial killer. Then it was something of a liability.

'I grew up in that general area, gorgeous country round there. Haven't been back for many years now, like.'

'Oh, it's worth going back if you can,' said Kitt. 'Nothing like the bracing air of the Yorkshire dales in your lungs, and of course the falls at Ravensgarth are something else.'

Ayleen shrugged. 'Not all the memories I have of that place are pleasant ones.'

'I'm so sorry to hear that,' said Kitt, her voice as gentle as she could make it. She needed Ayleen to think of her as a sympathetic stranger. Someone she might feel safe to confide in. 'I hope I haven't put my foot in it. It does, I'm afraid, seem to be my specialty.'

'No, you haven't. It's just . . . life,' Ayleen said with a sigh. 'Whitby's where I belong now. And there are much worse places to belong.'

'You're right about that. Lovely town. A personal favourite. Although, I did hear a bit of a disturbing rumour about the place the other day,' said Kitt. 'It left me a bit rattled.'

Ayleen seemed to cheer a little at Kitt's comment. 'Given it's a gothic paradise, disturbing rumours come pretty much as standard in this town. Go on, surprise me. What is it this time? A ghost at the end of the pier?'

'I wish it were that whimsical. It's just hearsay, mind. I listen to this podcast about the occult. I'm a librarian by trade and there's no subject that doesn't fascinate me, but someone had commented on the forum about the Vampire Killer.'

Ayleen shuffled on the spot. 'What did the comment say?'

'That the places where the killer had struck all seemed to revolve around Whitby, geographically speaking.'

Ayleen went quiet for a moment before responding. 'So, what are they saying, exactly? They think the killer has based themselves in Whitby for some reason?'

'That was the thrust of the comment, although unless

the killer already lived here I'm struggling to think what that reason might be. It's a beautiful town and all that but I don't think sunset aesthetics are necessarily the first thing on a serial killer's mind.'

Ayleen pursed her lips and ran a hand over her face, thinking. She opened her mouth to speak but then, seemingly deciding against it, closed it just as quickly.

'Is something wrong?' said Kitt, looking Ayleen's face up and down while trying to make sense of the odd expression that had fallen over it. The woman's eyes had widened and every muscle in her body seemed to be tensed. For a second Kitt wondered if she was going to faint, she didn't look too steady on her feet.

'Ayleen . . .'

'I think . . . the reason the killer's targeting Whitby,' she almost whispered. 'I think the reason might be me.'

ELEVEN

Kitt stood stock-still for a moment, her mouth hanging open. Was Ayleen about to confess to some involvement in the murders? Had Ruby been right all along? Was it a witch they were hunting for?

'What do you mean, exactly, that the reason might be you?' Kitt said, at last finding the words to speak.

'If she even looks like she's plotting something just say the code word and I'll be there in a flash to back you up,' said Grace.

Kitt would have taken more comfort in Grace's attempts at reassurance if they had chosen a code word that could be easily crowbarred into the conversation that was likely to follow. Kitt had suggested it should be 'Sherlock' after she learned from a quick skim of the opening pages of the biography she'd bought at Broomsticks, Black Cats and Books that Bram Stoker and Arthur Conan Doyle once attended the same school. She thought that might be the kind of fun fact she could bring up in a seemingly casual chat, given their location, and considering they had agreed to ask every potential suspect about the Creed of Count Dracula – what they knew about them and more importantly if they were affiliated with them in any way. This conversation, however, had not gone as planned.

'I—I shouldn't be talking about this with a customer,' Ayleen said. 'I'm sure it's nothing.' She tried to smile but Kitt could see it was a struggle for her to do so.

'I don't know what it is about me,' said Kitt. 'But I'm just one of those people that others meet and feel like they can tell me things. Maybe it's because I'm a librarian and spend quite a bit of my time listening to people so I can help them better. Whatever the reason, I don't mind a bit when people confide. So why don't you tell me? It's obvious something is bothering you. I can tell by the look on your face and I'd hate to leave here knowing you were struggling with something when I might have been able to set your mind at ease.'

Ayleen hesitated again, clearly still not quite convinced. Somehow, Kitt needed to show her that she assumed her to be in some kind of trouble, rather than the one causing it. Perhaps then she would let something slip.

'You know, I was mixed up in a murder case once. It was a serial killer too,' Kitt said.

'Mixed up how?' Ayleen said.

'My best friend was accused of murder. I was implicated and it was one of the most frightening ordeals of my life but in the end both of our names were cleared because we cooperated with the police and didn't withhold any information. If you know something, however small, about what's going on I would encourage you to step forward. Keeping important information to yourself only makes the police more suspicious of you, rather than focusing their energies on catching the true criminal. Take it from someone who knows.'

Ayleen slumped down onto a stool behind her counter and put her head in her hands. 'I didn't want to believe it was true. Maybe it isn't but it seems like too much of a coincidence.'

'What's a coincidence?' Kitt pressed.

'It's probably nothing,' Ayleen said, raising her head again to look at Kitt. 'But the thing is, I—I knew two of the victims who died.'

'Oh boy, that can't be good,' said Grace.

'I'm so sorry,' Kitt said, wondering if that could possibly be a coincidence or whether this was the starting point for a deeper confession. She thought back to her investigative training. She needed to handle this carefully. Make sure all of her questions were open and she didn't interrupt. Getting Ayleen into a state of conversational flow was the most likely way of finding out everything she needed to. 'Which of the victims did you know?'

'The first victim, Anna Hayes, and the third victim, Alix Yang.'

'Were you close to them?'

'No, no, I just did their tattoos.'

'Were they regulars?'

'I only did one tattoo apiece, but they were both definitely customers here.'

'I wonder why the police didn't pick up that connection when they looked at the victims' records, you'd think they'd be looking for all possible leads in a case like this,' said Kitt.

'Both of them had their tattoos done a long time ago now, so maybe they didn't look that far back.'

'How long ago are we talking?'

'Anna's tattoo was four years ago. Alix's was six years ago. Right away, I knew I recognized Anna for some reason when I saw her photograph online. I went back through my records, hoping to prove myself wrong. It's all digital now but in the first five years or so of opening the shop I couldn't afford to computerize everything so I kept all the details of what colours and designs I'd used for each customer in a card index alphabetized by name. And I found her in there. Later, when Alix was killed, and I saw her photograph on the news, I had that same feeling. Again, I went back to the records and there she was.'

'But you didn't know the second victim?'

Ayleen shook her head. 'When the first killing happened I thought it was just a terrible thing that befell one of my customers, you know? And then that older man died and I didn't know him. But I just knew I'd done a tattoo for Alix. My blood ran cold when I saw her face, even colder when

I found the file in the back office. After that, I checked for the name of the second victim in the files too, but I hadn't recognized him and his name wasn't there.'

'What about the latest target in York? What's her name? Ruby something, I think that's what the news said. Do you know her?' Kitt said, doing her best to sound as though she wasn't that up on the case, or in any way connected with the killer's next victim even though Ruby's neighbours had been talking to the press at every opportunity about the 'devilish woman who lives at number thirty-three'.

'I didn't recognize her from the photo I saw online,' said Ayleen.

'Well, then, surely it's likely to be a coincidence? A horrible coincidence for you, but a coincidence nonetheless,' said Kitt.

'Unless she's working with an accomplice and they take turns in picking out the victims,' said Grace, a thought that Kitt had just been pondering herself.

'Maybe not,' said Ayleen. 'When I was quite young my . . . my parents died and there's a whole chunk of my childhood I don't remember. What if I came into contact with those people then and don't recall? Maybe I'm connected to them and don't even realize it.'

'I'm so sorry to hear about you losing your parents so young. I imagine that could affect a person's memory so I suppose it's possible that you crossed paths with some people you now can't recall,' said Kitt. 'But why would a killer like this target you? It looks like you've got some occult interests, judging by your decorations, but it feels like for you to be at the centre of it all, there would need to be more to it than that.'

'You're right, I am a practising witch, but I don't think that's why the killer might be after me.' Ayleen paused then and took a long, deep breath. Kitt watched her closely and noticed her eyes flitting this way and that in a manner that made it seem as though she was making a calculation or perhaps weighing something up. 'A long time ago,' she said at last, 'I did something very foolish. I got mixed up with some people based in Sandersdale. It was sort of a . . . cult.'

'Sounds a bit scary,' said Kitt, while wondering how to ask for more information without arousing Ayleen's suspicions. 'Did it have a scary name?'

'Not really, or, at least, I didn't think so when I first heard of them. It was called the Children of Silvanus.'

'Silvanus,' Kitt repeated. 'Silvanus . . . isn't he a Roman god?'

Ayleen nodded. 'From what I understand he's sort of a protector. The name was supposed to make us feel safe, and I suppose it did, at first.'

'But then when you joined up, that changed?'

'It's difficult to explain. The leader of the group, he was charismatic, he could, I think, convince anyone of anything.'

'What was his name?'

Ayleen crossed her arms and looked Kitt up and down. 'Why?'

Kitt shrugged in as nonchalant manner as she could manage just then. 'I was just wondering if I'd heard of him, especially given I now live in Sandersdale.'

'Justin Palmer was his name – ring any bells?'

'No, I've not heard of him,' Kitt said.

'He and the other core members of the group purchased some old farmland out in the dales – they were based about twenty miles from where I used to live with my parents. Palmer had established rules that were designed to encourage obedience and fear in the group. It was his way of controlling us. Emotional manipulation was rife.'

'Did the abuse stop at an emotional level?'

'There were some physical altercations. Nothing sexual though, which I suppose is one small mercy. Palmer had a few mistresses, I think, but I was never one of them and it always seemed to me that they wanted to be with him. Looking back, like, that was probably all achieved through persuasion and manipulation too. Like everything else there.'

'How terrible that you got mixed up in something like that.'

Ayleen shrugged. 'I was young, still hadn't really dealt properly with the death of my parents and was lost. I'd been bouncing around foster parents for seven years by that point. Thanks to the internet, the more insidious among us were able to prey on the lost a lot more easily. I ran away from my foster parents and joined the group with little thought or hesitation and then found there was no easy way out.'

'How did you get away?'

'For a very long time, I didn't. When I finally escaped I found out I'd been there for six years. It had felt like for ever. One day, I discovered why time felt different there. Why everyone was more obedient than they might have been otherwise. It wasn't just Palmer's charisma. They were putting something in our food.'

'That must have been a shock,' said Kitt. 'What was it?'

'I never found out. But they had people they called godfathers and godmothers who oversaw the day-to-day running of the camp. I saw them mixing it into soups and stews. One of the rules of the camp was that you had to finish all food that was put in front of you. So I started to find ways of getting rid of it without our godmother noticing. After a few days I started to really sober up and realize what was going on. That was when I started to plan my escape.'

'As you're here, telling this story, I'm assuming you did manage it but from what you're telling me, it doesn't sound like an easy community to break out of.'

'It took some planning. The commune was in the middle of nowhere,' said Ayleen. 'I hoarded food in a backpack, nothing liquid, only solids so I could be sure it wasn't contaminated. I stole the thickest blanket I could find and crept out one night. The blanket was to throw over the barbed wire at the top of the gate so I could climb over it.'

'Smart girl,' Kitt said with a sympathetic smile.

'Not smart enough. Still got scratched to hell. But I didn't care about that. All I was interested in was making it out of there. As soon as I was over the fence, I hiked as quickly as I could to a road I'd been watching in the distance and managed to hitch a ride just as the sun was rising.'

Kitt paused for a moment before speaking, wondering why Ayleen wouldn't move further away from Sandersdale after her ordeal. Yes, it was a three-hour drive to the tip of Sandersdale from Whitby but that wasn't exactly difficult ground to cover if you wanted to find someone. Still, that was a question they could perhaps try and answer at another time. Right now, Kitt had to focus on the basics before Ayleen ran out of goodwill towards her. 'How come the police didn't come and shut the place down? People must have had some idea about what was happening.'

'Only people who were part of the cult were allowed in or out so there weren't any witnesses to what went on there. Once or twice the police visited after reports from locals who suspected some worrying behaviour but that's the thing, when you have real control over people, they'll swear to anything.'

'So you all told the police that you were part of a happy community,' said Kitt, shaking her head.

'Exactly. Plus the Children of Silvanus were self-sufficient when it came to food. It was one of the ways they made sure people didn't need to go in or out. There was a water supply and some livestock. So we were trained to say that we were a self-sufficient community family, farming off the land and living in peace. I'd rather not go into all the ins and outs of what went on there, but suffice to say that was only part of the story.'

'By the sound of things, it wasn't a particularly peaceful existence,' said Kitt.

'No, not everyone was as susceptible as they would have liked to what they were putting in the food, and they were taken away to be punished. The threat of punishment was always at the back of your mind.'

'What an ordeal,' said Kitt. 'I'm so sorry you lived through all that. It sounds terrifying. I would certainly have been terrified in your position. But what does it have to do with the Vampire Killer? Are you saying you think the killer is perhaps the leader of the cult? This Justin Palmer, coming after you because you escaped?'

'I don't know. It's been a decade since I escaped. I changed my name after that and lay low for several years. I didn't even have a website for this place until about two years ago. I haven't dared look into them online since I left in case I clicked on something and they were able to trace it back to me, but I think Palmer is probably dead by now. He was old back then. Long grey hair, had that wizened look about him, you know? I don't even know if the Children of Silvanus are still in operation. Probably not. At least not under the same name or the same leader. But the killer could be one of the people Palmer manipulated. Someone who was loyal to him and believed him to be their protector. He might have made them promise to go after anyone who escaped.'

'You've lived through an exceedingly frightening experience. And what you're saying isn't impossible but why wouldn't someone like that just come after you directly rather than target people you vaguely knew?'

'Like I said, the Children of Silvanus ran on manipulation. It's possible that they just want to scare the hell out of me before they strike. And truth be told, I have been scared. I managed to talk myself into the idea that I was just being paranoid but if what you say is right and the killer is based somewhere in the Whitby area, then it could be that they've come for me at last.'

'And instead of going at you directly, they've decided to torture you first with the idea that even after hiding for all these years you can't escape them, by picking off people in the periphery of your life, people who, in some cases, you don't even remember your connection to,' Kitt said with a nod. 'I take it you haven't told the police about this?'

'I came close more than once. I even dialled and hung up.

But it could be a complete waste of their time. The delusions of a woman driven mad by years of paranoia and looking over her shoulder. I don't want to distract from their investigation when they have so little time between the marks appearing and the killing taking place.'

'What if it's not a distraction at all? What if you could save the life of the next victim?' said Kitt. 'I think when it comes to this case, the police will want to hear about every possible lead. If there's even a chance your actions could save someone, isn't it worth giving it a go?'

'I know you're right,' said Ayleen. 'But I'm ... I'm also scared about what might happen if I go to the police.'

Kitt reached across the counter and patted Ayleen's arm. 'From the sound of things, I think it'll be worse if you don't. And I think I know just who you should contact. When I was mixed up in that case I told you about I met a detective in York, DI Malcolm Halloran. You should ring the police and ask to be put through to him. With the latest target being in York, he'll be part of the team working on this now and if anyone will listen with an open mind, it's him.'

'OK. I'll do that ... I'll ... Wait a minute.' Ayleen's eyes narrowed and she looked Kitt up and down. 'Before, you used my name, Ayleen. How did you know my name? I didn't tell you that.'

Kitt smiled to give herself time to think. 'I understand your natural suspicion given everything you've been through,' she said, praying the lie she was about to tell would stick.

'But I don't think you can make a spanking new website like the one you've got and not expect prospective customers to check it out before they get here.'

'Oh,' Ayleen said, her face relaxing a little bit but not quite completely. Kitt's cover story for her little slip-up didn't quite fit her original claims of feeling impulsive and deciding on the spot that she wanted a tattoo. When Ayleen's expression held onto some of the tension, it was clear she wasn't totally convinced. The best thing was likely to get out of there, pronto.

'Well, I suppose I should probably let you get onto the police about this right away,' said Kitt. 'Don't worry about my tattoo, you've got a lot going on right now. I can come back for that another day.'

'Nonsense,' said Ayleen. 'You've been so kind to listen to my sob story, and offered me some much-needed guidance. I'm a witch, remember, and no witch worth her salt believes in coincidences. The powers that be clearly sent you to give me a nudge at just the right time. You can have a small tattoo on the house. I'm sure I won't be on the phone long to the police, and while I'm doing that you can pick out your design. Just go and bob yourself on the chair in that side room over there and relax.'

Kitt tried to grope for a reasonable excuse as to why she shouldn't get a tattoo but found when she opened her mouth that no words came out. In part, because she was convinced another U-turn in her story would really raise

Ayleen's suspicions. As she nodded to the woman and followed her instructions to take a seat in the side room, all Kitt could hear, above Ayleen asking to be put through to the police over the phone, was Grace's almost hysterical cackles echoing through her earpiece.

TWELVE

After the many revelations Ayleen had shared with Kitt, she was in dire need of a sit down and a cuppa. Mercifully, Marie Antoinette's was just around the corner from Squid Ink. This delightful tea room served generous chunks of cake and soothing cups of lemon and ginger tea, which made a nice change from Kitt's usual choice of Lady Grey. All the chairs and tables were made of solid dark wood and with its displays of delicate tea sets and vintage homeware, it had an ambience that Evie would have very much appreciated if she were here.

'Still can't believe you got a tattoo,' Grace said, shaking her head and chuckling as she took her first sip of tea. 'Though it doesn't surprise me it was a Keats quotation.'

'I was trying to think of something short,' said Kitt, wincing at the dull throb the tattoo needle had left behind. 'It didn't hurt half so much as our Becca makes out when she gets one but I wouldn't have wanted it to go on any longer. "Truth is beauty" was the most succinct quotation I could think of.'

'And quite fitting for a hard-boiled detective,' said Grace.

'Ooh, I wish you'd stop calling me that,' said Kitt. 'It makes me sound old and bitter, and before you make any smart alec comments, thirty-seven is not old.'

'No, not at all,' said Grace. 'Forty, however . . .'

'Grace . . .'

'Well maybe I'll agree you've still got some life left in you if you tell me where the tattoo is. If it's somewhere adventurous then I can't really argue with that, can I?'

'No matter how many times you try to bait me, I'm not telling you that.'

'Why not?'

'Because that's for me to know, and for Mal to find out,' Kitt said, smirking, while imagining the sparkle in Halloran's eyes as he admired it. 'Anyway, you are always far too concerned with me and my dealings. I've never known anyone so young to be as obsessed with someone more than a decade their senior, as you are with me.'

'Well, you must admit, you are a bit of an anomaly,' Grace said, with an impish smile. 'Put it down to a hangover from my psychology degree – pure scientific curiosity.'

'What we need to be curious about are the people we've spoken to so far.'

'Yes, I did do a quick check into Arnold Sykes since we're following up on the leads he offered us.'

'And?'

'Nothing worrying to report. I did a thorough search of his online history going back ten years. According to his business website, and some local news articles I found, he opened the bookshop about eight years ago after a career change from working in insurance. There's nothing untoward on his personal social media accounts and there is the odd post here and there of him sponsoring local charities so he's above board.'

'Good to know, and thankfully as expected, but Ayleen is another matter. Obviously she's already phoned in her version of events to Mal. He texted me to say he's going to question her himself later at the local police station this afternoon, establish her alibis for all three murders and such. He'll join us at the guest house when he's done.'

'So glad that we didn't insist on adjoining rooms after all.'

'Thank you, that's enough of that.'

'I'm assuming that, since Halloran is establishing her alibis for the murders, you're not sure enough about her story to remove her from the suspect list.'

'Not as yet,' said Kitt, considering the many strands of the story Ayleen had told her. 'You know what I said to you about the purple paint on the walls in there. Not to mention the giant stencil of a vampire.'

'We are in Whitby, Kitt, vampires are a bit of a thing round here,' said Grace.

'Not like you could miss that fact,' said Kitt, thinking

about all the nods to Bram Stoker's novel they'd seen since they'd arrived just yesterday. Even some of the ice cream vans had rebranded strawberry sauce as 'Dracula blood'. Kitt imagined this was the kind of detail tourists loved but, to her mind, particularly given the case they were working, such culinary ingenuity didn't stir her appetite. 'But there's still a chance she's involved with the killer, or is the killer, and is spinning us a bit of a yarn.'

'Why bother to do that though?' said Grace. 'Why not just deny any involvement with the victims at all? Anna and Alix were customers of hers long enough ago that it's unlikely the link would've been discovered. You said it yourself while you were in there – the police didn't even pick up on it.'

'But the longer the case goes on the greater likelihood there is of it being discovered as the police dig deeper and deeper into the victims' lives and histories. According to the volumes I've read about serial killers, it is quite a common trick for them to admit to something small when being investigated by the police so that they can weave a narrative and evade suspicion for the bigger crime they are a part of.'

'So, in Ayleen's case, she's admitted to knowing two of the victims? Which on its own seems like a small confession while also giving the impression she's willing to be honest with us.'

'Exactly, and then she told us an elaborate but plausible story about this cult up in Sandersdale. This allows her to control the narrative, and her place in it, when it comes to these killings. Don't get me wrong, if she really went through all that she has my sympathies. There are some shocking examples of groups like this in British history and their impact on the individuals who found themselves at their mercy is not to be underestimated.'

'But you think she might have made the story up?'

'I suspect that if she is playing with the truth in some way, she hasn't told us a complete work of fiction. But we need to be sure, as far as we can be, that every part of her story adds up. If she's lied to us about anything, even a small thing, she could be lying about other aspects of what happened to her and her connection to the current murders. We'll need to do a lot of checking into what she's said to be sure. She could just be trying to play the victim when really she's the one behind it all.'

'I got a head start on verifying what she had to say while you were in the tattooist's chair,' said Grace.

'What did you manage to find? Does her story ring true?'

'Her parents' deaths were covered in the local news, there was an unexplained fire in their house in 1997. At least, I think it's the right family. You remember she said she'd changed her name? Anyway, this was the only story about a family dying in a domestic fire in Sandersdale.'

'It's likely it's the right family. I can't think that's too common an occurrence, at least not in recent history.'

'Ayleen's name was Jamelia Park back then; she was eight at the time her parents died.'

'A terrible thing for a child to live through,' said Kitt. 'Did the coverage say anything useful about the incident? Remember what Arnie said about some people believing she had a hand in it? Although, he seemed to be hinting at a supernatural power which – of course – I give no credence to. I wonder if any of the newspapers said anything that might suggest that Ayleen could have been responsible or hint that there was something strange about the occurrence. I don't understand why they weren't woken up by their smoke alarm.'

Grace shook her head. 'That is strange. I don't know what the regulations were on alarms in 1997, but not everyone follows the regs at any rate. Maybe they didn't have one? It's not mentioned in the few reports I found. They were really just short snippets reporting on the tragedy. Each cutting stated the same thing: that the cause of the fire was unknown. That the fire brigade suspected it was arson but weren't able to confirm it. Do you really think she had anything to do with it? Wouldn't the fire service have been able to figure out if there was foul play? What would be her motive for killing her parents anyway?'

'Though they can in many cases, the fire service can't always determine the cause of a fire. And the Vampire Killer, whoever they may be, obviously has psychopathic tendencies. The way in which they take their time to bleed the victim, carefully leaving a jar of blood at the scene, that's not the quick, vicious act of someone killing out of anger or passion. That's a slow process that would require a person to be pretty detached from what they're doing.'

Grace looked down at the raspberry topping on her cake with less enthusiasm than she had been before.

'So, what, you think she had a hand in the death of her parents and it was an early demonstration of her psychopathic tendencies? Why didn't she ever strike again? Why just that one time, until now? And why confess to you that she has links to the victims today?'

'Well, that's the part that makes me wonder if she's spinning us a yarn. But in terms of why she might have waited so long to strike again, I'm not sure. Perhaps she's been resisting the urges for a long time but can't resist them any longer? At any rate, I'm just saying it's a possibility. Unlike the local community, I don't think her status as a witch has anything to do with it but psychopaths are skilled at pretending to be normal. At veiling their true horror behind politeness or kindness. They can fantasize about things for years and then something will trigger them into making that fantasy a reality.'

'Isn't there also a chance though that she had nothing to do with her parents' deaths? That it was just one of those horrible flukes that happens from time to time but joining the Children of Silvanus changed her?'

'You mean, brainwashed her in some way?'

'Yeah, or conditioned her to carry out unspeakable acts. Or maybe she's trying to regain control after being controlled for all that time by the godfathers and godmothers at the camp ... ugh,' Grace said with a shudder. 'It's sickening, turns my stomach, it does.'

'We agree on that point. But until Halloran has checked out all of Ayleen's alibis, we can't draw any firm conclusions – even if her links to the occult, her strange past and the fact that she knows two out of the three victims somewhat count against her. There is still a chance she's innocent in all this.'

'When you list all the black marks against her name like that it doesn't feel like it.'

'I know. And I'm still not convinced we've necessarily got the whole truth out of her. But it might be less sinister than we're imagining. If she did have a hand in the fire at her childhood home, for example, she might not have meant it to happen. There's a chance it was a complete accident. And when her parents died she realized some part of her liked the feeling of power it brought.'

'But do people really jump to serial murder just because they've had a taste of it? If she's not a full-blown psychopath, wouldn't she have felt guilt as well as pleasure and tried to find another way of satisfying that desire? I just think, based on that theory, there's not much motive for her to go around killing people linked with the occult in quite the way the Vampire Killer is.'

'It depends on so many factors,' said Kitt. 'Even if she had nothing to do with her parents' deaths, she may have been affected by the trauma. Given her witchy leanings, perhaps she believes she has some kind of supernatural power that started the fire and is taking her self-hatred out on others who dabble in the so-called black arts.'

'Maybe. Her idea about someone from the cult coming after her is quite convincing though,' said Grace. 'From what she said, they do not sound like right-minded people.'

'I've already texted Halloran all the core details she gave me so he can check it against the statement she makes when he talks to her in depth. Did you manage to find anything on the Children of Silvanus online while you were waiting for me?'

'There isn't much about them, which I suppose is fairly typical of that kind of . . . organization. But I did find one thing. A Reddit post from someone looking for old members of the group.'

'How old was the post?' asked Kitt.

'Six years or so,' said Grace.

'Not recent then. If it had been posted in the last six months we might well have found our killer.'

'I know what you mean, but think about what Tremble said. Every detail of these murders seems to have been accounted for. Assuming they're not clairvoyant, as Peter suggested, they might well have been planning this, or fantasizing about these acts, for that long.'

'Good point. What's the name of the person who posted the Reddit post?'

'It's a handle rather than a name. SimonB666.'

'Ominous numerics.'

'I know. I might be able to run that username through one of our tracer services and see if they can track it down to an attached email address or social media account.'

'Yes, let's do that,' said Kitt. 'Based on what Ayleen told us about the cult, how difficult it was to get away from them and the fact she felt the need to hide from them all these years, SimonB666 might well be our killer on the hunt for his runaway witch.'

THIRTEEN

The Elysium Guest House stood at the top of Whitby's West Cliff, where East Terrace and North Terrace met. From the guest house bar, Kitt and Grace had been able to periodically look out over the harbour, which was bordered by stacks of red-roofed houses, as the sun slowly set and the sky became a palette of deep pink, orange and violet.

While admiring the view, they also contacted the Creed of Count Dracula to arrange an appointment with Stoke Bramley. They also called Seaview Care Home in Sandsend to start the ball rolling on organizing a chat with Cyril Armitage, just to well and truly rule him out. Additionally, it was agreed that Grace would do some of her notorious cyber-stalking and find out all she could about Joel Mendoza. Given that his only crime was being an artist with a pot of purple paint, Kitt didn't want to waste time tracking him down and interviewing him unless something more incriminating came to light. Once it had been decided that

Grace would report back tomorrow on anything untoward she found on his social media profiles, alongside making a list of any places he'd checked in on Facebook on the dates in their murder timeline, the pair had parted ways and made their way back to their respective rooms.

Though the guest house itself could do with a good paint and was filled from top to bottom with furniture Kitt's great-grandmother would have deemed old-fashioned, it was the best accommodation they could afford on their limited budget. Opening a detective agency hadn't been a cheap affair and corners had to be cut wherever possible. Frankly, Kitt was just grateful to have secured a place to stay in Whitby itself on the funds they had available, rather than in one of the outlying coastal villages. Particularly when their view of the harbour included the famous whale bones which not only harked back to the local whaling expeditions in the Arctic seas but beautifully framed the ruins of Whitby Abbey on the other side of the bay.

It was half past nine and long since dark when Kitt heard a hard knock on the door of her room. The knock sounded out in such a rhythm that she knew at once that it was Halloran. She smiled, made her way up off the bed and called to him through the door. 'What's the secret password?'

'Same as your safe word, isn't it?'

Kitt threw open the door at once, her cheeks burning. 'Mal, would you give over? Don't be saying things like that loud enough for the whole hotel to hear you. What will people think?'

'Who cares?' Halloran said, leaning in and cupping her face with both his hands. His lips were on hers before she could reply and she moaned contentedly as the kiss deepened. It was some minutes before Halloran paused to close the door behind him. When he turned back to resume the kiss, however, Kitt made a dash around a chest of drawers that was nestled at the end of the bed.

'Come here, you,' Halloran said, chuckling and taking a step towards her.

'Now, before things go any further, Inspector Halloran,' Kitt said with a demure smile, or, at least, the closest approximation she'd ever managed, 'I expect a full update on the case.'

Halloran stared at her for a moment. 'I can't tell if you're joking.'

'I'm most certainly not joking,' said Kitt. 'I handed you a strong lead on a plate today. You promised this exchange was going to be mutual. So I want to know if Ayleen's got alibis for the murders before we enjoy even so much as another cuddle.'

Halloran sighed. 'Is this what people mean when they talk about their partners using sex as a weapon?'

Kitt paused for a moment, thinking. 'Probably. But you can punish me later.'

Halloran laughed. 'I'll hold you to that.'

Kitt raised an eyebrow at him and smiled. 'So, come on, out with it, what do you think of Ayleen's story?'

Halloran, seemingly accepting the fact he wasn't going to get out of talking shop, took off his dark grey coat and hung it on a peg on the back of the door. 'Extremely sad, if it's true.'

'You couldn't be sure either then, if she was telling the truth?'

'I've got a pretty good nose for these things, she didn't give any of the usual tells people do when they're lying. But of course that could just mean she's good at it. From the way she behaved, I would say the bulk of what she's telling us is true but until I substantiate as much of the story as I can, I'm reserving judgement.'

'What about alibis?'

'She was a bit taken aback by that question when I asked. I told her it was routine but, I don't know, she still seemed put out by it. Which isn't usually the go-to for a psychopath. They're usually all too happy to provide full details to us. They tend to be overly polite, in fact, and usually very pre-pared. That's often how you catch them out. They're just a bit too helpful.'

'So the fact that she was unprepared for the question might also signal she doesn't believe there's any reason why she should be considered a suspect.'

'That, or she's even cleverer than we think and double bluffing us.'

'Could she prove her whereabouts on the nights of all three previous murders? That would certainly help us rule her out without having to analyse every last word and bodily response.'

'She could only provide an alibi for the middle murder of the three,' said Halloran. 'When Roger Fairclough was murdered she was out having drinks at a pub in town and then continued the party back at her house with a couple of her friends.'

'She doesn't have anyone at home with her?'

'No, she lives alone.'

'On the one hand I can understand that,' said Kitt. 'Given all she says she's been through. Trust wouldn't come very easily to a person who'd suffered that kind of manipulation and betrayal, so relationships would probably be more difficult to forge. On the other hand . . .'

'It means that she lives her life unmonitored. Anything could be going on at home and nobody would be any the wiser. If anything untoward comes up while verifying her story, I'll be applying for a search warrant like a shot.'

'Given that she can't provide an alibi for the days when the people she knew were murdered, I'd say that was a good call,' said Kitt. 'That seems like a concerning development.'

'It's certainly enough to keep her in the frame but we're going to have to go through her finance and phone records with a fine-tooth comb to find out whether it's likely that she really was at home asleep.'

'What about the dates when the doors were marked by the killer?'

'With those happening around dusk she has an alibi for all three. She was at work and is fairly sure she had clients in the shop. Financial records for the business should verify that, especially if we can get hold of the customers she served and confirm her whereabouts with them.'

'So it's just a case of making sure she's really telling the truth about where she was when the murders were committed,' said Kitt.

'CCTV footage from the local areas where the killer struck has already been scoured by the police in other districts and they haven't come up with anything useful so yes, it will be about other, smaller details.'

'And simply not being able to provide an alibi at that time of night won't necessarily incriminate her in the eyes of a jury, right? Even though she knew two of the victims?'

'Not a chance,' Halloran said. 'It's got to be proven beyond reasonable doubt. I need some hard evidence to attest to her involvement and until I have that it's just circumstantial. Many other people also knew the victims and couldn't provide alibis for all three murders. Given the time of day the murders have taken place, it's not surprising that she can't.'

'But were those other people linked to the occult in the same way Ayleen is? Were they practising witchcraft or anything like that?'

'Nothing has come up on any of the searches we've done

or interviews we've conducted with the victims' nearest and dearest. We're looking into that web name you mentioned, SimonB666, though, to see if we can track down the user.'

'We've submitted the name to one of our tracing services,' said Kitt. 'Here's hoping it's a genuine lead. Time is running out. How is Ruby doing? Have you heard anything from the safe house?'

'Last I heard she was giving DS Redmond a tarot reading, much against his will from the sound of things. I think he was just too scared of her to say no. I don't know what she's been saying to him but he seems really rattled by her.'

'Oh dear me,' said Kitt with a little chuckle. 'Sounds like she's giving him a run for his money, and likely Wilkinson too. Did you manage to follow up with Ayleen about why she didn't move further away from Sandersdale when she left the cult? I did find that a bit odd.'

'I did ask her about that,' Halloran said with a nod. 'She said that she moved down south for a few months while she changed her name but ultimately, she decided to move to Whitby because she had fond memories of visiting here with her parents. She thought the name change and a make-over would be enough to throw anyone off her scent.'

'I suppose that's plausible enough,' said Kitt. 'We've managed to set up an appointment with Stoke Bramley tomorrow so I'll let you know if there are any new leads on that score.'

'I won't hold my breath,' Halloran said with a teasing

smile. 'You're still going to talk to him even though the Boro nick have already had a crack at him?'

Kitt shrugged. 'You know as well as I do that sometimes people are willing to tell a civilian something they'd never dream of telling the police. I might be able to get some information out of him they couldn't.'

'Just be careful,' said Halloran. 'I don't have any concrete evidence that he's up to anything untoward otherwise I'd have had him down the nick in a snap, but according to the station at Boro his manner was . . . slippery.'

'Worry not. I'll be on coms with Grace the whole time I'm in there,' said Kitt, and with that she yawned and stretched her hands up to the ceiling, deliberately reaching high enough to make her T-shirt ride up. As they always did whenever they had the opportunity, Halloran's eyes roamed admiringly over her curves but Kitt had to bite her tongue to keep from laughing when she saw Halloran do a double take at the sight of the tattoo on her hip bone.

'Is that . . . did you . . . ?' Halloran looked from Kitt's face to her hip and back again several times, seemingly trying to digest the information. He moved closer, pushing aside her T-shirt to get a better look.

'Yes, that's right. I'm now officially a complete badass,' Kitt said with a nervous chuckle. She was pretty sure this was the first time she'd ever had cause to say the word 'badass' in her life. And given how awkwardly it had just rolled off her tongue, she didn't intend to make a habit of it.

'Well,' Halloran said, pushing Kitt backwards on to the bed and at once climbing to sit astride her. 'Shop talk is well and truly over.'

'Now, Mal,' Kitt said, adopting a mock serious tone as she started to slowly unbutton his shirt, bit by bit revealing the broad chest hidden beneath. 'Ayleen was very explicit, I'm not supposed to do anything that creates friction on the tattoo.'

Halloran grinned. 'Then I suppose we're just going to have to get creative,' he said, as his hands slid under her T-shirt and lifted it over her head.

FOURTEEN

The next day felt like the longest Kitt had suffered through in a long time. Not because they packed so much into it but because absolutely nothing of use or consequence happened at all. Their appointment with Stoke Bramley wasn't until sundown – well, what else would Kitt expect from a wannabe vampire? And the rest of the day seemed to be a frustrating waiting game on all other fronts. The trace service didn't come back with any further information about SimonB666, and the lovely ladies who worked at the acupuncture clinic in the new town both had alibis for all of the murders. The pair were so nice about providing said alibis that it seemed to Kitt the only thing those two could kill someone with was kindness.

As Kitt had expected, Grace hadn't found anything concerning whatsoever on Joel Mendoza's social media profiles, which at least meant he could be struck off the suspect list with little effort but that was hardly some grand silver lining. They didn't get a call back from Seaview Care Home where Cyril Armitage was a resident until right before they were due to set off for their appointment with Stoke Bramley so visiting him would have to be put off until the following day. And, to top it all off, Kitt was still waiting on the Sandersdale library and archive to get back to her about any documents they might hold pertaining to the Children of Silvanus.

Kitt could only hope she'd get something out of Stoke Bramley to save the day from being a complete write-off.

The Creed of Count Dracula was based in a stately home christened Twilight Manor which stood quite close to the cliff edge just a twenty-minute walk beyond Sandsend. There weren't any other buildings in the immediate vicinity, save an old farm barn on the horizon and a charming little crematorium with ornate pillars and a domed roof that they had passed on the walk over. Thus, with no obvious shelter available, Grace was given no choice but to hide behind some nearby bushes in order to stay close enough for the coms to keep working.

'You sure you want to go in there on yer own?' Grace said, eyeing the Gothic mansion from the spot she and Kitt had decided would be a safe enough distance to exchange their final plans.

Kitt again took in the towering structure that seemed to have been built with the darkest bricks the labourers could find and also boasted the ugliest gargoyles she had ever seen. They were huge hulking appendages with ghastly animalistic faces, furred and fanged. Some of them seemed to Kitt to be howling in pain while others looked as though they were snarling. From this distance, she guessed that, though they didn't have wings, the carvings were supposed to be reminiscent of bats. They were, however, certainly a lot less cute than the Instagram video of a baby bat Evie had shared with her a few months back. Overall, it was a building that seemed to revel in its ability to intimidate.

'I'm sure I'll be fine,' said Kitt, but even she could hear the uncertainty in her voice. 'Halloran knows where I am and will be back in town in the next hour or so. Bramley is aware I'm a civilian investigator looking to help the police apprehend a killer. Given how close that story is to the truth, he can't exactly catch me out. If anything goes wrong, you'll be on coms and can call for help.'

'Rather you than me,' Grace said.

'I'm sure those dark clouds overhead make the whole place look worse than it really is. It's probably lovely once you get in there.' Kitt nodded and then, holding her posture as straight as she could in an attempt to prove to herself that she wasn't afraid, marched towards the iron gates of Twilight Manor. As she pressed the buzzer and studied the name plaque etched in gold typography, Kitt wondered if this old place had been renamed before or after the success of Stephenie Meyer's books. Probably before. She imagined a true vampire enthusiast would find the romantic element of those books a little on the tacky side.

'Yeeees?' A Lurch-like voice droned through the speaker.

'Kitt Hartley, here. I have an appointment with Stoke Bramley.'

There was a beeping sound and the gates began to swing open. Kitt slid through as soon as they'd opened wide enough and made short work of the gravel path leading to the main entrance of the house.

No sooner had she climbed the few steps to the porch than the front door opened which meant, Kitt reasoned, that they likely had video cameras trained on the entrance.

At first it seemed as though the panelled oak door had opened of its own accord but then a man dressed in a black suit appeared in the door frame. Presumably he was the person who had spoken to Kitt through the telecom. He was an exceedingly tall man but was also very thin, with a wiry frame. What little hair he had was a dark shade of grey and, strangely, his skin seemed to have the same grey tinge to it. Likely a lack of vitamin D. Kitt imagined there wasn't much opportunity to be out in the sun when your employer believed himself to be a vampire.

On entering, Kitt couldn't help but openly gape at her surroundings. The colour scheme was almost entirely charcoal, of course, but it had been accented with marble and crystal. A large double staircase dominated the hallway and a giant chandelier hung above it, sparkling even in what little light was available. Various portraits hung on the walls in ornate silver frames but the subject of every one of them looked sour-faced and in some cases even depressed. Though the overall impression was quite morbid, there was no mistaking the expensive tastes of the owners. It was clear to see where all the membership money for the Creed of Count Dracula had been spent. And these people were paying for what, exactly? To be given external verification that they were real vampires? Halloran hadn't gone into detail about that. After what Ayleen had told Kitt about the Children of Silvanus, she intended to make sure everyone here was here of their own free will. If there was any hint of manipulation she'd be onto Mal about it like a shot. These kinds of organizations could only thrive when nobody spoke up about what was really going on and Kitt was no casual bystander.

'Follow me please, madam,' said the man Kitt presumed to be Bramley's butler.

Not much liking the idea of being lost on her own in this place, Kitt did as instructed, sticking close behind the old man while also making a silent promise to have a chat with him on the way out about how happy he was working for a man like Bramley.

After a short walk along an adjoining corridor, decorated in the same manner as the hallway, Kitt was shown into a room panelled with dark mahogany. As far as she could see there were no windows in the room. Just lines of shelves filled with strange trinkets and photographs. Kitt also noticed two goblets wrought in silver that made her wonder, just for a moment, if her host used them to drink blood.

The room was illuminated by several large candelabras that just about offered enough light to see by.

'The master will be with you shortly,' said Bramley's butler. 'In the meantime, do make yourself comfortable.'

Fat chance of that, Kitt thought, but offered the man a polite smile anyway before he took his leave. After all, it's not like Bramley's employees were responsible for the man's taste in decor.

A large painting on the wall caught Kitt's eye, and she moved in for a closer look. It depicted a dark-haired man, clearly a vampire, about to sink his teeth into a pale-skinned blonde woman whose dress didn't quite cover as much as it could have done. It was the kind of outfit that Kitt's mother would have told her she could catch her death in. Another painting further along the wall featured a cave full of bats all hanging from the ceiling, their eyes gleaming yellow in the mottled dark. All of a sudden Kitt felt a chill creep over her. Perhaps coming in here alone had been a mistake.

'Grace,' she hissed into the microphone which was safely hidden behind a silk scarf she had coiled and knotted around her neck. She waited but there was no response. Checking the door to make sure she wasn't about to be interrupted, Kitt tapped the earpiece and adjusted the microphone.

'Grace?' she hissed again. But all she received in return was static.

Oh dear.

Perhaps they hadn't chosen a close enough spot for Grace to stand in for the radio to work. Or maybe there was a fault in the equipment. Or maybe Bramley had equipment that blocked radio transmissions because he really was the Vampire Killer.

And she was trapped in his house.

Alone.

Better to live today and fight tomorrow, Kitt thought, making her way towards the door. She could tell the butler she was feeling unwell if he asked and let him know she'd call to rearrange her appointment as soon as she was better. Yes, that was a plausible enough excuse. Once she'd made it out alive, and they'd solved the coms situation, they could try again.

Just as Kitt reached for the door, however, it swung open and Stoke Bramley stood in the frame. It took all of Kitt's resolve not to cry out with the shock of seeing him there.

'Miss Hartley, I presume?' he said, with an unnerving smirk on his lips. He had tied his long dark hair back into a bun. With so few lines on his face it was difficult to be sure of his exact age, but he definitely hadn't hit thirty yet. Given that in literature looking beautiful for ever was generally deemed to be one of the perks of becoming a vampire, she imagined the youthful look played very well with his potential members.

His complexion was not the only striking thing about him. Even in the dimness of candlelight his green eyes seemed iridescent. Almost to the point that Kitt wondered if he was wearing contact lenses. With his tight black trousers and his ruffled white shirt, which hung loose and revealed more of his chest than Kitt would have preferred to see, it seemed he was of the Anne Rice school of blood-suckers. Quite appropriate, perhaps, given that this was almost literally an interview with a vampire.

'Are you going somewhere, Kitt?' he asked. Kitt presumed the smug look on his face and his sultry swagger was a result of Bramley overestimating his own attractiveness. Certainly he seemed to be enjoying some joke that she wasn't a part of and this attitude, along with the lack of coms, made her muscles tense.

Perhaps he was used to admiration. Perhaps most of the people who visited this place were groupies who found the notion of a real-life vampire alluring. If that was the case, she may have been wrong about the Stephenie Meyer reference at the door. Instead of a good name being tainted by pop culture, it could be a knowing, tongue-in-cheek reference meant to entice people who found vampires enthralling.

Luckily for Kitt, the idea of having her blood sucked by a demonic fiend did not send her pulse racing. Which meant that Bramley was vastly miscalculating his power in this situation, and the power he had over her. 'No, no,' Kitt said, steadying her breathing. 'I thought I heard a noise at the door and came to see what it was. It must just have been you approaching.' She made sure to keep her tone ultra-casual. Her explanation for why she'd been at the door only seemed to amuse Bramley all the more.

He breezed by her, passing closer than she'd like as he did so. Another cheap trick to assert dominance. Well, it wasn't going to work.

Steeling herself, Kitt followed him back into the room. When she spoke, she made sure her tone was as business-like as possible to avoid any misunderstanding.

'Mr Bramley, thank you for seeing me on such short notice. I won't take much of your time.'

'You can call me Stoke,' he almost purred whilst uncorking a bottle of red wine that had been standing on a table in the corner. He poured a glass. 'Won't you join me for a drink, Kitt?' he added, his green eyes gleaming.

'No thank you, I don't drink when I'm on duty,' Kitt replied, eyeing the glass dubiously. Was that one hundred per cent red wine or was there some truth to those disgusting rumours about animal blood? Halloran had said Bramley had denied any such accusations but of course he wasn't going to admit something like that to a police officer hunting for a killer who drained the blood of his victims.

Bramley took a big gulp of his drink and swallowed it,

hungrily. 'Let me guess, you're here to find out if I am the Vampire Killer?'

'As you're not in custody it would seem the police have already ascertained that you are not. I'd imagine yours would be one of the first doors they'd knock on when trying to solve a case like this,' said Kitt.

'You assume right in both instances. They knocked and found nothing. And yet here we are, me the leader of a vampire collective and you a civilian investigator. You must think that there's more to the story than I told the police. You don't seem like the kind of woman who wastes her time. And we all know the killer's next intended victim has but days left to live – five, by my count – unless the killer is stopped.'

'I don't know that there's any more to the story than you told the police but I think that sometimes when people are talking to someone who has the power to arrest them, they are more concerned with making sure it is understood that they're innocent than they are in conveying all the facts that might be relevant,' said Kitt. 'So I'd like to start by asking about what it is you really do here. As far as you're willing to tell me.'

'I have nothing to hide, Kitt,' Bramley said, taking a step closer to her. 'We are, as I said, a vampire collective. But it's not about drinking animal blood as some gossips would have you believe. It's about embracing the darkness.'

'Physically? Is that why you don't go out until sunset?'

'That's not a strict rule,' said Bramley. 'Our members have to function in society, when all's said and done. But a physical embracing of the darkness, spending more time with the night and other nocturnal creatures can help us contemplate the inner darkness that so many others fear or try to pretend isn't there. We all have a dark side, Kitt. Don't you?'

There was no way on earth Kitt was answering that question. Instead she moved the conversation on. 'And what does that achieve? Self-development or enrichment?'

Bramley smirked at Kitt, dodging the question, but he didn't seem surprised by it. 'Yes, I believe it does help with those things. Exploring our dark side, and the dark side of the world, can support us in living more enlightened lives. It also prevents us from fearing our own mortality; like most spiritual collectives we believe in life eternal, mirroring the life of a vampire.'

'So, you all sit around and discuss the ills of the world and how to make peace with them? Or something like that?'

'Something like that. But it's more ritualistic to give it significance. For example, we might ask members to write about a time in which they experienced trauma and burn it on a fire to free themselves. There are many things that we do here but none of them are nearly so terrifying as some would have you believe.'

'And there's no alarming initiation ritual you're not telling me about?'

'Define alarming,' Bramley said, his smile broadening further.

'Well, I'm not really well-versed in these things but off the top of my head I'd have to say anything that involves ritualistic slaughter, violence, coercion or abuse.'

'None of those things sound particularly legal,' said Bramley. 'And I don't engage in illegal activity.'

'What about the members of your group?'

'They know that if they are caught in an illegal act they will be expelled. The list of our terms and conditions for membership is considerable. Given how many people would love to see us shut down altogether we can't take risks and recruit bad apples. Most of our members went through a lot to become a part of the collective so they know better than to flout the rules.'

'Went through a lot? So the initiation is intense then?'

'The initiation is centred around a person proving they are truly willing to embrace their own darkness and whether they're willing to fully trust. A vampire has no physical reflection, so we ask participants to hold a mirror up to their own soul. To admit the things they've got wrong and accept responsibility for the life they lead. So many hold back and cannot be accepted into the group. They want to blame others for the ills that have befallen them rather than accept their own part in them or learn how to harness them for a greater good. We are none of us perfect and a vampire cannot be in denial of the darkness, that is where he truly comes alive.'

'Well that all sounds . . .' Kitt frowned, 'rather fascinating, actually. But you mentioned trust plays a part too. What's the trust part of the initiation?'

Gently, Bramley took Kitt's hand in his. 'Initiates agree to let me bite them, just here.' He drew a line with his finger across the skin just above her wrist.

'What?' Kitt said, pulling her hand from his. Everything up until then had seemed so immersed in philosophy she somehow hadn't expected that.

Bramley laughed. 'I suppose we just found out where you are on the trust spectrum.'

'I don't need to let a stranger bite me to prove I'm trusting, thank you.'

'I do not draw blood,' said Bramley. 'That's the trust part. The initiate has to trust that I would never do anything to harm them, which I wouldn't. If they can't trust me, then they have no place in this collective. Anyone I bite, and it is a mere playful nip, has consented for me to do so. And whenever I do, the response is always laughter, never torturous pain or trauma. In that moment the initiates see that placing a little trust in another needn't be such a big deal. And they laugh at how foolish they were to worry or build up the moment at all.'

'Seems like there are easier ways of establishing trust than that,' said Kitt, still put out by Bramley's comments about her trust issues. She had come a long way with trusting others since Mal had come into her life but being a private investigator and thinking the best of others didn't particularly go hand in hand.

'Easy isn't what makes us grow,' said Bramley, and grudgingly Kitt privately admitted she agreed with that.

'So,' Bramley continued, 'having heard what we do here, what do you think? Am I the Vampire Killer?'

'Right now I don't have any evidence that you are,' said Kitt. 'Other than the link between your vampire activities and the marks left on the victims' necks. But honestly, I think the link is too obvious. This killer has been meticulous in all of his dealings. It doesn't seem likely that he would so readily point to his true identity.'

'I agree it would be an act of astounding arrogance,' Bramley said.

Kitt suppressed a sigh. Arrogance seemed to be at the core of who Bramley was. And the fact that a link between the deaths and his organization was too 'obvious' may just be the perfect grounds for dismissing any allegations against them. They could argue with ease that they would never be so stupid as to commit violent acts that so readily pointed at them, when really they were simply relying on that line of argument to cover the fact they were the ones acting out these atrocities.

'What I was more interested in was finding out if there was anyone who wished your collective harm,' said Kitt, deciding not to challenge Bramley about the fact he seemed arrogant enough to believe he could get away with anything. It wasn't as though he was going to admit anything to her directly and the officers at Middlesbrough had already established that Bramley and his current membership all had alibis for the murders.

Bramley laughed a long and somewhat sardonic laugh. 'As the head of a vampire collective, one that most people have labelled a cult, I'm afraid that list is not a short one. It's strange really. We are very open about who we are and the fact we find creatures of the night so intriguing that we wish to emulate them. And we are labelled monsters for it. But true monsters do not reveal how sharp their teeth are until it is far too late. And something tells me you know that, Kitt.'

Try as she might, Kitt could not disagree with Bramley's hypothesis. It seemed, in so many cases, that the culprit had veiled their truly evil act behind a polite and manipulative mask.

'I'm not talking about idle gossip,' Kitt clarified. 'I am talking about threats, written threats perhaps, that you have received. Either through the post or through social media. Anyone who has made it clear that it is their intention to harm or even destroy you.'

'We have had such threats, but not for several months now. They come in periodically and we save them in case anything untoward happens but nothing ever has.'

'Until now,' said Kitt. 'It is quite possible that this whole situation revolves around implicating you.'

'I've considered that,' Bramley said, taking another step closer to Kitt. 'But I think if that was the case the killer would have drawn a clearer line between us and the victims. I handed over all of our records to the police – all the applications we received from people wanting to join us – but not one of the victims is part of what we do here, we have no link with them. If this was about us the killer would surely have targeted people who'd applied to become one of us, or had at least even visited us, to make sure the finger was firmly pointed in our direction.'

'Possibly,' Kitt conceded. 'But if it's all the same I would like to see those threats that you received anyway. If you show them to me and let me work on them I might be able to find out who the killer is and simultaneously remove all suspicion levelled at your organization.'

For the first time since the start of the interview, Bramley's face seemed to be smirk-free. By now he was only a pace away from where Kitt was standing. 'You may have the files if you think it will help. I'll do anything I can to put an end to these killings. Despite the suspicions against me and mine, I have no wish to see people killed in this way. My desires may be dark but they're not murderous.'

'I beg to differ on that point,' said a deep, familiar voice.

Kitt turned to see that Mal was standing in the doorway, his expression grave, his fists clenched. Grace was with him and Kitt could tell by the startled look on her face something was deeply wrong.

'Kitt, step away from him,' Halloran said. 'He is the person we've been looking for. He's our killer.'

FIFTEEN

As instructed, Kitt took a step back from Bramley and looked back at Halloran.

'Who are you? How did you get in here?' Bramley said, an annoyance Kitt wouldn't have expected from him ringing out in his tone. Up until now, it seemed nothing could ruffle him.

'I'm Detective Inspector Malcolm Halloran,' Mal said, holding up his badge. 'And I'd advise you not to take that tone with me. I have a warrant to search this property. More officers are on their way to ensure no stone is left unturned.'

The tightness in Bramley's face seemed to relax; he looked almost amused by the idea of Twilight Manor being searched. 'I'm assuming, since you've gone to the lengths of securing a search warrant, that you suddenly think that I'm involved with the killings?'

'I have reason to believe you're either responsible or working with one of our other suspects, yes.'

'What could possibly make you think that?'

'It has to do with an online alias of yours, SimonB666.'

'You're SimonB666?' Kitt said, her eyes widening as she took yet another step away from Bramley. If that was the case, he must be in some way connected with the Children of Silvanus and was either targeting Ayleen, or working with her.

For his part, Bramley frowned. 'I don't understand why that would be incriminating. I haven't used that handle in a very long time. Since before I changed my name and formed the Creed of Count Dracula.'

'You were Simon Baker back then,' said Halloran.

Bramley shrugged. 'Yes, that's a matter of public record. It's not something I've ever tried to hide. I ask my members to believe a lot of outlandish things, but even I have to admit that asking them to believe I was born with the name Stoke Bramley would be a bit of a stretch. I still don't understand what all the fuss is about. It's not illegal to change your name, or use an online handle. At least, not to my knowledge.'

'It's not illegal, but when we find evidence that you used that alias to reach out to a collective, as you would call them, involved in the case of the Vampire Killer, well, let's just say that's enough for reasonable suspicion against you.'

'I didn't know there were any other groups mixed up in this. What collective are you referring to?' Bramley said with a frown.

'The Children of Silvanus,' Halloran replied. Kitt noted

that as Mal said this his eyes were fixed on Bramley, carefully gauging his response.

All previous amusement and good humour disappeared from Bramley's face at once and his lips hitched in a snarl as he spoke. 'Why is that important? What have the Children of Silvanus got to do with any of this?'

Halloran's glare deepened. 'You tell me. You're the one with ties to the . . . group.'

'No, I'm not,' Bramley snapped, and, out of nowhere, raised his voice. 'I wasn't part of their cult. I would never have anything to do with a group like that. They were the closest thing to the devil this side of Scotland when they were in operation.'

In an instant, Bramley's whole demeanour had changed. He was panting after his outburst and if it were possible he looked even paler than he had before.

'If you feel that strongly, then why were you online asking questions about them?' Grace countered. 'From the message I read it looked like you were trying to connect with members of the group. If I felt that way about a group of people, I wouldn't go looking for them. I'd put as much distance between them and me as I could.'

At Grace's question, Bramley sighed and slumped into the nearest chair. His former bravado had all but evaporated. His voice was flat and full of defeat. 'I didn't have anything to do with them. But my sister, Penelope, she was a member of their group.'

'How did that happen?' asked Kitt, while noticing that Halloran had reached for his pocket book.

'We were foster kids. Pen never got on with our foster parents. She was a couple of years older than me so she had more happy memories of our birth parents than I did. I think on some level that made her less willing to accept our new reality. No matter what our foster parents did, as far as she was concerned they were always the villains.'

Foster kids? Just like Ayleen. Sounds as though the Children of Silvanus had a pattern when it came to who they groomed. Kitt tried not dwell too long on that point. Few things made her blood boil more than people exploiting the vulnerable but she had to stay focused on the matter in hand.

'So, somehow she became involved in the Children of Silvanus?' said Halloran, jotting down a few notes on what Bramley had said so far.

'One day, out of nowhere, she told me she had been chatting to these people online. She didn't say who they were in the beginning but I later learned they were the Children of Silvanus when they tried to recruit me too. They had invited Pen to become part of their community. She was almost eighteen. She knew I wouldn't let on to our foster parents where she'd gone and probably thought by the time they caught up with her she'd be an adult and there would be nothing they could do about it, even if they wanted to.'

'So, you lost touch with her and your online post was a bid to reconnect?' said Halloran.

Bramley shook his head. 'If only it was as simple as that. I didn't lose touch with her. She was deliberately cut out of my life by those people. One day, I tried to visit her at the camp and the guys guarding the gate wouldn't let me see her. No matter what I tried I couldn't gain entrance. They said only members were allowed inside.'

'Can anyone verify this?' Halloran asked, his tone a little gentler than it had been before.

'I reported it to the police at the time,' Bramley said, his eyes filling with tears, 'so there's probably some kind of record. But it was tricky. Technically no crime had been committed. As far as anyone could see, Penelope was there of her own free will. She'd had her eighteenth birthday by then so she could do what she wanted. Still, someone on the inside of that camp must have been worried about arousing suspicion because the police managed to gain access. They let them in willingly and made it look like they were cooperating.'

'Did they find anything? Anything worrying, I mean?' said Kitt.

Bramley shook his head. 'The officer who reported back to me said it all looked very calm and peaceful there. There were no signs that anything untoward was going on. But there was no sign of Pen. The leader of the group got one of the members to feed the police some story, that Penelope had left the camp two months prior, of her own accord. As if a group like that would just let someone go.'

'From what I've heard about them, I admit that doesn't seem likely,' said Kitt.

'Right then, I knew, something had happened to my sister at that camp. And I was determined to find out what. I tried to join up but they recognized me and guessed my game so refused to admit me.'

'So what did you do next?' asked Halloran.

'A few different things. I started to reach out online to find out if anyone had any information about Penelope. I knew a bit about the group's practices from when they first tried to recruit me and knew they expected members to kill animals. It was described as a necessity – to keep the camp a sustainable community but it seemed to me more akin to animal slaughter, so I thought maybe occult forums might be a good bet. I used the handle you discovered with the 666 at the end so that I looked credible. But of the few ex-members of the group I came into contact with, none of them had useful information about Penelope, and most of them wouldn't talk in any depth at all about their experiences.'

'I'm quite surprised you found any ex-members at all,' said Kitt. 'Did they manage to escape or something?'

Bramley shook his head. 'The cult disbanded in 2011, about a year after Penelope disappeared. There was a large fire in one of the barns and the leader of the group, alongside many of his followers, died in that fire. From what

I understand, those that were left either had wanted to escape for a long time or didn't want to be led by someone new. This meant that in the mid tens it was still possible to get in touch with some ex-members though it only seems to have got more difficult over time.'

'So, you never found your sister?' said Kitt.

'No. When reaching out online didn't work, I started to plan my own collective to see if I could draw someone out in the community who knew something. It took several years of strategy but as you can see I did it eventually,' Bramley said, gesturing to the room around him.

'The Creed of Count Dracula?' said Kitt. 'You mean, it's really a front to put you in touch with similar groups so you can find your sister?'

'It was to begin with,' said Bramley. 'But I've always been drawn to vampires and when I started work on the project, I got much more into it than I expected. I saw the opportunity to make a real difference.'

'And a lot of money, judging by the membership fee. Twelve thousand pounds per year,' said Halloran.

Kitt's eyes widened. She had no idea that the membership fee would be a thousand pounds a month. Exclusive was the word. No wonder Bramley didn't need to admit more than six people a year.

Bramley shrugged and a little of his former attitude returned. 'There are a lot of costs associated with running a group like this. And despite what you might think, I don't siphon off the money to spend on luxury items. I keep the manor to a standard the members expect when they come here for short stays and ritual gatherings. If there's any spare, I put it into my search for Penelope. But as I say, I haven't found her yet, or found out what happened to her. It's been ten years since she disappeared now, so frankly, I'm starting to lose hope that I ever will.'

'We will need to look into this story, Mr Bramley, and we'll still need to conduct the search regardless,' said Halloran.

'I have nothing to hide, DI Halloran, and you have to admit I have no real motive for committing these murders,' said Bramley.

'I wouldn't say that,' said Halloran. 'The culprit clearly gets a kick out of holding ritualistic power over people . . . similar to the kind of power you hold over your members.'

'Be that as it may, I've never hurt a person in my life. Any power I have is given to me with the consent of my members. I will cooperate in any way I can to see the killer brought to justice. Especially if it has something to do with the Children of Silvanus.'

'We don't exactly know what role they play in this as yet,' said Halloran. 'But their name has come up more than once in our enquiries. We would be grateful if you could share any information you have about them. Any names we could follow up on, for example.'

'The list of names of those still alive is short, I'm afraid,' said Bramley. 'I spoke to a man called William Brockley a few years back who told me that Justin Palmer kept a journal. That was a bit of a breakthrough. Knowing that out there, somewhere, there was a book that detailed everything Palmer did. In there, I thought I might find the answers about what happened to Penelope.'

'How did Palmer's journal survive the fire if most of the people on the camp didn't?' said Halloran.

'Brockley said he didn't keep the journal on his person. He buried it and had instructed a loyal few on where they could find it if anything happened to him. One of those loyal few survived. Brockley didn't know what had happened to the journal but he believed Palmer had had a son before he formed the cult. He thought the journal might have passed to the son. I have tried to track down Palmer's son but I haven't been successful. According to Brockley, the kid probably didn't know who his dad was until after he had died, and the rumours are that he went off grid. No phone, no computer, no contact with the outside world.'

'Probably not surprising that he disconnected with the world after that. It can't be the easiest thing to live with,' said Kitt. 'Learning that your father left the family to be a cult leader. It's likely he just doesn't want any reminders.'

'Or is worried someone from his father's past – an enemy perhaps – might find him,' said Grace.

'We'll see if we can track down Palmer's son,' said Halloran. 'If the Children of Silvanus are involved in this case then it's possible he might be too. Or that he might even be in danger. Is Brockley the only person you've managed to find in all your years of searching?'

'I have a suspicion I've crossed paths with others,' said Bramley, 'but they've always denied any involvement with the group. I'm guessing anyone still alive who had an affiliation with them likely regrets it. Their practices were . . . from the Dark Ages.'

'All right, if you don't have any other names for us, we'll start looking into Palmer's son,' said Halloran.

'Oh, wait. There is one other name I know because I've been specifically looking for leads on Penelope. The woman the police spoke to. Her name was Jamelia Park. She was a godmother, that's one of the roles they had on the camp, but I don't really know what it means other than that they each seem to have been in charge of a small group of the members. She was the one who convinced the police that Pen had left of her own accord. Claimed to have been good friends with her and sad to see her leave. All that kind of stuff.'

'Wait, Jamelia Park was a godmother?' said Kitt. 'Are you quite sure about that?'

'I'm certain,' said Bramley. 'That's what the police told me, anyway, and I've had so few leads in the time I've been looking it's not difficult to keep it all straight . . . why?'

Without a word, Kitt turned to Halloran and Grace. Their expressions were just as tense as hers. If what Bramley had just said was the truth, Jamelia Park, or Ayleen Demir as she was now known, had lied to them. She wasn't at the mercy of the obedience training and the drugging of the food, she had been one of the people in charge of it. And what if she'd enjoyed all that power and control she'd had over others too much? What if she missed it more than she realized she would? Could that unquenchable urge be motive enough to kill?

SIXTEEN

It was nearing midnight when Kitt settled herself into the small booth behind the double-sided mirror at Whitby police station. The local officers had understandably taken some convincing before they would allow Kitt to witness the interview, but luckily Halloran knew one of the officers, DS Sandra Drake, from his time working in Irendale. DS Drake had grey hair worn in a long bob that just met her shoulders and had a soft, round face that looked kindly enough. From her posture, however, Kitt got the distinct impression that she wasn't the type to stand for any nonsense.

Duly, even if she had known Halloran for some time, she wasn't entirely enthused about the idea of Kitt observing from the sidelines. Once he explained that Kitt was a civilian investigator who had already interviewed the suspect once and would thus be able to quickly spot any holes in the suspect's story, however, Kitt was discreetly shown into the back room. It was already late and nobody wanted to make this a longer job than it had to be. Especially given that after the stroke of midnight, there would only be four days left to catch the killer. If they could put this case to rest tonight, they could all sleep easier when they finally got to bed.

Grace was, of course, put out not to be permitted the same access as Kitt. But once she had accepted they couldn't breach protocol any further than necessary, she agreed to continue her research into *The Curse of James I, A Musical* – the play Cyril Armitage had performed in that he now seemed to be reliving.

As they were operating from a different police station, it was highly unlikely that Chief Superintendent Ricci would find out about Kitt's sneak peek into the interview. Even if she did, Kitt wagered that with so little time before the next murder was due to happen, Ricci would forgive this lapse in protocol if they managed to bring the killer to justice.

Though Kitt privately admitted that, just now, it was a big if. Ayleen Demir may have lied to them but they still had to prove she had means, motive and opportunity to commit the vampire killings. The means were taken care of with the tattoo needles, the opportunity – well, she had known two of the victims and didn't have an alibi for the nights they were murdered, so perhaps something further would be uncovered on that point. The motive, however, was the real issue. Had the death of her parents been her fault? Were they dealing with a long-term psychopath? Or had her experiences with the cult warped her mind in some irreparable way?

Beyond the glass of the two-way mirror Ayleen, or Jamelia, sat in a pair of jeans and a tatty grey T-shirt she'd thrown on when the police came knocking after she had already gone to bed. Her hair hung long and unkempt around her shoulders and the bags under her eyes betrayed the fact she hadn't been sleeping well. Was that because of guilt over whatever acts she had committed in Sandersdale all those years ago? Was it because she had been left tossing and turning and wondering when the lies she'd told to the police would catch up with her? Or was it because she was the person they had been hunting for all along? Kitt could only hope that in the course of this interview they would find out. She had sensed from the get-go that Ayleen might not have been telling the whole truth but even she had been surprised by the revelation that she was a godmother for the Children of Silvanus; that she had inflicted all of the pain she had claimed to have been victim to.

'She did my tattoo, you know?' Kitt said to Halloran and Drake. 'For that reason alone I'm sort of hoping you prove her innocent. Me being tattooed by a chief figure in a sinister cult is bad enough. If I've been tattooed by a serial killer, well, that is just the kind of information that sends Grace off onto a wild case of hysterics. And frankly I have to deal with enough of those as it is.'

'She lied to you, Kitt, and to me,' said Halloran. 'And not

about something small. She completely misrepresented her role in the Children of Silvanus. She sat there and painted herself as the victim. She didn't tell you about some of the things the godmothers did on the camp, and I was hoping to spare you the details. But there were beatings, members pitted against each other in hand-to-hand combat, there was some suggestion that ritual animal slaughter played a part too, and that was just the stuff she felt like telling me about. She made us believe she was on the receiving end of all this. But she was the perpetrator. That's a huge red flag in a case like this. We won't have the forensic tests that have been carried out at Twilight Manor for a few days but the team that searched the site didn't find anything on a first pass. Which means that, right now, she's our chief suspect. If she's capable of some of the things she described to me, she might be capable of much worse.'

'Halloran's right,' said DS Drake. 'If she's carried out that kind of behaviour in the past, there is a chance that she's escalated.'

'I know,' said Kitt. 'I think I'd just rather you proved I didn't lock myself in a private room with a serial killer for an hour with only Grace on coms as a fail-safe.'

'You seem to have survived the experience,' said DS Drake, with an admiring note to her voice the likes of which Kitt had never heard from DS Banks in nearly two years of knowing her. 'And now you're in a position to help us make sure that if she is responsible she doesn't get away with anything else. Listen carefully, and make a note of anything that doesn't seem in line with what she told you before.'

'Er, yes, what she said,' said Halloran, with a small reassuring smile. 'Let's see what she's got to say for herself, shall we?' Without another word he exited the booth along with DS Drake. The pair walked into the interrogation room and at once Ayleen's brown eyes were on them. Kitt could tell from her questioning expression that Ayleen was looking for some clue as to why Halloran and Drake had dragged her down to the station. She knew she had been brought in for further questioning under caution, of course. But she didn't know specifically what kind of questions might be asked. From her look of open curiosity, it seemed she was trying to figure out which lie had been unravelled, which left Kitt wondering how many lies she'd told them.

Neither officer spoke while they took their seats. After which they paused for a moment and fixed their stares on the suspect. Kitt remembered Halloran and Banks giving her much the same treatment the first time she had been in the interrogation room. It was the kind of moment some people, who think themselves tough, believe they would handle well. But in that small room, with just you and the officers, Kitt knew from personal experience that no matter how tough you were the pressure only mounted.

After a moment, DS Drake pressed the record button on the equipment sitting on a table.

'Interview with Ayleen Demir, Tuesday the thirteenth of

April at eleven fifty-four p.m. Present in the room is DI Halloran, DS Drake and Ayleen Demir. For the record can you confirm that you've been offered legal representation and declined it?'

'I don't need a lawyer,' said Ayleen. 'I've done nothing wrong.'

'That's the story you're sticking to, is it?' said Halloran, raising his eyebrows.

'Story? It's the truth. What's going on?' asked Ayleen, a note of surprise in her voice. 'I've already told you everything I know. What could possibly be so important at this time of night?'

'We have a source that tells us you haven't told us everything you know,' said Halloran.

Ayleen flinched at this revelation but tried to morph it into a frown. Kitt hadn't missed her reaction though and she knew that Halloran and Drake wouldn't have either.

'Why don't you explain to us again, for the record, your involvement in the Children of Silvanus?' said DS Drake.

Ayleen looked nervously between the two officers. 'Nothing much to tell. At least not that I haven't already told you.'

'Let's start from the beginning and see if we can jog your memory a bit,' said Halloran. 'Tell us again, why did you join the group?'

'But I already . . .' Ayleen saw the look on Halloran's face and trailed off. There was no getting out of this, and in that moment she knew it. Sighing, she obliged.

'When I was eight I lost my parents in a house fire. I spent several years in foster care. I never really got over the trauma that I'd experienced. I was into all sorts of things back then. I drank heavily. I experimented with ... substances that I really shouldn't have. I was looking for a way of just staying alive and then one day, on an internet chat forum, I met a member of the Children of Silvanus. The person at the other end of the line, they made it seem like they really cared about me. They told me lots about their family, as they called it.' Ayleen paused here, seemingly for effect more than anything else. 'A sense of belonging to a family, well, that was just what I was missing. So, not knowing what I was getting myself into, I ran away and joined them.'

'How old were you at this point?' asked Drake.

'Fifteen, almost sixteen.'

'And what did you do out there with them? Describe a typical day for me,' said Halloran.

Ayleen offered a dismissive wave. 'It was mostly just chores: cooking, cleaning, gardening and looking after the chickens. The camp was self-sufficient when it came to food but we all had to pitch in to make that possible.'

'Was there any other livestock, besides the chickens?' asked Halloran.

This struck Kitt as a rather odd question but she assumed Halloran must have had a good reason for asking it.

'There were a few other animals. A couple of cows for milk. Sheep for wool.'

'And did you ever eat any of the animals that you kept?' Halloran pushed.

'We, er, yes. Once in a while. Sometimes we killed a chicken or cooked grouse or rabbits that wandered into our enclosure.'

'And how were the animals killed?'

Ayleen looked at Halloran, her next words slow, cautious. She clearly suspected a trap but hadn't worked out yet what the trap was. 'One of the members would be asked to slaughter it so that the rest could eat.'

'Who did the slaughtering?' asked DS Drake.

'We took it in turns. Anyone who was over sixteen took their turn.'

'So, if you got there when you were fifteen and didn't leave for six years, you spent five years slaughtering animals at the behest of Justin Palmer?' said Halloran.

'Yes, but—'

'And did you only ever kill these animals for food?' said DS Drake.

Ayleen paused for a moment before responding. 'No. Sometimes they would make us kill the animals as a thanksgiving sacrifice to Silvanus.'

'Sounds to me like good preparation for ritually killing larger mammals,' said DS Drake looking at Halloran and speaking as if Ayleen wasn't even in the room. 'It might have been forced at first, but she probably came to enjoy killing defenceless little animals.'

Halloran nodded. 'And when it all stopped, she missed it. That feeling of power. It's not surprising that, after that, she moved onto killing humans.'

'Humans?' Ayleen repeated, and then suddenly realizing where this conversation was heading, she shook her head and slammed her hand down on the table. 'No, that's not true. I didn't want to. I didn't want to kill the animals. They made me do it. I can still hear the noises the poor things made when we killed them. I wouldn't have done something like that voluntarily.'

'But you did do it for five years,' said Halloran. 'And we're supposed to believe that didn't have an effect on you? Didn't give you a taste for killing?'

'I didn't kill anybody.'

'But you tortured them, didn't you?' said Halloran.

'What? No, I did not.' Ayleen had the gall to look outraged at the insinuation.

'Well, perhaps tortured is a bit too much of a strong word. Let's say you coerced and punished them. Gave them what you thought they deserved.'

'No. No. No!' Ayleen half-screamed.

'I don't believe you, Ayleen,' said DS Drake. 'And do you know why?'

Slowly, Ayleen shook her head.

'Because we know that you were a godmother at the camp. We've got it on record and we've got a person willing to testify to it. We know that you were the one putting strange substances into people's food. Intimidating them into killing animals, and into fighting each other. We know you were the one dishing out the punishments. We know what you did.'

Ayleen began to shake. 'Look. Look, I know I wasn't completely honest. And I . . . I may have done some things that I regret, but I'm not your killer.'

'If you really weren't trying to throw us off the track, then why did you lie to us about the killer coming after you because you escaped from the Children of Silvanus?' said Halloran.

'Because,' a tear slid down Ayleen's cheek, 'I didn't want to admit to the real reason the killer is probably after me.'

'And what reason is that?'

'They are probably after me for payback for what I did. All the things I did that I shouldn't have done.'

'How far did you take it?' said Halloran. 'Did you coerce people into killing animals? Into fighting each other to show their obedience and allegiance?'

'You don't understand,' Ayleen said. 'You don't understand how scary it was. If you disobeyed Palmer, if you didn't do as you were told, you disappeared.'

'Like Penelope Baker,' said Halloran.

Ayleen's eyes widened. 'You know about Penelope?'

SEVENTEEN

Halloran stared even harder at Ayleen than he had before. 'Yes, we know, but we want to hear the truth from you.'

'Is it just Penelope or do you know about the others too? Did you find them?'

'Never mind what we know. We want to hear what you know,' said DS Drake.

'I don't know where Penelope is, if that's what you're asking?'

'Then why did you tell the police at the time that you did know what had happened to her?' said Halloran. 'Why did you lie, again?'

Ayleen sat quiet and still.

'Lying seems to be something of a bad habit for you, Ayleen. If I were you, I'd come clean now and tell us what you really know about Penelope's disappearance.'

Still Ayleen didn't respond.

When DS Drake spoke again, her voice was soft and

warm. 'What happened to Penelope, Ayleen? You need to tell us. Her family deserve to know what became of her.'

'I can't tell you where she is because I don't know. But I can tell you part of the story. The bit that I saw. The bit that I—'

Kitt took a deep breath. From the sound of things, Ayleen hadn't just witnessed what had happened to Penelope, she'd had some part to play in it too.

'Go on,' Halloran pushed.

'It was a new recruit to the group. Jesse, his name was Jesse. There was something different about him, I knew it as soon as I met him but I did as I was told anyway. Initiated him into the group. Made him kill animals as sacrifices. Put him in hand-to-hand combat against other members. Nothing lethal. That part of the initiation wasn't about killing each other, it was about proving to Palmer that you would be willing to do exactly as he said. Failing to stop a fight on the order of a godparent was deemed by him as serious an offence as refusing to fight when ordered. It wasn't about violence; it was about control. About building allegiance to him.'

'And this Jesse, what happened with him?' asked Halloran.

'He joined around the same time as Penelope. He was always hanging around her. I think he was a bit obsessed with her. She had shown reluctance to complete the initiation of killing a grouse but had gone through with the task.

When it came to killing a rabbit, though, she couldn't do it. She started screaming that she was going to leave and tell everyone about what was happening at the camp.'

'What happened then?' asked Halloran.

Kitt shuffled on the spot, realizing she both did and did not want the answer to that question.

'Part of me was relieved, when I heard her scream like that. It was buried very deep by that point but there was still a part of me that wanted to escape and when I heard Penelope cry out it was the first time since joining the group that I really acknowledged it. That I felt that part of me had a voice – even if that voice wasn't my own. But the others around me didn't feel the same.'

'What did they do?' asked DS Drake.

'He was . . . just so clinical about it – Jesse. He walked over to her and without even blinking he punched her to the ground to stop her from screaming. He then screamed down at her that she was a disappointment to Palmer. That she didn't deserve to be part of his collective. This altercation didn't go unnoticed by the leaders closest to Palmer. They praised Jesse for his loyalty and took Penelope away. I knew then I would never see her again, and I never did. I also knew that if I stayed, one day that would be me. One day they would push me too far. And I would try to rebel. And that would be the end of me. I'd be gone like all the others. That's why I made my plan to escape.'

'We will need the names of anyone you can remember

from that time, especially the leaders closest to Palmer,' said Halloran.

'I will do that but I don't know who is still alive. It was a brutal existence up there.'

'It would have been better if you had come clean about all this in the first place,' said DS Drake. 'You've made it very difficult for us to believe anything you tell us by lying about your part in this group.'

'I didn't lie because I am guilty of the vampire killings. I lied because I'm ashamed of who I was, and what I did.'

'I understand the rationale,' Halloran said, his voice calm but stern, 'but you should know that given what you've told us, you won't be leaving this station without being charged for the crimes you've committed in the past. Misuse of drugs, coercion, animal cruelty, and that's just for starters.'

'But I did those things under duress,' Ayleen pleaded.

Halloran held up a hand to silence her. 'Any mitigating circumstances will be considered in full by a court. But we have to submit the necessary case work to them and let them decide the outcome.'

Ayleen lowered her head at Halloran's statement but offered no further pleas. She had done all she could over the last decade to escape the consequences of what had happened in that camp. It seemed to be finally dawning on her that there was no escape, she would be held accountable for her actions. Kitt shook her head, thinking about how young Ayleen had been when she'd got to the camp. Though she had been an adult when she'd left, by that point she had already endured six years of conditioning. At fifteen, did you really have the confidence to challenge adults over what they were telling you to do? Especially when everyone else was being so obedient. Kitt could only hope that the court would take the manipulation and victimization Ayleen had endured into account when deciding on any penalties.

'As for the vampire killings and any possible role you may have in them, this is not a case we can take any chances on,' Halloran continued. 'We will be conducting a full and thorough search of your business and personal properties. You will be held in custody while we wait for the forensic results. If we discover you have lied to us a second time, I will have you charged with obstruction of justice on top of everything else, do you understand?'

Ayleen nodded. It was a meek gesture. So slight as to be almost indiscernible. 'I think I'd better speak to a lawyer now,' she mumbled.

From this reaction alone, anyone would think she was nothing more than a helpless victim in all this, and she had been when it all started. But Kitt imagined that not everyone rose to the rank of godmother at the camp and until the police had thoroughly investigated Ayleen's involvement with the Children of Silvanus, they could take nothing for granted when it came to the true identity of the Vampire Killer.

EIGHTEEN

The next day, the sun rose at quarter to six and Kitt rose just a few minutes later. With just days until the Vampire Killer was due to strike for a fourth time, it was impossible to rest easy and sleep long. Instead, Kitt quickly dressed, gave Halloran his good morning kiss and took herself off for a walk on the sands near a long line of brightly painted beach huts. This, she reasoned, would give her the time and space she needed to think before Grace roused and they got down to the business of the day. The rushing swell of the ocean and the promise of sunshine beyond the clouds also took the edge off the morbid dream she had had the night before. A dream in which she had been buried alive.

It wouldn't have taken a qualified therapist to decode that one.

With so little time left before the Vampire Killer was due to take Ruby, Kitt was trying not to dwell on just how complicated the case had become. She had suspected the involvement of a cult when she'd arrived in Whitby, that's why she had insisted on interviewing Stoke Bramley. But she hadn't expected that a cult in operation more than a decade ago would play a part in the proceedings. If the Children of Silvanus really was at the centre of this case, then who knew how long the killer had been plotting their revenge? Right now, she was buried alive, all right, in clippings and notes from interviews and lists of possible weapons. And despite it all, she felt no closer to discovering who was really behind the murders.

'Kitt!' Halloran's call came from behind. She turned to smile and wait for him as he marched his way across the sands. Before she'd left for her walk, he had mentioned he had some early morning calls to make about the search on Ayleen's house and work, and the search conducted at Twilight Manor. He had promised to come out and find her as soon as he was done.

'All right, pet,' he said when he caught her up, kissing her forehead and taking her hand in his.

'What do you know then – anything at Ayleen's?' Kitt asked as they continued a slow walk across the sands.

'Nothing yet. They're making a thorough job of it and any forensics won't be back for a good two days at the earliest. We can hold her for ninety-six hours if totally necessary – and it has been known for tests to take that long, even in a high-stakes case like this.'

Kitt nodded. 'Ninety-six hours would take us up to the

night of the murder so if she is still in custody then at least she won't be able to get at Ruby by the deadline.'

'She can't but don't forget, it's highly likely this killer has an accomplice, given the complexity of it all.'

'So let's hope those tests come back quicker. If they find something, we'll need to break her and find out who her accomplice is as a matter of urgency.'

'I'm putting on as much pressure as I dare; hopefully the tests will be back before then.'

Kitt sighed. 'I know she might have done some terrible things, Mal, but I can't help but feel sorry for her. Losing her parents so young like that and then falling into the hands of a cult, no less. You heard what Stoke Bramley said about him and his sister, they were foster kids too.'

'I know,' said Halloran. 'It sickens me as much as it does you. The way people like that prey on the vulnerable. Unfortunately, when you do this job, you start to realize it's a bit of a theme. There's always someone out there ready to exploit people who don't have the means or the faculties to stay safe.'

'Which, I suppose, makes it even more important that people like you and me stand up for those they try to exploit.'

'Too right,' said Halloran. 'Even if she has nothing to do with these murders, Ayleen won't escape some kind of penalty for her past crimes. I'm sure, however, the fact that she was groomed will be taken into consideration, even if she wasn't a minor when she committed some of the crimes.'

'I hope so. Right now it feels like there's a darker story behind all this than we first realized. Any more news about Bramley?'

'We don't have the forensics back on Twilight Manor yet, but unlike Ayleen, Bramley doesn't appear to have lied to us. Or at least, we haven't found any evidence of it. Ayleen, on the other hand, was conditioned to lie as a survival instinct years ago. Because of that, she is the top suspect right now, but Bramley's been told not to go anywhere. We'll continue investigating other leads at the same pace as before. We cannot ease up even for a moment until we're one hundred per cent sure we've brought the true killer to justice. Banks is trying to track down Penelope Baker and has started work looking into Palmer's son.'

'You think Penelope's still alive?' Kitt said, quite taken aback by the idea. In her mind's eye, she could picture the kind of place the Children of Silvanus camp would have been, out there on that lonely moor top. She had been trying not to engage with this bleak image but, of course, after all that had happened in the past twenty-four hours it was inevitable that her mind would wander to that dark and isolated place. Ayleen had said Penelope wasn't the only one to have disappeared. Kitt hadn't consciously addressed what might have become of her and those like her who wouldn't obey. It wasn't an idea she wished to dwell on. But some part of her suspected that they might have been murdered and buried out in the dales. After so many years had passed, the odds of finding their resting places with no instruction from a knowledgeable party didn't seem high. The idea that Penelope might still be alive wasn't one Kitt had even considered. 'With all the money Stoke Bramley has thrown into finding her, don't you think he'd know if she was alive by now?'

'You're assuming that she wants to be found,' said Halloran.

'You don't think she wants to be reunited with her brother? Why? Because she might have done things at the camp she was ashamed of?'

'That's one possibility,' said Halloran. 'Being in that environment might have changed her. Might have made her bitter or vengeful.'

'You think she might be the Vampire Killer, don't you?' said Kitt.

Halloran nodded in response.

'I can understand the rationale but that only works if you believe Ayleen's story that the killer is trying to intimidate and scare her before he – or she – finally comes for vengeance. Ayleen only knows two of the victims – so far as she remembers – so I'm not sure we have enough evidence to support that theory.'

'I know, but now that we've discovered Ayleen played a key part in performing some of the more unethical acts that took place in that camp, somebody coming after her makes a lot more sense. Remember also, the killer has been smart about covering their tracks since the first murder took place. It could be that they just selected some people at random who had associations with the occult in order to mask their true target – Ayleen – when they finally get around to killing her. If they had gone after her first and she had been the only victim, we would have looked into Ayleen's past and likely discovered her involvement with the cult. This might have made the identity of the killer quite obvious – especially as so few people seem to have survived the fire at the camp.'

'So, if Penelope Baker is the killer, you think she blames Ayleen for what happened to her, and Penelope – or somebody who knows her – is taking revenge?'

'It is just a theory at present. We've asked Ruby if she knows, or has ever known, a Jamelia Park or Ayleen Demir. She doesn't recognize the names so she and the second victim don't seem to be acquainted with Ayleen. She hasn't heard of the Children of Silvanus either, which I must admit I was slightly surprised about. I didn't think there was anything weird out there that Ruby wouldn't be well-versed in.'

Kitt smiled at the thought of Ruby's eccentricity but just as quickly the smile disappeared. 'And yet we do seem to be led back to that group over and over again. But there's nothing about them online – except for Stoke Bramley's post on Reddit. So it's very difficult to find anything out about them.'

'Maybe for a civilian investigator,' Halloran said with a

twinkle in his eye. Kitt knew what he was doing. Baiting her to try and take her mind off just how many different strands there were to this case and how little time they had left to untangle them all. Still, just because she saw straight through his efforts didn't mean she didn't appreciate them.

'Oooh, give over, you and yours wouldn't even be in Whitby if it wasn't for Hartley and Edwards Investigations. You don't know that you'll get to the bottom of it before I do.'

'Want to make it interesting?'

'What do you have in mind?'

'How about, if you solve the case before me, I will be your unquestioning servant for twenty-four hours.'

'And in the unlikely event that you solve the case first?' Kitt said, just to see Halloran smile.

'You will do the same for me.'

'Well, that sounds like a win-win,' said Kitt, leaning in to kiss him. 'Ooh, I wish I had longer to spend with you,' she added, once their lips parted again. 'But I've got to get back to the hotel. Me and Grace have to get our questions in order for Cyril Armitage.'

'What? The bloke who thinks he's the reincarnation of James I?'

'I'm not sure that's quite what's going on. I'll know more after we've talked to him but either way the poor old chap sounds very confused. I can tell by your tone that you're not convinced it's going to be a particularly lucrative interview, and I'm minded to agree with you, but at least once we've spoken to him we can rule him out as a suspect and focus on Ayleen, Bramley, Penelope or whoever it is from the Children of Silvanus that is really pulling the strings here.'

'All right, I'm parked up on the cliff top so I'll part ways with you here,' Halloran said, pulling Kitt in for one last hug. 'You'll update me on anything you find out from Cyril?'

'Of course, how else will you crack the case if I don't help you?' Kitt chuckled. With that, she blew Halloran a kiss and turned back towards the guest house. She had only travelled ten paces or so and was just wondering which details she should add to Ayleen's file after the interview she had witnessed last night, when all of a sudden she heard an ear-splitting crack from above. She looked upwards and her eyes widened in terror to see a large block of stone hurtling off the cliff towards her.

'Kitt, look out!' she heard Halloran bellow. She started to run but couldn't be sure she was fast enough to move out of harm's way. A second later Halloran knocked her off her feet and rolled her over several times in the sand before an almighty thud sounded out as the hunk of rock landed mere inches from where they lay.

Kitt felt as though there was no air in her lungs at all and she gasped and gasped to catch her breath. Her whole body was shaking like it never had before.

Halloran held her face in both of his hands. 'Are you all right? Kitt? Are you all right?'

She nodded. Not yet able to speak.

'I just looked back at you one last time and I saw a figure on the cliff top, holding the rock above his head. For a second I couldn't believe what I was seeing but it quickly became clear you were standing right below him and something in me – I don't know ... I just knew you were in danger. It ricocheted off the side of the cliff as he threw it over. If it hadn't been for that I probably wouldn't have got to you in time.'

'Are ... are you saying somebody knew I was walking down here and they threw the rock at me deliberately?' said Kitt, her eyes filling with tears.

'I'm ... I'm afraid so,' Halloran said, running a hand through her hair.

Kitt could barely digest what this meant. Someone had tried to put her out of the picture, possibly for good.

Catching her breath she rolled over to take a look at the rock that had almost crushed her to death. As she did so, she cried out.

'Kitt, what is it?' Halloran asked.

But she couldn't find the words to answer him. She blinked, checking she really was seeing what she thought she was seeing. The piece of rock was long and a garish face had been carved into it. The carving was of a devilish creature with a tortured expression that Kitt recognized at once. There was no mistaking it. This wasn't just any old hunk of rock. It was a gargoyle from Twilight Manor. And the unnerving animalistic face wasn't the only thing carved into it. Along the top, someone had scratched a single word into the stone.

Die!

NINETEEN

'I am going to kill him. Just you wait til I get my hands on him,' said Halloran, who was pacing up and down, seemingly intent on completely wearing out the grass near the bench at the end of Henrietta Street on the other side of the harbour from where Kitt had been attacked. Below, the East Pier was bathed in mid-morning sunlight and the red-roofed buildings of the town beyond seemed to be stacked on top of one another, built, as they were, between the two steep cliffs on either side of the Esk river.

'Mal, come on now, for goodness' sake calm down, will you? said Kitt.

'Yeah,' Grace chipped in. 'Calm down, Halloran. If you kill him it will cost you your badge. If I kill him, I'll go to jail, but it'll still be worth it.'

'Stand down, the pair of you,' said Kitt, her voice sterner this time. 'I'm really not convinced that yet more cold-blooded murder is the answer to our problems here. And besides, Stoke Bramley is not behind this.'

'But you said the gargoyle was from Twilight Manor,' said Grace. 'It's not quite a smoking gun but it is near as dammit, if you ask me. I knew that guy was too smug for his own good, he's been plotting this all along.'

'And don't forget, there's the timing, Kitt,' said Halloran. 'Ayleen's in custody so she couldn't have done it – or at least not directly. We just conducted a major search of Bramley's property. Perhaps this is an attempt to scare you off because if we keep digging we're going to find what we're looking for. Evidence that he really is the Vampire Killer. For all we know, these victims have something to do with his sister's disappearance and he's taking revenge. Or Penelope is the real killer and he's trying to protect her.'

'I agree that a lost sister, or protecting one's sister, would be motive for revenge killings,' said Kitt, knowing that if anything happened to her sister, or indeed any member of her family, she would stop at nothing to see justice served. 'But if you wanted to get someone out of the way would you use a weapon that incriminated you? Because that's what that gargoyle is. It's designed to make you think that Bramley wants me dead or at the very least in hospital for the foreseeable future. If it really had been him, I think he would have found a more subtle way of scaring me off.'

'I'm not sure if you noticed,' said Halloran, 'but subtlety isn't exactly Bramley's strong suit.'

'Be that as it may,' said Kitt, 'unless a witness steps forward who got a good look at whoever was on top of that cliff this morning, and until forensics come back on that gargoyle, nothing is certain.'

'Someone might have seen something. I'll be canvassing nearby houses and hotels,' said Halloran.

'Given that it happened just after half past six in the morning a fair way down the beach I think you'll be lucky to have any witnesses,' said Grace.

'Won't stop me trying to find some,' said Halloran.

'If you really think about it, what happened this morning was a good thing,' added Kitt.

Halloran frowned. 'Forgive me for not quite yet being able to see the silver lining.'

'The fact that this has happened simply means we're getting close to the truth. We wanted to smoke the killer out. Prompt them into doing something rash that might get them caught. And that's just what they've done.'

'You almost getting crushed to death by a falling rock is not what I had in mind,' said Halloran.

'Well, I'm sure I wouldn't have been crushed to death. Maybe I might have sustained a head injury I couldn't have recovered from but . . .' Kitt trailed off, noticing the thunderous look on Halloran's face. 'That's not a comfort to you, is it?'

'I know it all happened really quickly but you didn't notice any details that could help us track them down?'

Grace said to Halloran. 'When you looked up there, I mean. At the time, I know you will just have been focused on Kitt's safety. But in retrospect, you don't remember anything about their clothes?'

Halloran shook his head. 'They were dressed in black. They were possibly – possibly – wearing the same hoodie as the person who spray-painted Ruby's door. But I couldn't even say that for certain. I'm trained to notice details but it all happened so quickly and I could see what was going to happen to Kitt if I didn't move fast.'

'I'll never make fun of you going for your morning jogs again,' Kitt said.

'Really?'

'Well, no, not really. If you insist on going out with a northern lass you have to suffer the banter, I'm afraid. But I'm obviously very grateful that you're so quick on your feet.'

Halloran paused his incessant pacing long enough to smile at her. After a moment, however, his smile evaporated as his mind switched back to thoughts of Bramley. 'The second we get confirmation that it was him I am taking him in to the nearest nick and I will not be going easy on him in the interrogation room.'

Kitt closed her eyes for a moment, taking a deep breath and being thankful that she was still in a position to do so. Both Halloran and Grace were already so wound up about her brush with death she thought it prudent to downplay the effect it had had on her. She couldn't deny it had rattled her. Someone wanted her out of the way. Someone didn't want her interfering. Whether it was somebody they had already spoken to or an acquaintance of one of their interviewees, Kitt could not be sure, but one thing was clear: somewhere along the line she had hit a nerve. And whoever she had provoked, they certainly didn't lack in confidence. A murder attempt in broad daylight, even that early in the morning when so few people were around, was a bold move.

'You said yourself, Mal, we can't discount the fact that Ayleen might have an accomplice,' said Kitt.

'Or either Ayleen or Bramley have someone who wants to protect them,' said Grace. 'And that's who threw that rock.'

'Hm, yes,' said Kitt. 'I would wager that someone like Stoke Bramley has quite a few admirers.'

'And what exactly makes you think that?' Halloran said, raising an eyebrow.

Kitt just about managed to hold in a chuckle at his reaction. Halloran's jealous streak was well worn in. It greatly amused Kitt that he thought anyone could hold a candle to him in her eyes, and at the same time made her more determined to keep showing him that could never be true. 'He thinks so much of himself and I can't think that much bravado comes from ego alone. Plus, this is Whitby, home of the goth weekend, and I imagine quite a few people who frequent the event are somewhat drawn to the vampire aesthetic. He's probably beating them off with a stick at this time of year.'

'So, you think one of his many admirers might be trying to protect him?' said Grace. 'Hoping to win his affections?'

'Well, if he happened to mention in passing that he had been questioned by a detective when he was innocently trying to find his long-lost sister, if whoever he told was possessive over him, they might have taken matters into his or her own hands.'

Halloran nodded. 'Assuming Bramley or Ayleen are clever enough to understand that pulling something like this the day after we've interviewed them would incriminate them – and I'm not saying I'm giving either of them that much credit, especially Bramley – then the idea that somebody wanted to protect one or both of them is more plausible. Besides anything else, I just don't know if Ayleen or Bramley would be able to pull off what this killer has, at least not alone. Given the fact that neither have successfully kept their past aliases a secret, perhaps it's more likely that this is the work of somebody else. Somebody behind the scenes that we're just not seeing.'

'Like Palmer's son?' said Kitt. 'You heard what Bramley said, he's gone off grid. No phone. No computer. Nobody knows where he is. Bramley thinks that he has access to his father's journal. He could be using it to target people involved with the cult. People like Ayleen and even Bramley himself. He tried to go after the cult after Penelope disappeared. It might have felt enough of a threat for Palmer to record it in his journal.'

'Well, Banks is looking into Palmer's past partners now to see if we can get a lead on his son. It's not a quick job as we don't exactly know when he founded the cult and he clearly wasn't short on girlfriends.'

'I didn't get a chance to tell you earlier because of the near-smushing incident,' said Grace. 'But I may have another potential suspect for our list related to Cyril Armitage.'

'Who's that?' asked Kitt.

'Stella Hemsworth,' said Grace.

'Stella – the director at the amateur dramatics company?'

'The person who wrote and directed *The Curse of James I, A Musical*,' said Grace. 'There are some clips from the rehearsals on YouTube. There's a scene in which one of the witches has their blood drained and the witches all have marks put on their door when the witch hunter comes after them. Not a V, I admit, but when I was watching the clips these elements did seem to stand out.'

Kitt frowned. 'Yes, that doesn't feel like a coincidence.'

Halloran pulled out his phone. 'I'll ask Banks to start looking into her too and see if he can find anything dubious in her records. She won't thank me for the extra workload right now, hunting down Palmer's son is a job and a half in itself, but we can't afford to overlook any potential suspect.'

At that moment Kitt's phone rang. It wasn't a number she recognized.

'Ms Hartley?' said a plummy voice at the other end of the line when she answered the call.

'Speaking.'

'Veronica Miles here from the Sandersdale library and archive.'

'Oh, yes. Thank you so much for getting back to me. I know it was a bit of a strange request. Any luck on that name I gave you?'

'I am afraid there is absolutely nothing in our archive about a group called the Children of Silvanus. Are you sure that's the right name?'

'Yes, that's definitely the one,' Kitt said with a sigh.

'Oh dear, I am sorry. I did think it was a long shot. I'm afraid we had a terrible fire here a couple of years back. We lost most of our paper records and I suspect that any documents pertaining to the Children of Silvanus would have been in those files, if indeed any existed.'

'I'm so sorry to hear about that. What caused the fire?' Kitt said, feeling cold all of a sudden.

'It happened late at night when there were no staff around so the cause was never confirmed. It was a proper blaze. We lost so much.'

Kitt could hear the pain in the archivist's voice. As a librarian, she understood that pain. 'Again, I am terribly sorry to hear about that. I do appreciate you trying to help anyway.'

There was another minute of mutual commiseration

before Kitt hung up the phone. Despite the fact that both Halloran and Grace were shooting quizzical looks her way, Kitt didn't speak. She simply sat still and rigid on the bench.

'What's going on?' Grace said after a moment or two. 'You've got that look about you. The look that means you've just learned about something terrible, I know it well enough by now.'

'The library and archive at Sandersdale lost a great deal of their records in a fire a couple of years ago.'

'OK,' said Halloran. 'That's sad news, pet, and I know you take the destruction of books very seriously but—'

'Oh, Mal, will you give over?' said Kitt, shaking her head at him. 'Of course I'm not ecstatic about that news from a cataloguing perspective but it's more than that. They couldn't find the source of the fire.'

Grace's eyes widened, the realization dawning on her. 'Just like the fire at Ayleen Demir's house when she was young. It was suspected arson but the cause of the fire was unknown.'

'Exactly,' said Kitt.

'Those fires happened almost twenty years apart,' Halloran said. 'Are you really trying to insinuate they're connected?'

'But those aren't the only fires we've heard about,' said Kitt. 'The Children of Silvanus camp . . .'

'. . . also burned down in 2011.' Halloran finished her sentence. 'It's still quite a long time between each instance, though they are all in the same area of Sandersdale. So perhaps there is something in it.'

'I don't think we can dismiss the possibility,' said Kitt. 'I know it might seem like a long shot, but to me it just seems too much of a coincidence that nobody knew what caused the fire at Ayleen's childhood home, or the fire at the library and archive in the place where she used to live, and then on top of that a fire finished off the Children of Silvanus.'

'Well, when you put it that way, I suppose I can see the link,' said Halloran.

'Which gets me thinking about the gossip we learned when we first got here,' said Kitt. 'There is some specula-tion in this town that Ayleen was the one to start the fire that killed her parents. What if she did the same with the library? And the Children of Silvanus camp?'

'She said she was ashamed of what she'd done,' said Halloran, recalling Ayleen's words in the interview he had conducted the night before. 'That she didn't want anyone to find out.'

'And she was willing to go to the lengths of lying to the police about what she'd done,' said Grace. 'What if she started that fire at the library and archive so that anybody who checked in the future wouldn't be able to find any record of her or what she got up to there? What if even before that she went back to the camp and started a fire to kill off the remaining witnesses to what she'd done and end the cult for good?'

'I suppose that is a possibility,' Kitt said with a nod. 'Given that she's already lied to us once, there's a good chance that we still don't know the worst of what she got up to all those years ago.'

TWENTY

'You've got some visitors, Cyril,' said Benji, the care worker with whom Kitt had arranged their visit at Seaview Care Home in Sandsend. If Kitt had to guess, based on his baby-fresh skin, she would have said Benji was in his early twenties. He had his hair shaved short in a way that emphasized all of the bones in his skull which somehow further accentuated the babyish look to his face. He spoke to Cyril in that slightly too loud way that some did with all people over the age of sixty. Although Kitt had read that hearing loss was becoming an even bigger issue for people now than it had been in the past, she sometimes found the extremes people went to, in terms of over-enunciating, quite patronizing.

Cyril, who was sitting in an armchair near the window in his surprisingly spacious room, turned when he heard his name mentioned. As soon as he acknowledged he had company, Benji offered a nod to Kitt and Grace before dismissing himself, likely to attend to other residents. Seaview Care Home was much bigger than Kitt had imagined. Three storeys high and from the signage she'd seen on the way in, long enough to accommodate two rows of private quarters on every floor. This was, of course, good news for the amount of stimulation guests were likely to get as there were a greater number of residents to interact with. Kitt had noticed in the short walk from the reception area to Cyril's room, however, that the staff seemed to be run off their feet. Almost all of them looked like they could have done with more sleep the night before and several of them hadn't seemed to really know if they were coming or going. Being understaffed when you were caring for this number of vulnerable people was no joke.

Kitt was quite surprised by how robust Cyril seemed. Arnie from the bookshop had described him as frail. While he was in no way a muscled Adonis, he was stocky enough in his stature that Kitt guessed he might be capable of considerable physical strength. Perhaps Arnie had been more focused on Cyril's mental faculties. When people display symptoms of mental illness, those around them sometimes interpreted that as frailty on every level, especially if the symptoms were severe.

'Do . . . do I know you?' Cyril asked in a soft voice as he looked between Kitt and Grace.

Kitt smiled at him. 'No, you don't. We are visiting Seaview because we're doing a local history project.'

This, she and Grace had agreed, was the kindest lie to tell Cyril in an attempt to get him to talk openly without confusing him too much. They were, after all, pretty much here to eliminate him from the list of suspects. There was no point in offering the full context when it may upset Cyril and possibly trigger his symptoms.

'It is nice to see such young people engaging in local history,' Cyril said, offering Grace a charming, wrinkly grin.

Kitt had hoped that she might be included in the young people bracket but Cyril did not extend his smile to her. Well that's it, lass, Kitt thought to herself. Thirty-seven and you're past it.

'Did they tell you that me memory isn't so good now?' Cyril asked.

'Yes, we are aware of the challenges you're managing, Mr Armitage,' said Kitt. 'Don't worry, if you don't want to talk to us you certainly don't have to.'

'Actually, I'd like to talk to you for as long as I can,' said Cyril. 'Don't have any kids of my own, or siblings, so I don't get many visitors. There's just our Alan, really.'

'Alan a good friend of yours, is he?' said Grace, taking a seat in a chair opposite the man as he indicated that she should. Kitt did the same.

'A distant cousin,' said Cyril. 'Haven't seen him in a little while now. He gets very busy, you know? It's funny, I didn't even know he existed till about three years ago. Even when you think you've got it sussed, life is still full of surprises. But I've been glad of 'im. It'd be quite lonely otherwise.'

'I'm pleased to hear you've got some company – outside the other people who live alongside you, of course,' said Kitt, wondering if she should be suspicious about a long-lost cousin just reappearing like that.

Cyril groaned and curled his upper lip. 'Oh, I don't bother with any of that lot. I keep myself to myself in here. A lot of the other residents are much older than me, see? So it can get me down if I spend too much time with them. Reminds me that I've sort of got old before me time.'

'I can understand that,' said Kitt. 'And I'm sorry for what you're going through.'

Cyril gave a dismissive wave. 'Never mind, I spend enough time talking about that with the doctors. Let's get onto happier subjects. What kind of local history do you want to talk about? I've lived in Whitby most of my life, you know? Seen a lot of change in that time. It's not like it used to be. Well, at least not in the new town.'

'I'll bet,' said Grace. 'We are particularly interested in the cultural community here in Whitby, and we understand you've done some amateur dramatics in your time.'

'Oh aye, I have done quite a lot over the years. With not having a family or any kids, I decided to join the local drama club to meet some new people, you know, feel less lonely.'

Kitt couldn't help but notice that Cyril had described

himself as lonely twice now. And that by his own admission, he had no family to speak of – save his long-lost cousin. Alongside his distaste for mingling with the other residents, he did seem to fit the loner profile she, Grace and Evie had discussed before the investigation was moved to Whitby. Cyril seemed so sweet and gentle, she couldn't imagine him having a dark side but in the interests of exploring all lines of investigation, she had to keep an open mind.

'What kind of plays were you in?' asked Grace.

'Ooh, all sorts. Our previous director wasn't the most imaginative so we did our fair share of *Salad Days* and *Oliver Twist* but when Stella took over that changed. She started her directorial leadership with a play she had written herself. It was so different to everything else we'd done.'

'Oh yes,' said Grace, affecting an innocent expression. 'I think I read about one of the plays she wrote: *The Curse of James I, A Musical*?'

Cyril's face lit up at the mention of this play and there was no mistaking the shimmer of excitement in his eyes. 'Oooh, yes, and I got to play the lead role! That was my favourite part. In that one, I got to inhabit the body of James I himself, a difficult challenge, that. I had to do a lot of research into it. He was a complicated person, you know?'

'Oh I don't doubt it,' said Kitt, studying Cyril closely and waiting to see if this conversation was going to trigger anything for him. She had been instructed to call for a member of staff if this happened and she was not going to jeopardize the man's mental well-being for the sake of a hunch. She intended to follow the guidelines to the letter.

Cyril, however, continued to talk without any hesitation. 'I didn't mind doing the research. It was probably the juiciest part I ever had. It is so much fun stepping into the shoes of a historical character.' He beamed. 'Having the opportunity to bring them to life and put your own take on it.'

'I can imagine,' said Kitt. 'And your director, Stella Hemsworth, isn't it? From the reviews I read of the play, she must have been pleased with how it all turned out.'

The light in Cyril's eyes dimmed and he shook his head. 'I'm not sure about that. We were grateful to her for taking a more creative line with the plays we put on but she seemed to take that play very seriously. That was the only thing that took the fun out of it a bit for me. I think I could have been . . . I could have been . . . er.'

Kitt offered Cyril a sympathetic smile that she hoped was a comfort to him. He was having difficulty remembering his next word. This was something that had happened to her grandfather quite regularly when he was managing his dementia symptoms. A small prompt usually helped.

'A world-class actor?' Kitt ventured.

'Aye!' Cyril said. 'I could have been Sir Ian McKellen himself and she would still have given me notes after every performance, and the rest of the cast had it just as bad.'

'That sounds like a bit of a downer,' said Grace. 'Can't have been much fun to be getting critiqued all the time.'

Kitt couldn't tell if Grace was making a cheekily pointed comment about the number of times a day she had to rein in her assistant's antics but if she was she managed to keep a straight face.

'Oh well,' Cyril said, brightening a little, 'we all got used to it after a while. Stella was a perfectionist at the best of times but the whole cast thought she took it to extremes with that one. But we didn't let it get to us too much. We assumed that one was special to her, you know? Because she wrote it and it was her debut and all. She had a creative vision and we just weren't meeting it to her satisfaction. As I say, like, I'm not sure even the most seasoned actors would've done.'

'Sounds like your director might have been described as somewhat obsessed with achieving her vision,' Kitt said, shooting Grace a look as she did so. From Grace's almost indiscernible eyebrow raise, it was clear she was thinking along the same lines. Kitt wasn't sure why Stella Hemsworth was so fascinated with the idea of witch trials that she'd written a play and been obsessive about its execution on the stage, but after this conversation she was keener than ever to find out. Did Stella's obsession stop on the stage?

'The play was all about his fixation with witches,' Cyril explained.

'Yes,' said Grace, 'I believe he hated them with a passion.'

'It's true,' said Kitt. 'Must have been such a fascinating character study to explore. Mind you, I must admit, when

I was reading up about it I thought how lucky it was that the play was produced a good three years ago. I'm not sure you could put it on at the moment with all that's going on. You've probably heard about it on the news, about the Vampire Killer. Some bloke going around offing people who dabble in the occult. It's a bit like a modern-day version of your play come to life.'

Cyril's smile faded and his body stiffened. 'Yes, I am aware of the killings.'

'Don't worry,' said Kitt, concerned that the turn the conversation had taken might be unnerving the man. She coupled her words with a chuckle in an attempt to keep things light and set him at ease. 'We know you were just playing a part in that play. We won't ask for your alibi.'

Cyril started to breathe heavily and seemed to be breaking out in a sweat just at the mention of the word 'alibi'.

'Cyril, are you OK?' said Grace. 'Should I go and fetch Benji?'

Cyril closed his eyes for a moment. When he opened them again he seemed much calmer than before. His voice was almost robotic. 'I don't want to hide it any more.'

'Hide what?' asked Kitt, wondering if he was referring to something to do with his illness, or if he was having an episode and she just wasn't familiar with the kind of thing he might say during such a time.

'I don't want to do it any more.'

'Do what?' asked Grace. 'Talk to us? You don't have to talk

to us if you've had enough, Mr Armitage. We'd never want you to feel uncomfortable.'

'Too many people have died,' said Cyril. 'I don't want any more to. Please. Don't let me do it.'

Kitt frowned and her heart quickened. Was she understanding Cyril right? Surely not? 'Cyril, what are you trying to say?'

'I should have gone to the police the first time it happened but, I just couldn't believe what I'd done,' Cyril said, his eyes watering. 'But then I did it again, and again.'

'Did what, Cyril?' Kitt said in the gentlest tone she could.

'Killed those people. It's me. I'm . . . I'm the one they're after.'

Kitt shook her head and stood. She needed to get Benji back in the room now and verify what was going on here. 'I fear we must have confused you, Mr Armitage. I'll go and get Benji so we can clear all of this up.'

'There's nothing to clear up.' Cyril said, easing himself out of the armchair and walking over to the closet. He opened the doors and pushed all the neatly pressed shirts and trousers to one side. 'Here,' he said, pointing at a wooden box in the shape of a coffin that was sitting at the back of his wardrobe.

'Open it,' he added, his voice hollow and monotone, all feeling gone. 'You'll soon see what I mean.'

Slowly, Kitt and Grace approached the wardrobe. Kitt nodded at Grace to do as instructed and open the box. Cyril seemed lucid and sincere but she wanted to keep a close eye on the man in case this was some kind of strange trick or in case he suddenly took a turn for the worse.

Kneeling, Grace removed the lid from the box and at once gasped at the contents. She looked up at Kitt who, for her part, felt her mouth drop open as she cast her eye over a pack of medical needles, cans of purple spray paint and small vials Kitt would bet her first editions were doses of Xylazine.

Those weren't the only things that caught Kitt's eyes though. The box had been resting on something, a slab of dark stone with a garish face carved into the end – it was another of the gargoyles from Twilight Manor. And next to it, a large black hoodie. Kitt could just make out a symbol printed on the back of it: it was a pentacle.

TWENTY-ONE

Standing outside on the steps of Seaview Care Home, Kitt took in some deep breaths and tried to steady herself. The home certainly lived up to its name, overlooking the silver blue of the North Sea as it undulated on the horizon. Several ships sailing off to less troubled waters were dotted here and there in the distance. The sun was starting to set and the sky was full of thick pink cloud. Usually Kitt would find such a vista just as soothing as anyone else, watching ships sail off into the adventurous unknown at dusk, but the revelation that Cyril Armitage had confessed to the vampire killings was a shock she hadn't been prepared for. Not to mention the fact that, given the presence of the gargoyle from Twilight Manor, he also seemed to have been the person responsible for the attempt on her life early this morning.

Or, more likely, somebody else wanted it to look that way.

'I thought you both might want a cup of tea,' said Benji,

offering plastic cups first to Kitt and then to Grace as they watched DS Banks secure Cyril Armitage in the police car. He was cooperating but Kitt hadn't missed the lost look on the poor man's face. Though she had seen the evidence with her own eyes, this all felt so wrong.

Kitt stared at the dark brown liquid before remembering her manners and accepting the cup from Benji. 'So kind, thank you.'

Tea was a pretty universal cure-all in the county of Yorkshire but she wasn't sure some lukewarm, over-stewed version of her favourite beverage was going to be of much comfort just now. She nursed the cup, looking for a nearby plant to water when Benji wasn't looking.

A moment later, Halloran exited the building. 'Benji, we're waiting on a list of employees here that have contact with Mr Armitage on a regular basis. Would you be so kind as to see if it's ready for us? I'd rather not leave him sitting in the car any longer than necessary. I believe someone's also going to accompany Mr Armitage to the station?'

Benji nodded. 'Our duty manager. I'll just go and see if she's ready to go and I'll chase that list up for you too.'

'I appreciate it,' said Halloran as Benji hurried back inside.

Halloran turned back to Kitt and Grace then. 'Are you both all right?' It was the first opportunity he'd had to properly check in with them since he and Banks had arrived thirty minutes ago.

'We're fine,' said Kitt. 'Somewhat surprised and confused but otherwise fine.'

'He's all strapped in, sir,' said Banks in her sharp Glaswegian accent. 'I've managed to keep him calm but it just about broke my heart, the way he looked at me there. He reminds me of my grandad.'

'What's going to happen to him?' asked Grace.

'Based on what we found in his room, there's a strong possibility that he is going to be charged with murder,' said Halloran. 'Or at the very least as an accomplice. On closer inspection it is not just the needles, the hoodie and the gargoyle. We found three Kellington's jam jars filled with blood at the back of his wardrobe, just like the jars found at each crime scene. I'm fairly sure the blood is going to match the three victims', and if it does, this is pretty much going to be case closed as far as our superiors are concerned.'

Kitt shook her head. 'I'm sorry, I know what you found and I know what I saw but . . .'

'It doesn't feel right?' said Banks.

Kitt nodded. 'We've been in circumstances like this before. Where all the evidence points to someone we know in our hearts hasn't done it. There are too many questions. Starting with, how did Cyril get hold of the gargoyles from Twilight Manor?'

'I've already contacted Stoke Bramley about that,' said Banks. 'After what happened to you this morning, Halloran wanted to question Mr Bramley but it was decided it was best if I spoke to him.'

Kitt offered Banks a weak smile. She could imagine how that conversation would have gone. Mal would have been hell-bent on talking to Bramley himself and Banks, in her wisdom, would have had to talk him down. Luckily, Banks's no-nonsense attitude often gave Mal pause for thought. They were perfect partners in that way; Mal helped Banks investigate hunches she otherwise wouldn't and Banks, well, she was the reason Halloran hadn't been kicked off the force for rogue behaviour years ago.

'What did Bramley have to say for himself?' said Grace.

'Allegedly, the gargoyles were added to the manor by member vote and sponsorship. According to Bramley, when they were commissioned, they decided to have a few extra made so they might be auctioned for charity.'

'Aw, such thoughtful wannabe vampires,' said Grace.

Banks shook her head. 'Don't even get me started on how weird this case is. I suppose I should expect nothing less of something that revolves around Ruby Barnett. But it's all been even weirder than I thought it would be.'

'So, Stoke Bramley is claiming the gargoyle that almost killed me was one they sold at auction?' said Kitt.

'You guessed it,' said Halloran. 'But, of course, with them being a strange vampire cult, the bidder was anonymous and the fee was paid in cash.'

'Can't they remember what the person who paid the fee looked like?' said Grace.

'The cash was sent through the post and at the time they had no reason to keep the envelope,' said Halloran. 'It was agreed that the bidder would pick the gargoyle up from a local stone worker, so we'll be talking to them to get a description. We'll also be looking at Cyril's bank account to see if there have been any large cash withdrawals.'

'So, we're supposed to believe that Cyril bought these gargoyles so he could frame the Creed of Count Dracula for his crimes?' asked Grace.

'From the look of things, that's the gist of it,' said Banks.

'But why would he want to do any of this?' said Grace.

'I don't know,' said Banks. 'Initially it seemed as if we were supposed to believe that he felt compelled to carry out the murders because of his delusions and wanted to make sure there was a scapegoat in case suspicions were raised about him. But he's just told me and Halloran in there that he played up his dementia symptoms and that he's not really that sick at all.'

Kitt wasn't known for keeping her temper at the best of times but this revelation was more than she could stand. 'I've just spoken to that man – he is vulnerable and there's no doubt about it. He exhibited very similar ticks to my grandad when he suffered from dementia. I think I'd know if he was putting them on. And when he confessed, there was something not quite right about the way he spoke. It felt like a practised line, sort of robotic. Someone is manipulating him. Also, if he was really out at midnight on three separate occasions on his own, six different outings if you count the marking of the doors, the home would know about it. His absence would have been noticed.'

'I take your point, Kitt, I do. I agree that there's something off about the way he's talking and behaving, and I don't think it's linked to his condition,' said Halloran, before lowering his voice. 'We can't rule out that it's not someone at the care home yet. That's why I've asked for the list of people who regularly work with Cyril. The more likely explanation is that someone who works with him, who has access to his room and his closet, planted those things there.'

'Even if someone is manipulating him, he confessed in such an open manner,' said Grace. 'Why would he do that if someone else had planted the gear in his wardrobe?'

'There's a chance that it goes deeper than someone else manipulating him,' said Banks. 'That he's confessed because he has convinced himself that he is guilty and can't bear the thought of hurting anyone else. His dementia might have played a part. He couldn't have been getting clothes out of his wardrobe all this time without noticing those things at the bottom. Perhaps one day after they were planted, he found them and that added to whatever manipulation he'd been experiencing and he finally believed himself to be guilty.'

'There's all sorts of ways that the person who planted the evidence could have planted some seeds in his mind. Told him he was missing on the days of the murders, for example, and asked him where he was,' said Halloran.

'Pretty much the first thing he said to me and Grace was that he had trouble with his memory,' said Kitt. 'But you can't plan when a person's going to have a memory lapse. What if he could remember what he'd done on the nights the murders took place? Surely— Oh . . .'

'What is it?' said Halloran.

'Arnie said that Cyril was on a lot of medication when he visited the bookshop. A buffet, Arnie called it. He thought from the way Cyril was acting the doses were too high.'

'Any medication to temporarily alleviate symptoms would be prescribed by a doctor,' said Banks.

'But it's administered by the staff here,' said Kitt. 'If the Vampire Killer works at this care home and has carried out all of these terrible acts, including framing an innocent and vulnerable man for their crimes, making that man pretend he's not as sick as everyone thinks, no less, then I doubt they'd be concerned about messing around with Cyril's dosage to make him believe whatever they want him to believe. I've read a couple of books in my time about brainwashing protocols in the secret service around the world. Drugs always play a part in manipulating a person's mind.'

'This is too sad,' said Grace, blinking back tears. 'All that evidence against him, and I know he's going to confess to you as soon as you get him to the police station, just like he did to us. He thinks he did it.'

'He's not a well man, Mal, you're going to have to tread very lightly when you question him. I'm really not sure how he'll handle a police interrogation. It might be too much.'

Halloran stroked Kitt's arm to reassure her. 'I've no intention of taking a hard line with this bloke. Given his mental health status he will be granted a representative in the room with him to offer as much support as he needs. All I'm interested in is establishing the facts. If there are any holes in his story, we'll be able to poke at them until we get to the truth – whatever that may be. But I've got a feeling this is going to be a long process. We're not going to be able to hold him at the station the whole time, he's too vulnerable for that, and we won't be able to keep him in interrogation for hours on end, he won't cope. So, we'll have to do it in stints, verifying anything he tells us between each session.'

'Well, while you're questioning Cyril we won't sit idle,' said Kitt. 'We're going to track down Stella Hemsworth and find out why she felt compelled to write a play about the witch trials for her directorial debut.'

'It's good to rule out every possibility,' said Banks. 'But you should know there were no red flags in her financial or phone records. I didn't have time to look very far back because I've been focused on trying to track down Palmer's son, but certainly there's nothing in the last three months while the Vampire Killings have been taking place.'

'I appreciate you letting us know,' said Kitt. Banks was usually incredibly tight-lipped about confidential information. Clearly she didn't want to see Cyril go down for these killings any more than Kitt did. 'But if we don't go and talk to her face-to-face it will nag at me. Cyril described her as having a bit of an obsession over that play she wrote about James I. Her behaviour did not sound very balanced. As far as I know he still takes part in the amateur dramatics group so she still might see him on a semi-regular basis, which might give her the opportunity to manipulate Cyril if she does have anything to do with the murders.'

'All right, I don't know when I'll next get a chance to catch up with you on the task ahead. We're still in the middle of further investigations into Bramley and Ayleen, too, so there's unlikely to be even a minute to spare, but I will let you know if Cyril's going to be charged,' said Halloran.

'Oooh, one thing you must ask him about, if you can, is this long-lost cousin who mysteriously presented himself,' said Kitt.

'Yes, Alan Jenkins,' said Halloran. 'He's Cyril's only visitor. I asked for a list of people who he had contact with and other than his carers, Jenkins is the only person who visits him.'

'Did you get a description or even information on whereabouts he lives?' said Grace. 'If I know who I'm looking for, maybe I can look him up online.'

'Apparently he's a man in his late forties. He has blond hair and quite a thick moustache,' said Halloran.

'Sounds like a man in disguise to me,' said Banks. 'But then again, I always think anyone who wears a moustache is probably in disguise. Sir just about gets away with it because there's a beard attached.'

'Well, thank you for the style approval there, Banks. I will be sure to come back to you next season when I am ready to change my look,' Halloran said with a wry smile.

'I suppose one thing to be grateful for is that one way or another this is a breakthrough,' said Kitt. 'I don't think for a second that Cyril is guilty but he is somehow connected to whoever is pulling the strings. Which means we're probably closer to finding out who the real killer is now than we've come before.'

TWENTY-TWO

Early the following evening, Kitt and Grace were sitting in the Hook, Line & Sinker Inn, which stood on the seafront between the Dracula Experience and Whitby pier. The building itself couldn't be more quaint with its mock-Tudor beams, stained-glass windows and thatched roof, but given all that had been revealed at Seaview Care Home the previous afternoon, this was no social outing.

By the time she and Grace had got back to the hotel the night before, Kitt had been exhausted. Perhaps it had been the attempt on her life catching up with her. Or the fact that she hadn't really slept properly since the case began. Whatever the reason, she had barely kept her eyes open and, once they had found a lead on Stella Hemsworth's whereabouts, she had promptly retired to bed.

She had hoped to wake to a message from Halloran to say he'd had some major breakthrough based on information provided by Cyril, but no such luck. Halloran's morning text message merely explained that he was still verifying all of the information Cyril had relayed to them in interview and wouldn't be back until later that evening. Consequently, with the killer due to strike in just three days, Kitt and Grace had spent the day in full research mode. Firstly, looking further into Peter Tremble's history to make sure he'd never had any business in the Sandersdale area that might link him with the Children of Silvanus – which as far as they could see he hadn't – and swotting up on their next potential suspect, Stella Hemsworth.

Luckily, Stella Hemsworth, writer and director of *The Curse of James I, A Musical*, had been an easy person to find online, and it seemed that, much like the Vampire Killer, she had a flair for the dramatic. She was a regular performer at pubs in the area and tonight was no exception. She stood on a small stage in the corner of the inn, wearing a black sequinned maxi-dress and black feather boa, even though she was performing to an audience of no more than fifteen people in a pub on Whitby seafront on a Thursday night. Moreover, given the audience's somewhat overzealous reaction to slightly off-key show tunes of yore, most of the audience seemed to know the performer personally.

Kitt and Grace had endured almost forty-five minutes of Stella's questionable renditions and as she warbled out the last few notes of 'Call Me Rusty' from *Starlight Express*, Kitt prayed to all the lost librarians in the sky that an interval was nigh. If she and Grace had thought this plan through they would have been fashionably late to the beginning of the show and thus could have dodged the unforgettably patchy performance of 'The Rum Tum Tugger', amongst many others.

'Thank you, my darlings,' Stella purred through the microphone. 'I'll be back in twenty with my *Les Misérables* medley. So don't go away.'

Inwardly Kitt prayed they would get all the answers they needed before the second half of the show resumed. Stella's manner on stage was embarrassingly overblown. She couldn't imagine that the melodramatic histrionics of *Les Misérables* would do anything to temper that.

Stella tottered down from the stage in a pair of black sequinned wedge heels that Kitt wasn't entirely convinced the woman could walk in. Before anybody else could swoop on her, Kitt and Grace approached.

'Ms Hemsworth,' said Kitt, taking in the sight of the seasoned showgirl up close. From a distance, Kitt had thought her about the same age as herself. Up close, however, she could see just how much face powder she was wearing. Little pockets of it sat in several deep wrinkles around her eyes. Her revised assessment was that Hemsworth was in her early fifties but likely told people she was still in her forties. Kitt always felt rather sad about people who tried to hide their true age. Perhaps it was because she had seen so many lives cut short in the time she'd been involved in criminal investigations, but she had come to think of growing old as more and more of a privilege with each passing year. 'We're sorry to bother you but we are very big fans of your work and couldn't resist coming to say a few words to you.'

'Well, well, well,' Hemsworth said, placing a hand against her chest. 'It's always wonderful to meet a person who describes themselves as your fan.'

'Oh, we've kept track of your output for quite some time now,' said Grace. 'We always loved you in that advert for Stomach Settlers. We really believed you were in gastric distress. We've followed your work ever since on screen and stage.'

'Well, I'm surprised I don't recognize you. I always try to make as much eye contact with the audience as I can to show my appreciation for their support.'

'We . . . tend to sit further back,' said Kitt. 'It can be intimidating, you know, being up close and personal with a star of the stage.'

'Oh!' Stella said, patting Kitt's shoulder in what she thought was a somewhat overfamiliar manner given she'd only met the woman two seconds ago. 'I know just what you mean. I met Kenneth Branagh once and hardly knew what to say for myself. Would you like a photograph with me? Something to show your friends and family?'

'Well, maybe in a moment,' said Kitt. 'But we actually finally plucked up the courage to talk to you because we're a bit concerned about something we heard today.'

'Really? Oh dear, what was that exactly?'

'We ... apologize for bringing up morbid topics when you're in the middle of a performance but you've probably heard about the Vampire Killer on the news?' said Kitt, studying Hemsworth's face carefully.

'Oh yes, a terrible business indeed. Just shows you what can happen to you if you get mixed up with a dubious crowd. The town likes to make its money from the goth weekend but there's a consequence for getting mixed up in dark things like that – in fact I wrote a play about that very idea a few years back now.'

'We know,' said Grace. 'That's part of the reason we're worried about you.'

Hemsworth frowned and shuffled around a bit. 'Why is that?'

'Someone we know said that some members of the cast in that play are being interrogated by the police in relation to the killings,' said Grace.

'What? Which cast members?'

'We don't know exactly who, it was a conversation we overheard in one of the tea rooms here. But the people who were talking about it said that the police had decided to interview anyone involved with the play because of its link with the occult,' said Kitt.

'Apparently the police are desperate to catch the killer because he is due to strike again on Sunday evening. So they're leaving no stone unturned,' Grace chipped in.

'As soon as we heard that, we were worried for you. As the

director and writer of the play we thought you were likely to be the one the police were really interested in,' said Kitt.

'I haven't heard anything from them,' Stella said. She didn't sound half as concerned as Kitt needed her to be for the plan to work. Their plan involved a great deal of risk if Stella was the true Vampire Killer but with so little time left before the eleven days were up, they had no choice but to throw caution to the wind.

It was time to lay it on a little thicker.

'Well, of course you haven't,' said Kitt. 'They'll be going around the cast members first, getting all their stories on record.'

'Stories?'

'Yes, details on how you behaved during the production, anything you told them about why you wrote the play or chose that subject matter,' Kitt clarified.

'And when they've got all the stories from the other cast members, they'll pull you in for questioning to see if your story matches,' said Grace. 'That's how the police work. They try to catch you out.'

'Oh, I can just hear it now,' said Kitt. 'They will try to argue that the fact you wrote this play shows an unhealthy obsession with the occult. And let's not even start with what they'll do with the scene in which a witch gets her blood drained.'

'It will be a literal witch hunt,' Grace said, shaking her head. 'The police are desperate to make an arrest because it's hurting business in the area. And from the sound of things, we think you might be their next target.'

'But . . . but . . . but . . .' Hemsworth stammered. Her face was flushed and it was visible even through all the powder she'd applied. 'Oh dear, I don't quite know what to do.' She paused for a moment before speaking again. 'I should have known something like this was going to happen. You don't get anything for nothing. That's a lesson I learned early. I knew it was too good to be true. I'm being framed. Oh, framed! I'm too young for my career to be over!'

'Framed? By whom?' asked Kitt, trying to temper her surprise at Hemsworth's unexpected outburst and somewhat disorientating rambles.

Hemsworth looked between Grace and Kitt. 'I'm . . . not sure I should say anymore.'

'Oh, well, we wouldn't want to pry,' said Kitt. The prospect of prison hadn't rattled Stella quite as much as she needed. Perhaps a touch of reverse psychology was in order. 'We just thought you might want the help of two people who admired you. I've been accused of something I didn't do by the police before and really found out who my friends are. But, if you'd rather deal with this without our help, we understand. Come on, Grace.'

'Wait . . .' said Stella, her eyes darting left and right as she considered her options. She was quiet for a moment and then jerked her head in a way that indicated she wanted them to follow her over to the side of the room where they were less likely to be overheard. 'Can you keep a secret?'

'Of course,' said Kitt. 'We're your fans, we'll do anything if it helps you.'

'Good, good. That's who I need on my side right now. True fans who understand what it means to be discreet.' Stella paused and took a deep breath. 'Look, the truth of it is, I didn't actually write *The Curse of James I.*'

'Oh . . . then who did?' said Kitt.

'I . . . Well, I don't know exactly. One day, I received the script alongside a letter from an anonymous admirer of my work. They said they had written a script that they thought I would bring great directorial flair to and if I agreed to produce it they would pay me a handsome sum of money and let me take full writing credits.'

'How much is a handsome sum of money?' said Kitt.

'I'd rather not disclose the exact sum,' said Hemsworth, looking Kitt up and down. 'But we are talking thousands of pounds, not hundreds.'

'What was the catch?' said Grace.

'I asked the same question in my reply,' said Hemsworth.

'So you have an address for whoever sent you this letter? I mean, you had a place to send a reply to?' said Kitt.

'I can remember the area, at least. It was a place out in Sandersdale,' said Hemsworth.

'Sandersdale?' Kitt repeated, her stomach churning at even the mention of that name. Somehow, even this part of the investigation was leading back to the Children of Silvanus, or so it seemed. Surely it couldn't be a coincidence that this person, whoever they were, had been based in the same area as the cult? 'But you don't have the full address?'

'I might be able to remember some of it if I really think hard about it. But burning all correspondence once the money was paid was part of the deal and I didn't make a separate note of the address. The only record I had was on the letters themselves.'

'And you never ventured out there to find out who this mystery admirer was?' said Kitt.

'I thought about it,' said Hemsworth. 'I didn't like the idea of doing any kind of deal with someone I didn't know, even someone claiming to be an admirer. But the letter was so gushing in its praise for me and my work – well, I suppose part of me just wanted it to be a genuine offer. I was instructed that I could reply to any letters I received via that address but if I turned up or otherwise tried to find out the identity of my admirer, the offer would be withdrawn. He said he was too shy to ever meet me and that's why he had chosen to communicate in this manner.'

'And you didn't think it was odd that he wanted you to burn the letters afterwards?' said Kitt.

Hemsworth shrugged. 'Not particularly. He said it was to make sure they weren't dug up by a family member if something happened to me. You know, like if I was in a car accident or something and my family went through my belongings. He said he wanted me to take full writing credit and the only way to ensure that was to get rid of any evidence that he had any hand in writing it.'

'So what did you do?' asked Grace. Though Kitt was fairly sure she knew the answer to that question, it was important to hear it from Hemsworth in her own words.

'I double-checked with him that there would be no catch, no later claim to copyright if the play ended up being a huge success. And then, when it seemed as though all of my questions had been answered, I agreed to produce the play. The money came in the post in several instalments and I burnt all of the correspondence . . . well, almost all of it.'

'You kept something?' Kitt said, her hopes once again rising that there might be some way of tracking this person down. The letter might have the correspondent's DNA on it and this mystery correspondent was more than likely the real Vampire Killer – or at the very least an accomplice for them.

Stella paused for a moment, seemingly suddenly realising that she was revealing rather a lot to two people she'd only just met.

'If you kept something, you might be able to clear your name,' Kitt added quickly. 'And it would bring us great peace of mind to know that our favourite performer wasn't going to be wrongfully prosecuted for a horrible crime like this.'

'I can only hope it doesn't get that far,' said Hemsworth, her focus back on self-preservation. 'But there's nothing in the portion I kept that would help with identifying who this person was. Despite the reassurances, I didn't trust that he wouldn't crawl out of the woodwork and try to sue me for lots of money at a later date if the play went on to be a stunning success. So I secretly kept the page where he renounces all rights to the play. I decided he would never know that that one page wasn't in the stack of pages I burned. But what if I was wrong? What if he knew I didn't do as I asked and this is my punishment? Being framed for murder? Oh my!'

'I don't think that's what's happening here,' said Kitt, doing all she could to keep Hemsworth's melodramatic eruptions to a minimum. 'I think whoever this person is, framing you was part of their plan all along.'

'Dear me,' said Hemsworth. 'I knew I never should have taken that money. But you know, when you're a woman and you get to . . .' Hemsworth paused to whisper the next word as though it were some forbidden mantra, 'forty, well, the only place for you on the stage or screen is as the mother of someone so much younger than you are. Roles are hard to find. The money I was offered, well, it was enough to keep me in the lifestyle I'd become accustomed to and the opportunity opened up a new avenue in my career. Direction!'

As she listened to Hemsworth's explanation, Kitt couldn't help but feel a small pang of pity for poor Stella. Your livelihood relying on your ability to stay for ever youthful hardly seemed fair. Kitt frowned then, remembering something she'd thought about Bramley when she met him. Kitt had wondered if his youthful look was part of the lure for his potential members; that they were attracted to vampires because of their eternally beautiful appearance. What if Hemsworth had become bitter about her acting career coming to an end because she wasn't twenty-two any more? What if some twisted part of her had decided to get people's attention another way? Kitt had read about such behaviour in other cases, people committing serial murder simply for the attention and fame it brought. Perhaps Hemsworth didn't feel she'd done quite enough yet to reach the level of fame she was looking for and this mysterious admirer she had described was nothing more than a fabricated scapegoat, a twist in the story she would tell after she was ultimately unmasked as the true Vampire Killer.

'It seems to me your best bet is to take all this information to the police before they come to you asking questions,' said Kitt. 'Being proactive and cooperative will definitely put you in their good books. But it would help if there was some way of verifying who your admirer really was. There was nothing in the letters you received that might speak to his identity?'

'Nothing,' Hemsworth said, shaking her head. 'Except that he signed every letter with two initials. A.J.'

Kitt and Grace looked at each other, frowning. Did their list of suspects include someone who matched those initials? Kitt quickly ran down the list in her head. Ayleen Demir,

Peter Tremble, Stoke Bramley, Cyril Armitage, Penelope Baker, none of those were a match. They didn't know the name of Justin Palmer's son . . . but then Kitt's eyes widened as she did think of a mysterious figure mixed up in all this who did go by those initials.

Alan Jenkins. The long-lost cousin who had conveniently reappeared in Cyril's life just after he was diagnosed with dementia. If he wrote the play and was responsible for the killings, he may have planned to use Stella as his scapegoat. But then he experienced a stroke of luck that he never could have planned. The man who played the leading part began to suffer with dementia and became a more pliable patsy than Hemsworth ever would have been. Kitt could only hope that Mal had managed to obtain contact details for Jenkins while interviewing Cyril. Kitt didn't believe for a moment that he was really Cyril's long-lost cousin but, whoever he was, she was almost certain now that he was the one behind all this.

TWENTY-THREE

The next morning Kitt awoke to Halloran's hand stroking the side of her face. She smiled absent-mindedly for a moment, still caught in that dreamy place between sleep and wake. After a few seconds, however, her eyes sprang open as she remembered Halloran hadn't made it home the night before.

She had texted him the information about Alan Jenkins and had received a message in return that explained that Halloran was in for a long night and she shouldn't wait up for him to return to the hotel.

'Are you OK? What happened with Cyril? Did you get a chance to look into Alan Jenkins? He's the key to all this, I'm sure of it. I—'

'Kitt,' Halloran said, 'slow down. I've got a lot of news, and I'm afraid you're not going to like what I've got to say any more than I do.'

'What's going on?' Kitt said, her voice small. She sat up,

only to realize she was still in last night's clothes and there were papers strewn across the bed. Papers that had seemed so important and integral to catching the Vampire Killer, until she had just heard the tone of Halloran's voice. She knew that tone. It always meant the worst had happened.

'It's Cyril, pet. We've finished verifying all he's told us.'

'And?'

'And it all checks out. Right down to the last detail. It doesn't mean I'm convinced that he's the killer, but I've poked and poked at his story for nearly two days and I can't find any holes in it. At the very least, given the evidence on display, my superiors are going to insist he's charged as an accomplice to these crimes.'

Kitt swallowed hard, trying to digest what Halloran was saying. Cyril was being manipulated. They'd all agreed on that. How could the police be charging him with anything?

'Are you saying the care home verified he was missing on the nights the murder took place?' said Kitt. She couldn't just accept this. If she did an innocent man was going to be charged with conspiracy to murder . . . or maybe, ultimately, even worse.

'No . . . they weren't able to do that exactly,' said Halloran. 'But they were able to verify certain facts that support the explanation Cyril's offered us.'

'But the killer was striking all over the region. How did he even get to those places?' said Kitt. 'Is he able to drive in his condition? Does he have access to a car?'

Halloran shook his head. 'Remember, he's telling us that he played up his symptoms. But he says he took public transport. He's still got the tickets he purchased for the buses and trains.'

'How did he pay, by card?'

'No, cash.'

Kitt's eyes narrowed. 'I can just about see public transport working for Scarborough and Middlesbrough. I think the last bus to Scarborough gets in just before nine o'clock. The last one to Boro gets in just after eight so assuming he was the killer he would have had a couple of hours to prepare before he struck.'

'That's ... impressive working knowledge of the local bus network.'

Kitt shrugged. 'Yes, well, the fact that something like that impresses you is probably the reason we're together. But actually the timetables have barely changed in the last twenty years and growing up in Boro, Whitby and Scarborough were regular summer daytrips. So yes, I think it's possible he could have used public transport for those two places. But Malton is another matter altogether. It's not impossible to get there from here, of course, with the York to Scarborough train stopping there, but you have to get to either York or Scarborough first.'

'In that instance he took the bus to Scarborough and then the train from there to Malton,' said Halloran.

'But none of those routes run that late – certainly not till midnight when the murder took place.'

'He took the first trains and buses back to Whitby the next morning. In the case of Middlesbrough and Scarborough he was back in the care home by nine o'clock. In the case of Malton he was back in there by ten, so he says.'

'And nobody at the home noticed he was missing?'

'Understandably, once Cyril received his diagnosis he was watched quite carefully to make sure his symptoms didn't result in harm to himself or others but there's a couple of factors at play. Firstly, as you may have noticed, the home is quite significantly understaffed.'

'I did spot that, difficult to miss,' said Kitt. 'So he's claiming he got away with it because everyone was too busy to notice?'

'That's part of it, but one of the reasons Cyril chose Seaview is that they're very committed to resident privacy and dignity. So although a close eye is kept on them, each resident has a sign they can hang on their door handle when they don't want to be disturbed, a bit like in a hotel. After the evening meal, that's what Cyril did. He bundled some pillows up beneath the sheets on the off-chance anyone gave him a look-in. His room is on the ground floor so he was able to just climb out of the window when the coast was clear and catch the last bus to his chosen destination. He says he caught the first bus back bright and early the next morning, waited until the receptionists switched over from night shift to day shift, and then walked in claiming he had just been out in the garden because he wasn't able to sleep. All residents are allowed in the garden between six in the morning and dusk so nobody was any the wiser.'

Kitt paused for a moment. 'But if his dementia isn't causing him to re-enact parts of the play he appeared in, if he isn't as sick as he says, what is his motive supposed to be?'

'Cyril said that he has had an unhealthy obsession with witches and the occult from a young age because he was brought up in a very religious household. He was taught such people were working with the devil and for a long time he had a sort of fantasy of killing those who he was raised to believe were evil.'

'Is there any way of confirming that?' said Kitt.

Halloran shook his head. 'His parents are dead and he doesn't have any siblings. He was baptized and confirmed as a Catholic but that hardly counts as evidence at a forensic level. But when you have a confession from a killer, you don't really need it. A jury will take the confession as evidence of the killer's motive.'

'What about the gargoyles then?' Kitt said, still determined to find some hole in the theory that Cyril was responsible for these deaths. 'Was there any evidence that he was the anonymous bidder?'

Halloran nodded. 'Benji said late last year the pair had taken several trips into town. Cyril had insisted on going to the cash machine every time and taking out what he thought was a sizeable amount in cash. When he asked what all the money was for, concerned he might be being victimized by some kind of scammer, Cyril confirmed it was for a local charity auction that he'd bid on and won. Benji asked for further details to try to make sure he wasn't handing his money over to someone suspicious but Cyril would only confirm with him that his cousin Alan knew all about it and it was a bit of fun between them. We're hoping to confirm with the stone works today that Cyril was the person who picked up the gargoyles from the workshop.'

'So, if I'm understanding right, I'm supposed to believe that Cyril was the man on the cliff top yesterday morning. The one who nearly killed me? Can he even lift one of those blocks?'

'I got him to do it down at the nick,' said Halloran. 'He's surprisingly strong. I told him to lift it over his head and he did just that. Banks was making cracks that he was able to lift the thing easier than I had.'

Kitt sighed. 'What was his rationale for buying them?'

'He told us that he was going to plant them at one of the crime scenes if he ever thought he was close to being caught. His plan wasn't to use one in an attempt on your life, but when the care home arranged a visit with you, he checked into you online and saw that you ran a private investigation agency in York. He assumed, since the last victim he'd marked was in York, that you were here about the case and didn't want you sniffing around. He said he threw that rock at you to avoid having to sit through your questions. He wanted me to tell you that he never intended to kill you. Just scare you off the case. He wanted to avoid talking to you because, he said, he knew if he did he'd end up confessing to what he'd done.'

'Well, all right, fine, he can lift one of those gargoyles over his head but how did he carry it all the way from here to the cliff edge without anyone seeing him, and without a car?' said Kitt, a triumphant note in her tone.

'He put it inside one of those shopping trollies on wheels and pushed it there. The spot where you were attacked is actually not very far at all from where Seaview is in Sands-end. It's less than a ten-minute walk, even if you were taking the pace easy. He had found out from Benji that you were staying at the Elysium Guest House, he'd just asked innocently if you were coming from far away, and once he knew where you were staying, he crept out of his window at first light and pulled the trolley case with him.'

'And he just happened to know I'd feel like a walk down on the beach that morning?' said Kitt, her tone dubious.

'No, he never planned to throw it off the cliff, actually. His plan was to leave it outside your hotel room door as a frightening message, that's why he scratched the word "die" into the top of it. But when he saw you down on the beach, he decided that having something like that thrown in your direction would likely send a much stronger message.'

'Well, he's not wrong about that. Oh, he's got an answer for everything,' said Kitt, slumping in exasperation.

'Yes, funnily enough I haven't been sat twiddling my thumbs for almost forty-eight hours. That's exactly what I've been making sure of.'

Kitt sighed. 'Do you really believe all this?'

'I believe he believes it,' said Halloran. 'But no. I'm not convinced, despite all the evidence. There was something about the way he told the story . . . he had several moments in interview where he was very hesitant about answering the questions. And not in the way perps usually are. Not in such a way that it seems obvious they're just biding time while they think of a plausible excuse. He was having to search his mind for the answers. There was something really off about it. And he was displaying several of his dementia symptoms throughout so I don't believe he isn't sick like he says. I think someone has convinced him to say that.'

'Whoever they are, they'd better hope you get your hands on them before I do. Conditioning a vulnerable man suffering with a mental illness, it's enough to . . . to . . . to make you want to do things you can't do when you're going out with a police inspector.'

'I know,' said Halloran. 'The sad thing is how resigned he is to the fact that he's really the killer. When I explained after everything he'd told us that he'd likely be charged as an accomplice, he said he was just relieved that he couldn't hurt anyone else.'

Kitt shook her head, thinking for a moment. 'And nothing came of the list of people who work with Cyril at the care home?'

'We interviewed the people on that list while taking breaks from interviewing Cyril. All of them have alibis for the murders – most of them were on shift at Seaview, and they can also vouch for their whereabouts when the victims' doors were marked. Cyril's medication has been properly administered as far as we can see but there's still a strong likelihood that the medication he's on has made it easier for whoever's really behind this to manipulate him.'

'What about Alan Jenkins then? If the initials are anything to go by he wrote the play Cyril appeared in, and then he just magically turns up in Cyril's life as a long-lost cousin? Did you track him down?'

'We've been calling the number Cyril has for him but the phone is out of service. Untrackable.'

'Isn't that suspicious in itself? And after all Stella Hemsworth said about the fact she was paid to make that play.'

'We asked Cyril about that. He said he wrote the letters and gave Stella the address of a man he knew out in Sandersdale. According to Cyril he's just an old friend who used to live in Whitby. Glen Tucker is his name. Cyril said he told the guy he thought the care staff were going through his mail and asked if he could have the letters forwarded there. This enabled him to communicate with Stella without her knowing it was him.'

'And what reason did Cyril give for writing a play like that in the first place? Is he claiming he was trying to frame Stella for the crimes he intended to carry out?'

'He said that despite what he had been told growing up, he knew that the murderous impulses he'd been experiencing towards people aligned with the occult were wrong. So he wrote the play as a way of channelling some of the fantasies he had and given how ashamed he was of thinking about such acts he didn't want to be associated with the play in any way. He auditioned for the main part to try to exorcize his own inner demons, and he got it, but when the play was over, the impulses he'd had before the play were even worse than they had been. That, he said, was when he started planning the murders.'

'I suppose that's a plausible story,' said Kitt. 'Have you got confirmation from the guy who let him use the address that it was really Cyril sending out those letters?'

'We're going to go and get it today. There's no phone at the address so we'll have to go in person. But Kitt, you need to understand something. No forensic evidence was found at Twilight Manor or at Ayleen's property. They tested every long, sharp item in Bramley's mansion for the blood and, ironically, given his status as a wannabe vampire, they didn't find a drop. The chief has ordered Ricci to accept Cyril's confession as an accomplice. An announcement is going to be made about him being charged in the hope of restoring public faith in the police to solve these murders. You know how desperate they've been for a breakthrough on this case. They are not going to turn down a confession from a man whose story checks out. Especially when all the forensics we could ever need was found in his private quarters. It more than passes the threshold for evidence.'

Kitt sighed and scraped her fingers through the front of her hair. 'So what are we going to do?'

'We're going to Sandersdale to verify Cyril's story about the friend he has out there. If that's the point at which his story unravels, it might be enough to get the chief to think twice about his press release. And is highly likely to bring us closer to catching the real killer. We've had to release Ayleen but both she and Bramley are being surveyed until Sunday night when the eleven-day window is up. Given the number of times we've been led back to the Children of Silvanus during this investigation, I think the answers we're looking for are most likely to be found in Sandersdale.'

TWENTY-FOUR

Kitt tried not to shudder as Halloran's car passed a sign for Sandersdale village. From what she understood, the property they were on their way to was situated a couple of miles outside the settlement. Which meant that, after a tense three-hour car journey, in the space of just five miles they would find their next clue in their investigation to apprehend the real Vampire Killer.

In an attempt to distract herself from what might be waiting for them, Kitt stared out of the car window, taking in the rugged view of the dales, marbled green and brown by farm fields yet to be kissed by the summer sun, and being thankful that at least the day was bright and the sky was blue. It took the edge off what would have otherwise been a deeply foreboding journey.

Grace, who was sitting in the back seat, had been uncharacteristically quiet since they had set off from Whitby three hours ago. She had, of course, insisted on coming along even though Kitt had given her an out. Not travelling well over such hilly terrain, she'd cracked a window for some fresh air, so queasiness might well have been playing a part in her unusual levels of restraint. But perhaps the reality that they were possibly on course to visit a serial killer's lair was also dawning on her. If the killer had had post rerouted there, who knew what else they might find at the property? Certainly, Grace's expression was more serious than Kitt could ever remember it being.

Halloran's phone buzzed with a message.

'Take a look at that while I'm driving, pet, will you?' said Halloran.

Kitt grabbed the phone off the dashboard and scrolled to the inbox. It was a message from Banks.

'Oh no,' Kitt could barely believe what she was reading.

Halloran, splitting his concentration between Kitt and the road, frowned across at her. 'What is it?'

'It's the name and address that Cyril gave you for Glen Tucker,' said Kitt.

'Yes, what about it?'

'Banks has been looking into the property details and in the early eighties it belonged to a Mr Justin Palmer.'

'The leader of the Children of Silvanus?' said Grace.

'Banks says the property was joint owned by a Melissa Tucker before it was passed on to Glen, her son. Mal . . . if I'm reading this right, Banks seems to think that Glen Tucker's father was Justin Palmer.'

At this news Halloran checked his rear-view mirror to make sure nobody was behind them and then slammed on the brakes, bringing the car to an abrupt stop.

He rubbed his hand over his face and looked at Kitt.

'We're on our way to a house belonging to the son of Justin Palmer?'

'That's right.'

'Glen Tucker, the man Cyril said he was friends with, that's Palmer's son?'

'Yes.'

'No,' said Halloran. 'I can't take you two there now, knowing that. This could be a trap.'

'But Ricci said she couldn't give you any more resources,' said Grace. 'Everyone's tied up with other parts of the investigation, keeping an eye on Bramley and Ayleen and all that.'

'Grace is right,' said Kitt. 'The alternative to us not coming is either waiting who knows how many hours for what is likely to be very little back-up to arrive, or you going in there alone. I think we can all agree we don't have time for the former and there's no way I'm going to agree to the latter. There are three of us. Safety in numbers. We've all got our phones with us. If it comes to it and there's some kind of emergency, I'll dial 999.'

Halloran took in a deep breath and accelerated again. 'Here's what we're going to do. Kitt and I will approach first. If things escalate or we don't come out of there in fifteen minutes, Grace, you need to dial for help.'

'But—' Grace started.

'No arguments on this one, you are our only back-up. If all of us go in there's nobody to get the distress call out if something goes wrong,' said Halloran. Kitt noticed his hands clenching the steering wheel tighter than usual. He was scared. And, she had to admit, so was she.

Everyone was quiet for the remaining two miles of the journey. What was there to say? Nothing that would bring any of them comfort. Kitt had been so preoccupied with the story Ayleen had fed her about the cult that she hadn't stopped to consider that the killer might not be someone wanting vengeance for what happened there at all. It might be someone trying to continue Justin Palmer's work – or some twisted version of it. But this time, instead of sacrificing animals to Silvanus, he was sacrificing people.

'I think that'll be it, based on the GPS,' Halloran said, pointing at a house situated some way down a long, narrow dirt track.

He indicated and the car rocked as the wheels hit terrain left uneven by tractor tyres, horse hooves and jagged stones that lay strewn across the path, blown there by the wild dale-side winds.

If Kitt had not been told who lived at the property, she would have thought it rather quaint. It was one of those houses one often sees out on the dales, made of old brick with small square windows and a solid wooden door for keeping the worst of the winter gales out. She noticed at once, however, that unlike so many of the similar houses she'd seen on day trips, in this case the front garden was terribly overgrown. Kitt imagined there was at least a few months' growth there and the weeds had been left to run wild.

'Grace, wait here, OK?' said Kitt, unbuckling her seat belt and opening the car door without waiting for a response.

'And whatever you do, keep all the doors locked, do you hear me?' Halloran added.

Grace gave him a nervous nod.

Satisfied that her assistant was going to, for once, follow instructions, Kitt climbed out of the car and set off down the small path that led up to the front door. At once, she found herself doing up the top button on her coat and tying her scarf a bit tighter. Even with the sun, the surroundings never reached a clement temperature on the dale top at this time of year.

The path to the house was paved with stone but was overgrown on all sides by the untamed garden. Halloran was right behind Kitt. She glanced back to see him inspecting the grass as they walked. As if he suspected Glen Tucker might jump out on them from a place of hiding.

Kitt did all she could to put that thought from her mind. She had no idea what to expect from Tucker. How did one live with the fact that their father abandoned them for a different kind of family? One which brought so much pain and suffering to so many? Bramley had said he had gone 'off grid' and didn't communicate with anyone. Certainly, isolating yourself in this part of the dales wouldn't be difficult. It was miles to the nearest house. When Bramley had first mentioned that Palmer's son had cut himself off from the world, she had assumed that this might have been out of grief, or fear that one of Palmer's old disciples might find him. But maybe there was another reason. Maybe this house was really a hideout. One way or another, she was about to find out.

Kitt knocked on the door and waited a moment.

No response. Not so much as a creak or a shuffle from inside.

Halloran knocked this time, heavier and louder than Kitt had before.

'Doesn't look like anybody's home,' said Kitt after a minute.

'But the car's here,' said Halloran.

Kitt shrugged. 'Maybe he has two cars.'

Halloran knocked a third time. Then tried the door handle and rattled it. It didn't budge. 'Worth a try,' he said.

Doing her best to avoid a particularly large thistle, Kitt manoeuvred herself through the grass so she could look in at the nearest window. It was quite dim inside but she could just make out the most striking contours of the room. A Welsh dresser on the right wall full of what looked like small trophies and plaques. A modest bookcase on the left, too small for Kitt's tastes but certainly big enough to hold a decent number of volumes. There was a sofa near the window and towards the back of the room, Kitt was fairly sure she could make out a table. It was on examining this part of the room that Kitt let out a cry of shock.

'What is it?' Halloran said, striding over.

'There's someone in there, I can see him. A silhouette. Sitting in one of the chairs in the dining room. I can't see his face. But there's definitely someone there.'

Halloran knocked on the window. 'Hello, Mr Tucker,' he called through the glass. 'It's the police. I'd just like to ask you a few questions.'

The man in the chair didn't so much as flinch.

'Something's wrong, Mal. Why isn't he responding?'

'Let's try round the back,' Halloran said, nodding to the side of the building.

The back garden was as overgrown as the front and with the man inside not responding, Kitt was starting to get a terrible feeling about whoever was sitting at the kitchen table. The figure had made no movement even when they knocked and called.

And then she smelled it.

Kitt looked at Halloran and could tell by his expression he could smell it too.

A smell that was both sweet and sour all at once. The smell of a body, slowly decaying.

Halloran pressed the handle down on the back door.

It was open.

'Wait here,' he murmured.

'I will not,' Kitt hissed, crossing her arms. 'If that man's dead, his killer might still be in there. You can't go in alone. I'll let you go first, that's the best I can offer you.'

Kitt watched as Halloran made the unfortunate calculation in his head and came to the same conclusion she had: that going inside this building alone was not wise.

Nodding, he pushed the door wide open and waited.

The smell of decay worsened, and Kitt covered her nose with her arm, trying to fend off the worst of it. The room was icy cold. There was clearly no heating on in the building. She could see her breath in the air, despite the weak April sun doing its best to warm things outside.

When no immediate sound or movement could be heard from within, Halloran stepped over the threshold into the kitchen and through to the dining room.

He held Kitt back with his arm as she walked to stand by his side. A gasp rose to her throat when she saw the man she presumed to be Glen Tucker propped up in a chair at his dining room table. As expected, he was long dead. Kitt had never seen a dead body that had been left sitting for so long and tried not to dwell too much on the details. One thing she couldn't miss, however, was the way in which the man's head hung limp to one side, revealing two red marks on his neck. The same red marks that had been found on the three other victims of the Vampire Killer.

TWENTY-FIVE

'The police announcement about Cyril being an accomplice of the Vampire Killer is all over the news,' said Grace, three hours or so later when she and Kitt were seated back in the car.

On the discovery of Glen Tucker's body Halloran had ushered Kitt out of the house at once and called the nearest constabulary for support with conducting an initial search of the property. Ricci wasn't able to give any resources from York but a dead body found in their jurisdiction at once seized the attention of the most local station which was in the middle of Sandersdale, nearly a ninety-minute drive from Tucker's residence. As yet, however, Halloran hadn't had time to come back to the car and report on what all this meant for the case.

'I'm not sure what this discovery really means or if they'll be announcing anything else as a result,' said Kitt. 'It sort of depends on what they find in the house but I'm not convinced that we're going to have all the information we need in time to help Ruby.' Kitt had been keeping a careful eye on the position of the sun while waiting to hear more from Halloran. It had already started its descent in the west which meant the day was nearly over and the day after tomorrow the Vampire Killer was due to strike again.

A few moments later Halloran climbed into the driver's side of the car and put his seat belt on.

'Where are we going?' asked Kitt.

'Back to Whitby,' Halloran said, a note of weariness in his tone. He started the engine and turned back onto the dirt track they had followed a couple of hours ago, leaving the officers from the local station to finish up with their search.

'They're not going to retract the charges against Cyril, are they?' said Kitt reading the frown on Halloran's face.

'Not a chance,' he said. 'As far the chief's concerned this only proves Cyril's role. Banks has questioned him again and he has confessed to the murder of Glen Tucker. He said he didn't confess to it before because he didn't realize that we would visit the property in person.'

'Did he know who Tucker was? That he was Justin Palmer's son, I mean?' said Grace.

'He says he didn't,' said Halloran. 'He said he's never heard of the Children of Silvanus. He just saw a lonely house on the dales where he could operate from while setting everything up. He'd passed the house many a time on walks before he moved into Seaview and he never remembered anyone going in or out. He actually thought it was empty. When he found Tucker there, he befriended him, tricked him out of a great deal of money and then ultimately killed him. That's the story he's told Banks anyway.'

'So the link to the Children of Silvanus, we're supposed to believe that's just a coincidence? That can't be true, not after all we've learned.'

'So far, the story checks out. There were several large sums of money in Cyril's finances that he couldn't account for – or should I say *wouldn't* account for when we questioned him yesterday. We found evidence on Tucker's online banking account that large sums had been withdrawn in cash.'

'And you think Cyril used that money to pay Stella to put on the play?' said Grace. 'But that was more than three years ago.'

'I know. We think that the killer was perhaps reimbursing themselves for the money they'd spent bribing Stella and buying the gargoyles, or, of course, were just using it as another way of framing Cyril,' said Halloran. 'I explained the link to the Children of Silvanus to Ricci but with none of the other victims having any obvious connections with the group other than a couple of them getting tattoos from Ayleen, the chief has chalked this up as a coincidence.'

'Oooh,' said Kitt. 'Parnaby just wants Cyril to fit the bill no matter what. He just wants his golden media moment.'

'Unless . . . maybe the Children of Silvanus aren't a part

of this,' said Grace. 'I'm not trying to knock off work early or anything but we've been basing this whole Children of Silvanus angle on Ayleen's statement and after what she did she's understandably paranoid. Maybe there is no link between them and the Vampire Killer.'

'I suppose it's possible,' said Kitt. 'But I'm still not convinced Cyril's the man we're looking for. You remember how we felt about this killer when we started the case? We didn't know if we could solve it because the killer seemed to have thought of everything. At the beginning it seemed as though they had gone to great lengths not to get caught. Are you telling me that that same killer, the one we doubted we could outwit, leaves all the evidence the police could ever need sitting at the bottom of his wardrobe? Why would you leave all the evidence in plain view?'

'Maybe he thought because he was seen as an older man suffering from a difficult illness people wouldn't suspect him,' said Grace. 'People are always underestimating the older members of society. Ask any of them and they'll probably tell you how little credit they get for anything. Maybe he never expected to have his room searched.'

'But we didn't search his room,' said Kitt. 'He admitted it and opened the wardrobe voluntarily. Giving himself up, just like that, after all the pains he had allegedly taken to cover his tracks.'

'But he did have a rationale for that. He said he was relieved to get caught,' Halloran argued. 'It can sometimes work that way. That people who carry out acts like this are petrified of getting caught in the beginning and cover their tracks but then later, when the strain of deception is really getting to them, they feel differently. When an opportunity to bring it all to a close presents itself, they come to recognize the relief of being apprehended. They know they won't be able to hurt anyone else. Contrary to popular belief, not every serial killer enjoys the experience of killing. For some of them it is a compulsion and for those people, being caught knowing they are never going to hurt anyone again can be an alluring prospect. That said, I do take your point about all the evidence being on plain view. It's hard to believe that nobody caring for him caught a glimpse of any of those items in the last three months. But, as yet, there have been no red flags on any of the phone records or financials for people working at Seaview.'

'What are we going to do?' said Kitt. 'If we don't find the real killer soon I wouldn't put it past Parnaby to make sure Cyril takes the fall for this completely. And even besides that, we need to find a way of keeping Ruby safe.'

Halloran was about to answer, and likely reassure Kitt that they would think of something, when his phone rang.

'Banks?' he said, as he answered the call. 'What? When?' Halloran shot a look at Kitt that at once made her shoulders tense.

'Well, she can't do that, she—' Halloran listened for a

moment and then in a softer voice replied, 'No, you're right. Jesus. OK, I'll see you then.'

'What's going on?' said Kitt,

Halloran took a moment to answer. 'York Police Station have received a letter pertaining to be from the killer.'

'A letter? The killer's never sent a letter before. Are they sure it's from the killer?'

'There's no way they can be sure but given the contents of it and the fact there are just days before the next murder is due to take place, they've got to assume it's for real.'

'Why . . . what does it say?' asked Grace.

'That if we don't release Ruby from whatever safe house we're keeping her in, he's going to kill someone at random instead.'

Kitt sighed and raked her fingers through her hair, trying with all her might to keep calm. 'So no matter what we do someone is likely to die here?'

'It gets worse,' said Halloran. 'On learning of the letter, Ruby has insisted that she can't let someone else die in her place. She's determined to come to Whitby tomorrow. She wants to use herself as bait and draw out the killer.'

'What? She can't do that,' said Kitt. 'That's practically a suicide mission.'

'We can't hold her at a safe house against her will, or tell her where to go. The good news is she's agreed to let Banks and Evie drive her to Whitby. They'll meet us at the hotel tomorrow and together we'll devise a plan.'

'A plan?' said Kitt. 'You mean, you're going along with this? You're really considering using Ruby as bait?'

'I have to, pet. I have to consider all avenues right now. If we don't find a way to work with Ruby she might go off and get herself into trouble of her own accord, and even if we could talk her out of it, well then, another innocent person will die and we'll be left in a position where we have no idea who the killer is, or when they will strike.'

TWENTY-SIX

The news that the Vampire Killer's accomplice had been caught had made for a flurry of last-minute Saturday night bookings at the Elysium Guest House, and no doubt most other hospitality establishments across the county. The announcement had come just in time for the start of the spring goth weekend and it seemed regulars to the event needed no other incentive to make a dash to their favourite cultural gathering than a bit of reassurance that the police had the matter in hand. Ultimately, this meant that the only room left available to Evie and Ruby when Banks delivered them to the Elysium Guest House on Saturday afternoon was their most expensive one: a deluxe suite situated in an extension to the original guest house building at the back. Reception were happy enough to put separate beds in there so Evie and Ruby could share and, given the price of the room, at least when compared to the humble quarters Kitt and Grace had secured, it was no surprise the management were so obliging.

As it was a newer part of the building, the fixtures and furniture weren't quite as old-fashioned as in the other rooms. The deluxe suite looked as though it had last been remodelled in the nineteen nineties rather than the eighteen nineties, and thus still satisfied Evie's vintage tastes. It was adorned largely with luxurious coffee and cream shades that Laurence Llewelyn-Bowen would surely have approved of. Ruby, who seemed almost giddy at the prospect of no longer staying in the safe house, sat on the end of her bed, threw the large carpet bag she'd been carrying down next to her and sighed. 'What a week, what a week,' she said. 'Oooh, I've never been so happy to have fresh sea air in my lungs. Mind you, I had hoped all this would be over by now.'

'We thought it might be,' said Halloran. 'But the letter posted to York Police Station was received while Cyril was in custody, which means, whether he's using Cyril as an accomplice or not, the real killer is still out there, and we need to be very careful about any public appearances on your part. We only want the killer to know you're here when it suits us and we have half a chance of apprehending him.'

'Oh no,' said Ruby fanning herself with her hand, 'tell me I'm not confined to this room until then. I felt so cooped up at that safe house I thought I was going to scream. DC Wilkinson didn't seem convinced by any of my stories so my only entertainment was seeing how many tricks I could play on DS Redmond. If he asks, I've got the power to raise zombie bats.'

Everyone chuckled at the idea of Ruby convincing DS Redmond of such things. And that Wilkinson, who was some years younger than Redmond, had exhibited less naivety.

'Redmond needs to get a clue,' Banks said. 'Honestly don't know how he passed his training sometimes, given how gullible he can be.'

'On a serious note,' said Halloran. 'It would be better if you could stay here at least until we launch our plan to apprehend the killer tomorrow night.'

'Can you – er – make me stay in 'ere, like?' Ruby said.

'No,' Halloran admitted. 'If you choose to go outside that's up to you but it does make it more likely the killer will discover your hiding place.'

'Well, I'm not being funny but we all know tomorrow could be the last day I'm alive. I won't do anything rash like stand at the bandstand with a megaphone . . . although now that I think about it . . .'

'Ruby . . .' Kitt said with a small smile.

'I told you I'm not afraid to go if my time is up, lass, and I'd rather not spend me last day here staring at the same four walls. In this life, you've got to make the most of every minute while you can.'

'I believe I have a solution to your dilemma,' said Evie, pulling her suitcase up onto her bed and unzipping it.

Kitt watched closely as her friend pulled a long, black wig out of her suitcase and turned around to the group with a wide satisfied grin.

'Your Morticia Addams wig from three Hallowe'ens ago?' said Kitt. 'How is that going to help anything?'

'It's a disguise,' said Evie, plonking the wig down on Ruby's head and rearranging it until it sat straight.

'I hardly think that's going to convince anyone,' said Kitt with a chuckle.

'Well, unless you want to stay indoors for the whole of tomorrow you'll have to come up with something similar,' said Halloran. 'Ruby isn't the only person being targeted by the killer. Or have you forgotten the attempt on your life?'

'I'm not staying inside at a time like this,' said Kitt, suddenly sympathizing a little more with Ruby's resentment over being coddled.

'Don't worry,' said Evie. 'I'll give Kitt a makeover worthy of the goth weekend. Nobody will recognize her once I'm through.'

'Oh, thanks a bunch for putting that idea in her head,' Kitt said to Halloran.

Banks chuckled at Evie's antics but a moment later she'd corrected her expression. 'Sir, although we're focusing on the letter sent by the killer just now, you should know something's come to light that I think might be relevant to the whole Children of Silvanus angle.'

'What is it?' asked Halloran. 'Something to do with Penelope Baker? Have you found any leads on her yet?'

'No, sir,' said Banks. 'After she left her foster parents she seems to have just disappeared off the face of the planet. I will keep looking into it but what I have found out is to do with the second victim, Roger Fairclough.'

'The ex-police officer?' said Halloran. 'What about him?'

'With the Children of Silvanus being dispersed for some years, I went back in the victims' address history to see if there was any crossover with the group.'

'Things like that haven't already been looked at by other stations when the killings have happened in their areas?' said Kitt.

Banks shook her head. 'It's incredibly rare for a murder motive to stretch back as far as this one would have to for the Children of Silvanus element to be significant. When a murder takes place, most of the time we focus on the victims' more recent activity and relationships. On the whole that's where you're going to find your evidence. But in light of Glen Tucker's body being discovered yesterday afternoon, and Penelope's disappearance a decade ago, I went back much further than we would ordinarily and found that in the late eighties and early nineties Roger Fairclough had lived out on the dales and worked in Sandersdale. He left the area before either Penelope or Ayleen joined the Children of Silvanus but we don't know exactly when the group was founded.'

'So Roger Fairclough could have been working in Sandersdale when the Children of Silvanus were active?' said Kitt. 'Did he have any run-ins with Justin Palmer?'

'I don't know yet,' said Banks, 'the files are not digitized. They'll be at the nick in Sandersdale.'

'I'll put a call into them and see if they can send over what they've got,' said Halloran. 'With Palmer's son dead and Fairclough being linked to Sandersdale, it looks as though we can't quite rule out the idea that the Children of Silvanus might yet play a part in all of this after all.'

'Especially given that the letter we received was postmarked in Sandersdale,' said Banks. 'And I got Stella Hemsworth to hand over the fragment of the letter she received. The paper and the handwriting are a match.'

'Any DNA?' said Halloran.

'We're still waiting on results from the letter we received yesterday, sir. I doubt we'll hear anything back before tomorrow night but if we apprehend someone and there is DNA on the letter, we'll be able to make a match.'

'Ruby, are you all right?' Kitt interrupted. The woman had an extraordinary expression on her face. More extraordinary than usual, and when it came to Ruby that was really saying something. If Ruby thought she was getting messages from the beyond, her face could often contort in ways both unexpected and alarming, but Kitt had never seen her look like this before.

'What does Justin Palmer have to do with this?' she asked.

'We don't really know yet,' said Grace. 'Other than he was the leader at the Children of Silvanus. Why? Do you know him?'

'So he set up a cult?' Ruby said, shaking her head sadly.

'Have you come into contact with this man?' Halloran pushed.

'Not in forty years. But even after forty years, that name is burned into my memory.'

'Why?' said Kitt. 'How did you know him?'

'I used to read his tarot cards back then. That kind of thing was still hush-hush in those days. Occult people knew how to find each other – usually by wearing a piece of jewellery with one symbol or another – but there weren't all these online forums and organizations like there are now. Anyway, I forget exactly how, but I crossed paths with Justin Palmer at some little meeting or other and he wanted to have his cards read. So for a while, once every couple of months he'd slip me twenty quid and I'd lay out a spread. I had quite a few clients back then on the quiet, before the age of internet psychics.'

'Did something happen between you?' said Kitt. 'Something that might make one of his admirers come after you?'

'Not that I recall,' said Ruby. 'When I first started reading his cards, he was friendly enough but over time I started to notice some worrying trends in the cards that came up, or the interpretations he wanted to draw from them didn't sit right with me. He'd always take his ideas to the extreme. The last reading I did for him was one of the most frightening I have ever done. It still strikes terror into me heart now as I stand 'ere.'

'What did the cards say?' said Evie, completely involved in Ruby's story. Kitt did her best not to roll her eyes. Though she had no doubt Justin Palmer was an intimidating presence, Ruby could be quite dramatic when it came to describing her 'psychic' experiences.

'The cards were plain as day. I'll never forget them. First he drew the Emperor reversed. Then the King of Swords reversed. And lastly the Chariot reversed.'

'And that's . . . bad?' said Banks who, unlike Evie, had had a distinctly dubious look on her face ever since Ruby had started talking about tarot cards.

'He'd mentioned he was interested in setting up a spiritual group. He hadn't got a name for it yet, I suppose it must have become the Children of Silvanus. And all of the cards were about abuse of power and a subversion of the greater good. Authoritative power taken too far to the point of cruelty and extreme manipulation. I warned him that setting up his collective would send him down a dark path. One that he wouldn't easily be able to turn back from once he'd started on that course.'

'What did he say?' asked Grace.

'Well, that was the scariest thing about it all, really,' said Ruby. 'That's the reason I haven't been able to forget him. If you delivered news like that to most people, they'd be shocked or worried about it. At the very least they'd seem concerned.'

'But Justin Palmer didn't?' said Kitt.

'Ruby shook her head. 'Quite the opposite. He just smiled as if he already knew what I was talking about and as if that was exactly what he wanted to hear. We argued about what he should do next. He wanted to see the path through wherever it led. I told him it could only lead to pain for all concerned, but he didn't listen.'

'Did you see him again after that?' asked Halloran.

'No, I told him that there was no point in us continuing the readings if he wasn't going to take on board the advice that came with them. He left and I never saw him again. I wondered from time to time what had become of him. It's not much of a surprise that his next step was to become a cult leader.'

'Why didn't you mention this sooner?' said Banks.

'I didn't know you were looking for Justin Palmer. You asked about the Children of Silvanus – who I'd never heard of. Same for Jamelia Park. But nobody asked me about Justin Palmer.'

'Redmond did the questioning on that score, sir,' said Banks, 'and he has been a bit on edge around Ms Barnett.'

Halloran shook his head, exasperated.

'An unfortunate oversight but, Mal,' said Kitt, 'if Fairclough did come into contact with the Children of Silvanus and Ruby came into contact with Palmer, that does heighten the odds that the Vampire Killer is selecting his victims based on their association with the Children of Silvanus. I am wondering now if we go back through the victims' personal histories if we'll find a link somewhere in the last twenty or even forty years to the Children of Silvanus. If that's the key it might help us understand who the real killer is.'

'If Ruby did that reading forty years ago and the killer has waited all this time to act on their vengeful tendencies, we can assume that Cyril is much more likely to be a victim than an accomplice,' said Halloran.

'How can you be sure?' said Grace.

'Cyril said he was brought up in a religious household and that he's had long-running desires to hurt or kill people of occult belief systems. But he also said that he had never heard of the Children of Silvanus and the sheer number of links back to this group are too many to ignore. Whoever is behind this either lived the history of the Children of Silvanus for themselves or has done a lot of research. Given that all of the documents relating to the Children of Silvanus were destroyed, I'm assuming it's the former.'

'But remember Bramley mentioned that he thought Palmer had a journal that was passed onto his son,' said Kitt. 'Has anything like that turned up at Tucker's house?'

'Not that I've heard,' said Banks.

'Maybe the killer has it. And that's what they're using to select victims. And there's a chance the killer started the fire at the archive and library too. Making sure they had accumulated all the information they needed first before destroying it so that nobody else could follow in their footsteps. It's not like the Children of Silvanus are a branch of the local council – given the strange and antisocial nature of their organization, people would just have assumed that there wasn't any record of them.'

'If the fire at the library was started by the killer,' said Halloran, 'there's also a good chance that the fire at the camp and at Ayleen's house was started by the killer. What if Ayleen's parents had some strange connection to the Children of Silvanus that we haven't yet understood?'

'I'm already way ahead of you on that one,' said Grace, staring wide-eyed at her phone. 'It was what Banks said, about going further back into people's pasts. Ayleen's parents used to run an estate agency. It operated in Sandersdale and they specialized in selling farmland. Justin Palmer had to have bought that land he used for the commune from someone. What are we betting it was through the Parks' estate agency?'

'But a fire doesn't fit the Vampire Killer's MO,' said Evie.

'Not as we currently know it,' said Banks. 'But killers can evolve in their methods. If for some reason some extremist took against the cult, they might have started with arson.'

'Killing people who they felt were responsible for the Children of Silvanus,' said Kitt. 'First the people who sold him the land, then the leader himself, and any followers still with them in the fire that brought their collective to an end. Then the library that offered insight into who they were. And there may be more instances. We don't know.

We don't have a list of people who were affiliated with the group.'

'That'll be in Palmer's journal which, I have to agree with Kitt, is probably in the hands of the killer,' said Banks. 'Otherwise, how would they know who to target? How would they know about a tarot reading Ruby did for him forty years ago? That's the kind of information you don't find in a newspaper. The other victims must have links to Justin Palmer or the Children of Silvanus.'

'All right, here's the plan,' said Halloran. 'Tomorrow, at midday, we're going to make a press announcement that we've released Ruby from police protection now that we've caught the accomplice and are close to cracking the case. It's important that the killer knows we've abided by his request so that we have a chance of drawing him out on our terms. We know the killer strikes at midnight, so they're likely to want to get their hands on her late afternoon, early evening. We'll wait until just before dusk. Ruby, you can wander casually around the old town. And perhaps down to the seafront where it's more open and you're more likely to be spotted. We'll all be trailing you from different angles and I'll make sure I put a tracking device in your bag just in case. When the killer makes his move, we'll close in.' Halloran paused, looking at Ruby. 'What do you think? Are you sure you want to go through with this?'

Ruby was quiet for a moment before speaking. 'Aye, I would. You see, I'm not afraid to die, truly I'm not. But I just got new knees six months ago. The doctor said they'd last me twenty years. It'd be a real shame if we just sat back and hoped for the best and then the killer got to me anyway after I've only 'ad 'em a few months. It'd seem like such a waste.'

'Oh, Ruby,' Kitt said with a chuckle, though there were tears in her eyes. 'The world really wouldn't be the same without you in it, would it?'

Ruby, somewhat surprised by how emotional Kitt had become, smiled and patted her shoulder.

Remembering that there was no time to waste on sentimentality, Kitt cleared her throat and sat up a little straighter. 'Yes, well, come on, Grace. Now that's all settled we'd best get back to our research on links to the Children of Silvanus. We need to be as prepared as we possibly can be tomorrow. Ruby's life depends on it.'

TWENTY-SEVEN

'Ta-da,' said Evie, as she dragged a reluctant Kitt out of the en-suite bathroom the following afternoon.

Grace, who was taking a sip of a gin and tonic she'd bought downstairs in the hotel bar, spat her mouthful of drink back out again as she took in the cut of her boss.

'Right, that's it. I don't care what you say, Evie, I'm looking in the mirror,' Kitt said. If Grace's reaction was anything to go by, she would stand out rather than blend in to the crowds milling through Whitby's backstreets for the goth weekend.

Kitt strode over to the full-length mirror hanging by the door and jumped back a step when she caught her reflection. No wonder Evie wouldn't let her look in the bathroom mirror whilst the makeover was in progress.

Evie had almost completely emptied the white powder compact in order to get Kitt's usually rosy complexion looking deathly pale. She'd applied a thick layer of emerald-green eye shadow and the lipstick she had picked out was decidedly blood red. As if all this wasn't bad enough, the black lace dress she was wearing was a bit tight and thus Kitt's ample curves bulged out in places where she was fairly sure they shouldn't. The only thing that didn't distress her was the black collar she wore. She had a feeling Mal might quite like that bit, behind closed doors. Everything else, however, was a literal horror show.

'I look like I've had a makeover from Alice Cooper, for goodness' sake,' she said, turning back to face Grace. In the time she'd been eyeing her reflection, Grace had whipped her phone out of her pocket and begun taking photographs.

'Stop that,' Kitt said, snatching the phone out of Grace's hands. 'If even one of those photographs turns up on social media you can find yourself another job.'

'All right, all right,' Grace said with a chuckle, raising her hands in mock submission. 'Let's finalize the plan, shall we?'

'For the best, I think,' said Kitt. 'Evie, I know you and Ruby went for a potter around Whitby in disguise yesterday afternoon but the announcement was made about her release about thirty minutes ago so you'll need to mind her until dusk while Grace and I get any further briefing from Mal and Banks. Keep all of the doors and windows locked and, no matter what, don't let anyone in. In the meantime, we'll continue looking into any links Anna Hayes and Alix Yang might have had with the Children of Silvanus.'

'Got it,' said Evie. 'There's still a couple of hours till then. If you don't mind, we'll stream a movie on your tab to keep our minds off everything.'

'Yes, yes, yes, that's fine,' said Kitt, and then after a moment added, 'Nothing lewd though, Evie – that's going on my credit card.'

Evie held her palm against her chest, pretending to be outraged. 'Would I?'

Kitt shook her head at her friend, she didn't need her to answer that question.

'At dusk, we'll make sure the tracking device is securely on Ruby's person, and Mal and Banks will meet us here,' said Kitt. 'From there, he'll instruct Ruby on which streets will afford her maximum visibility – not that I'm really expecting her to follow instructions to the letter, you know what she's like. We'll all split up and follow her from different angles and directions while making sure we have regular check-ins over coms. We'll keep each other appraised of our location and Ruby's at all times.'

'If anything happens, Halloran and Banks will call for backup,' said Grace.

'Although I'm a bit scared about what might happen this afternoon, I must admit I'll be glad when it's all over,' said Evie. 'Charley has been out of her mind with worry about this case. She's used to having more to go on than this.'

'Mal's been in a spin about it too, even before someone threw a hunk of rock at me with the word "die" carved into it,' Kitt conceded. 'Whatever we do, we need to keep Ruby safe.'

'I will. I'll go and give her a knock now. Hopefully she's finished whatever religious ritual she wanted her privacy for,' said Evie, walking towards the door. Before she closed it behind her she added, 'Kitt, be careful, won't you, old chum?'

Kitt offered her a reassuring smile. 'Always, but less of the "old" if you don't mind.'

Chuckling, Evie closed the door behind her.

'Right, Grace, I know we've cracked some pretty tricky cases before but nothing quite like this. For both our safety, I don't want any of your distracting and dangerous antics tonight. Clear?'

'Distracting and dangerous? Is that how you see me? Probably the best compliment I've ever had.'

'Grace . . .'

'Oh all right. I'll be on my best behaviour,' she said, teaming her words with a cheeky little salute.

'If you could aim for a cut above your idea of best behaviour, I'd be even more grateful,' said Kitt.

'Doesn't sound like much fun,' Grace said with a smile. Kitt joined in but then her smile fell away. 'Any word from Halloran about the files at Sandersdale station?' Grace added, likely noticing Kitt's solemn demeanour.

'Nothing specific yet. He said there was too much to sum up in a text message so he'll brief us about it when we meet him. He's on his way here from York now so he should be back in good time to brief us and then carry out the plan. He says he's making sure the surveillance of Ayleen and Bramley steps up a notch tonight. Just in case it's one of the two of them. And he's got eyes on Tremble. Just a precaution. Meanwhile, he and Banks will be following Ruby, with our support, in the hope of drawing the killer out.'

'Just so long as you and Halloran don't engage in any mushy talk over coms. Or any sexy talk for that matter.'

'And provide you with yet more ammunition to facilitate your non-stop stream of cheek? I don't think so,' said Kitt.

Grace looked as though she was just about to offer a sassy retort when the door to their room flew open and Evie stood breathless in the frame.

'Something's wrong,' she said. 'The door of our suite is locked from the inside and I can't get Ruby to answer.'

'What?' said Kitt. 'She's probably deeply involved with some alternate psychic plane and just not heard you knocking.'

Evie shook her head. 'Ruby's a lot of things but hard of hearing isn't one of them. I was braying the door in like there's no tomorrow and there wasn't a sound from the other side.'

Kitt shot Grace a concerned look. All three of them rushed out of the room and hurried down the stairs to the back of the property where the deluxe suite was located.

'I've already told reception we're worried about her,' said

Evie. 'They're just looking to see if they've got something they can use to jimmy the inside lock now.'

'Ruby,' Kitt called, knocking hard on the door. 'Ruby!' she called again when nothing stirred. She tried the handle just to be sure but as Evie had already said, it was locked from the inside.

'Still nothing?' the receptionist said, with a sympathetic grimace.

Evie shook her head. 'If she was in the bathroom or something I'm sure she'd have heard us by now.'

'I've been at the desk downstairs most of the afternoon and haven't seen her leave through the main doors,' said the receptionist. 'The owner of the guest house usually takes care of any handiwork and would probably be able to jimmy the lock but he's out for the afternoon and won't be back for another couple of hours. Have you tried the patio doors at the back?'

'No – I didn't think of that!' Evie said, dashing towards the hotel entrance, closely followed by Kitt, Grace and the receptionist.

When they arrived at the back of the building a feeling of dread settled in the pit of Kitt's stomach as she looked at the patio doors. They were ajar and one of the windows had been broken. Someone had forced entrance.

'Oh no,' Evie said, tears forming in her eyes. 'I was only gone half an hour, if that. I shouldn't have left her.'

'Sssh,' Kitt soothed Evie. 'Wait on a moment. The intruder might still be in there.'

Kitt walked towards the door. The receptionist stood close behind her. Kitt pushed the door open. 'Ruby?' she called.

'Ms Barnett?' the receptionist echoed. When no response came the pair looked at each other and stepped over the threshold into the room.

'Oh my God,' said the receptionist, as she stared into Ruby's hotel room. Her mouth hanging open. Her eyes wide.

TWENTY-EIGHT

'What the bloody hell's been going on in here?' said the receptionist, finally finding the wherewithal to speak.

It seemed in the short space of time Ruby had been resident in the hotel room she had decided to redecorate in her own unique style. Fake cobwebs hung from almost every available surface. A thick black rug printed with a giant pentacle covered most of the carpet. And an assortment of candles, crystals, wind chimes and feathers had been strewn everywhere.

'Yes, I'm sort of with the receptionist on this one, Evie,' said Kitt. 'What has been going on in here?'

'Don't get at me!' said Evie. 'All I've heard from Ruby since last night is that today could be her last day alive and I am not in a position to argue with that, am I? When somebody might be nearing their final hours you let them decorate the room however they want.'

'Last day alive?' said the receptionist. 'I'm sorry, is your friend ill?'

'No,' said Kitt. 'Someone wishes her harm. And by the looks of things they've got to her.'

'She's not in the bathroom,' said Grace.

'Oh God, she's been taken. I was supposed to look after her,' said Evie, while starting to pace. 'But how would the killer have known to look for her here? They've only just made the announcement that she's been released.'

'Do you have CCTV cameras in the car park out back?' Kitt asked the receptionist.

'Yes, we've got a couple of cameras in case anyone tries to park there when they're not a guest with us.'

'Can you please check it for the last hour and call the police about the break-in? Let them know a woman is missing. Whoever has taken her, it's broad daylight so it's not like they could drag her somewhere against her will. The odds are that she's been taken away in a vehicle.'

'I'll check right away and report all this,' said the receptionist, unlocking the front door to the room and hurrying out.

Quickly, Kitt whipped out her phone and sent Halloran a text message updating him on Ruby's disappearance and letting him know they may yet have CCTV footage on their side.

'I still don't know how the killer would even know we were here,' said Evie.

'Well, Ruby did insist on venturing out yesterday afternoon after she'd unpacked,' said Kitt. 'Where did you go?'

'She was wearing the disguise, so I didn't think anyone would recognize her. Plus there's lots of people out and about for the festival. I just thought we'd blend in. Let's see. We had a walk along the pier. Visited Rainbow Gems on Haggersgate. Then we went into the old town for an ice cream. Visited the occult bookshop and Whitby Glass. Then walked back to the guest house. We can't have been outside more than a couple of hours and it was dark for most of the time.'

'After all we've done to try and protect her it's bloody hard luck to have failed her now,' said Grace.

'We're not beaten yet,' said Kitt. 'Remember. The other killings didn't take place until midnight. It's not yet half past one. We've still got time to find her. I wonder if there's a clue in here as to where she has been taken. Quick, take a look around.'

For several minutes everyone spent their time opening drawers, looking under the beds, checking inside the wardrobes and inside the bathroom but there was nothing of consequence. Sighing, Kitt slumped down on Ruby's bed.

'This is exactly what I was afraid of happening,' she said, her eyes fixing on a volume sitting on Ruby's bedside table. It was a copy of *The Whitby Witches*. On top of it was the receipt from Broomsticks, Black Cats and Books, alongside the change from Ruby's purchase. Kitt couldn't say why she was so fixated with the coins. There was something odd about them. 'That's a bit weird,' she said, when she finally realized what was bothering her.

'It's been a bit of a week for that,' said Grace. 'You're going to have to narrow it down. What's a bit weird?'

'These coins, Ruby's change from the bookshop.'

'What about them?' said Evie.

'They were all minted in 1991.'

'What, all of them? That is weird,' said Grace. 'There are six or seven different coins there. What are the odds of that?'

'I'm no mathematician, but almost non-existent I would imagine,' said Kitt, hurrying to open her satchel. She didn't carry much cash on her these days, most places accepted cards even in small fishing towns like Whitby. The small amount of change from her own purchase in the bookshop was still sitting in the front of her purse. 'Oh my word,' she said. 'This is my change from the same bookshop; again, all the coins have been minted in 1991.'

'OK,' said Grace. 'There's no way that could be a coincidence. Why would Arnie be giving out change only in coins minted in 1991?'

Kitt shook her head. 'It's very odd indeed. Arnie was the one who put us onto Ayleen and Cyril . . . but we checked into him and he seemed all above board.'

'Nothing untoward came up in any of my searches,' said Grace.

'So what's with all these coins from 1991?' said Kitt.

'I don't know, in fairness I didn't find anything about Arnie from 1991. Most of the search results were from the last ten years. Anyroad, I'm going to find out. Something freaky is going on here,' said Grace, pulling out her phone and tapping away at the screen.

'Anything?' said Evie after a few seconds.

'Not sure. "Occult 1991" has brought up too many results. None of them seem that relevant.'

'Try "occult Yorkshire 1991",' said Kitt.

Grace obliged. She scrolled down for a few moments and then her eyes widened.

'Arnold Sykes wasn't always a bookshop owner,' said Grace. 'And I know why nothing untoward came up in any of our searches before: his name wasn't always Arnold Sykes.'

'What?' said Kitt 'Well you did say he had a career change from insurance. But there was nothing about a name change.'

Grace shook her head. 'He's built a whole new identity for himself. In the nineties he was a farmer, in Sandersdale and his name was Victor Greenwood. Look, this is him in the picture, I'm sure of it.'

Grace turned her phone to Kitt. Sure enough, the article Grace had found was headed up with a picture of a man who looked just like Arnold Sykes, only thirty years younger.

'Sandersdale . . . Oh no,' said Kitt. 'And being a farmer . . .

that means he would likely have had access to Xylazine. And Victor . . . V.'

'That's why none of the lists of recent prescriptions for Xylazine have been any good to the police,' said Grace. 'He's been hoarding it for decades.'

'But why?' said Evie. 'Why would he kill all those people?'

'Looking at the headline on that news article,' Kitt said, 'I'd say we've got his motive. In 1991 almost all of his livestock were killed.'

'Let me guess,' said Evie, 'the Children of Silvanus were the ones who slaughtered his animals, in ritual killings.'

'The article doesn't name the cult,' Grace said shaking her head. 'Otherwise it would have come up in earlier searches that we've done on them, but it says that the slaughter meant bankruptcy for Sykes. He lost his farm. He lost everything.'

'He wasn't insured?' said Kitt.

'It says here that his insurers wouldn't pay out, that kind of act wasn't covered under his policy,' said Grace.

'Sounds to me as though Arnold Sykes – or Victor Greenwood as he was known then – found out it was the Children of Silvanus behind the slaughter and started systematically targeting anyone who was even remotely involved with them in revenge.'

'Starting with Ayleen's parents all those years ago,' said Grace, 'if our theory about the fires is correct. And I'll bet Arnold Sykes and Alan Jenkins are one and the same too.'

'But if Arnold Sykes is the killer and has gone to all these lengths to cover his tracks, why would he hoard coins minted in 1991 and give them out as change when it could – and has – led back to him?' said Evie.

'I can't be sure,' Kitt admitted. 'But it's likely it was a compulsion, or a way of making himself feel cleverer than everyone else. Leaving such a small detail in plain view. Knowing the full story was under everyone's noses if only they looked close enough. Still, there's no time for theorizing now. It's clear Arnold Sykes is our killer,' said Kitt. 'We've got to find him at once. He's got our Ruby and if we don't catch up with them she won't see the other side of midnight.'

TWENTY-NINE

Without waiting another minute Kit and Grace hurried out of the guest house leaving Evie to receive the police, scrutinize the CCTV footage and inform them that as a matter of urgency they needed to find Arnold Sykes's home address. The only place Kitt and Grace could immediately link him to was his business and so they agreed they would start the search there. It was highly unlikely that they would find Sykes at the bookshop now that he had been bold enough to kidnap somebody in broad daylight but it was the only starting point they had.

Due to the crowds of people who had gathered for the goth weekend it took them twice as long to navigate their way between the West Cliff and the East. Sure enough, when they got to the bookshop there was a sign on the door that said: *Family emergency. Closed early. Sorry for any inconvenience.*

'Family emergency my foot,' said Kitt.

'What now?' said Grace.

'I don't know, I— Wait, Grace, isn't that him there?'

Grace turned to see the same thing Kitt had. Arnold Sykes standing twenty feet ahead of them in a black hoodie. He had been watching them and had a frightening leer fixed on his face. Without warning he pulled the hood over his head, turned on his heel and began to run.

'Quick, we've got to catch him!' said Kitt, before breaking into a run. A moment later Grace gave chase. Kitt was not a natural runner and had to work hard to keep up with her assistant. All the time, she kept her stare fixed on that black hoodie with the white pentagram as he sped through the cobbled back streets of the old town towards the harbour. As they approached the swing bridge, Kitt heard a sound that would usually bring a smile to her face. The bell that meant pedestrians had to clear the walkway because the bridge was about to open to let a ship through.

Sykes just managed to dodge around the gate as the operator closed it to cut off pedestrian traffic. Knowing that if they waited for a boat to pass through they would undoubtedly lose Sykes, Kitt did something she would never normally do: she broke the rules and climbed over the barrier. Not an easy feat in the ridiculous dress Evie had picked out for her. She was in no doubt she was putting her wares out on display in the process but frankly, there was far too much at stake to be concerned with matters of modesty. Grace followed closely behind her. As they ran towards the middle of the bridge they felt a sickening lurch as it began to swing.

'Quick,' said Kitt, jumping over to the other side just before the two sections parted and grabbing Grace's hand so she had no choice but to follow.

'Oi, you two!' the operator shouted as she and Grace hopped over the barrier at the other side

'Ever so sorry!' Kitt strained to call back, though she barely had the breath to do so.

Turning onto the promenade at the other side of the bridge, Kitt suddenly realized she had lost sight of Sykes. She hurried along through the crowds, checking the face of anyone wearing a black hoodie. None of the faces were Sykes and all of them were angry or perturbed at being jostled by a woman they didn't know. When they reached the end of the promenade and still hadn't found him, Kitt was just about to concede that they'd lost their subject when Grace picked up his trail.

'There,' she said, pointing up to the steps that ran up the side of the West Cliff.

'We're going to pass our guest house,' said Kitt. 'Do you think he's leading us back there for some reason?'

The pair didn't have time to discuss this theory. Instead, they crossed the road as carefully as they could and ran up the steps. Once on the cliff top, Kitt could see Sykes a little way in the distance running towards a fairground that had been set up especially for the goth weekend.

Kitt and Grace followed as closely as they could but they

were tiring from the chase and Sykes had managed to get a bit of a lead on them.

Entering the fairground, the two women looked around, panting and squinting through the crowds to try and locate their target.

'Over there,' said Kitt. 'He's . . . he's going into the Mirror Maze.'

'Oh no,' said Grace. 'Can't we just wait for him to come out the other side? We'll never find him in there.'

'According to that banner there are six different exits, we can't cover them all,' said Kitt, shaking her head. 'We'll have to go in and just do our best to follow him.'

Grace had a few coins in her pocket and paid herself and Kitt into the attraction. No sooner were they inside, however, than Kitt knew at once this was a big mistake.

They were surrounded by glass on all sides to the point that it was difficult to work out even where the openings to the main maze were. Indeed, the first thing she did was walk into a pane of glass, not realizing the corridor was behind her. Ordinarily this would have drawn hoots of laughter from Grace but it seemed even she understood the seriousness of the situation.

'I don't understand, a couple just went in before us and they're nowhere to be seen,' said Kitt. 'Finding a way into this thing can't be that difficult.'

'Maybe they've done it before,' said Grace. 'Some people come here every year, you know?'

Feeling their way along and stretching their hands out to avoid any more bumps, they did what they could to navigate their way forward. Kitt could hear giggles echoing around the maze from other people in other parts of the attraction. Knowing there was a serial killer on the loose in there only made the sound of their merriment more eerie. They had no idea they were trapped in here with someone with the capacity to kill. Kitt and Evie turned two corners before they came face to face with Arnold Sykes.

Kitt jumped back in surprise. She thought he had been trying to escape from them. Why would he be stood here waiting if escape was his plan?

'We know you're behind the killings, Arnold, it's over. Just come out of here quietly. There's no need to make anything worse than it already is.'

'I'm afraid I can't do that,' said Sykes. 'And it isn't over. Not until you catch me.'

Arnold turned to run again. Kitt reached out to grab his arm but her hand only hit glass. 'What? What?' she said, realizing she had been speaking to Arnold's reflection all along. She turned to see what she was pretty sure was the real Arnold running in the opposite direction. She and Grace began to follow but then realized there were two different corridors and they weren't sure which one Sykes had run down.

'You go this way and I'll go that way,' said Grace.

'Splitting up is not a good idea,' Kitt argued.

'We don't have time to debate it,' said Grace. 'If Sykes escapes now it will mean the end for Ruby. He's not going to kill me in the mirror maze. The risk of being caught red-handed by another visitor is too high.'

Reluctantly agreeing with her assistant, Kitt nodded and began to make her way down the first corridor, all the while praying she would be the one to find Sykes. For a couple of turns she didn't see anything except her own reflection. For a few moments she contemplated working her way back to where she'd left Grace, fearful that she might be having a showdown with Sykes and that she wasn't there to help her. Then she caught a glimpse of something. A black shadow, small and fleeting. Kitt followed it until she had Sykes back in her view. She increased her pace then and Sykes increased his. Once or twice she hit glass and realized Sykes was running in the other direction. There was no doubt that Sykes knew his way around this maze. Had he planned this? If so, why lure her here? She didn't have time to consider that now. Keeping visual contact with Sykes was all that mattered and to her credit she never once lost sight of him after that until they emerged on the other side of the maze. Sykes didn't ease up, however. He just kept running, away from the fairground, away from the crowds, in the direction of Twilight Manor.

Kitt followed him, her breath ragged, her feet aching, the thought of what might happen to Ruby the only thing that kept her going as she manoeuvred around a small hedge.

Once on the other side, though, she realized she could no longer see Sykes. No sooner had that realization hit her than she felt a sharp prick to her neck and within seconds the world around her started to distort. Her vision blurred. She could no longer stand and fell to her knees.

'What have you done?' she tried to say. She had no idea if the words ever reached Sykes's ears but deep down she knew she already had the answer.

Sykes had injected her with Xylazine and given that she could barely keep her eyes open, she would wager the dosage was high.

A single tear slid down Kitt's cheek as she wondered what would become of her, just before the world went black.

THIRTY

When Kitt began to awaken, the first thing she sensed was a searing heat. An utterly confusing sensation given that some part of her remembered that the day hadn't been that warm. Whatever was creating the heat wasn't close enough to burn her but it was nearby. Nearer than she'd like. Slowly, she opened her eyes but that didn't help her in ascertaining where she was. It was dark. The only thing she knew for sure was that she was lying down. She tried to move but in doing so found that her hands and feet were bound and she couldn't see with what.

Taking a deep breath in a vain attempt to remain calm, she reached her hands out, spreading her fingertips as wide as they would go until they met something solid.

It was wood.

Kitt took a sharp intake of breath and tried not to give in to the tears that threatened as she released it.

In that moment, she knew exactly where she was.

Frantically, she began twisting her body and running her bound hands along any surface she could reach. Surely she must be mistaken. Surely she was just imagining the worst. But no. She was surrounded by wood. She was in a wooden box.

Or, to be more specific, a coffin.

Tears threatened again at that thought but again Kitt choked them back. Crying wasn't going to help her and she was sure she could hear some scuffling sounds beyond that suggested one small mercy: she hadn't been buried . . . yet.

She didn't know where the coffin stood but currently her only hope of escaping was that someone may be outside, a friend rather than a foe, and that they might hear her if she called.

'Help!' Kitt cried, and began to beat her fists against the wood as loud and as fast as she could. 'Help me, please!' she cried out again and again, hitting harder and harder as she became more panicked. She knew, like everyone else, that she would one day have to face her own mortality. But she wasn't ready to do that yet. There were still so many things she hadn't done. So many places she hadn't seen. Being something of a workaholic, she'd not got around to quite as many of those things as she would have liked and had always taken for granted that there'd be plenty of time. Suddenly, the odds of doing any of them seemed frighteningly slim.

'Help!' Kitt called out again, and continued her banging

even though, after the effect of the drugs, the noise made her head feel as though it would split in two.

Kitt couldn't say how long it was before the lid of the coffin was lifted. Probably no more than a minute but it felt like a lot longer.

Light returned to her world.

It was only candlelight but in comparison to the darkness of the coffin it felt like a bright summer's day.

Any relief Kitt might have felt was at once drained away when she saw where she was and who she was with. Craning her neck she could see she was in a crypt of some sort, built of dark stone. A furnace was ablaze right next to where she lay and it was that detail that helped her understand where she must be: in the crematorium she had noticed on the way to Twilight Manor. And for company she had Arnold Sykes, leaning over the coffin and staring down at her with a mix of mild confusion and cold calculation.

'I'll be honest, I didn't think you'd wake up after the dosage I gave you. That wasn't part of the plan. You must be strong.' Sykes sounded almost bemused as he spoke. 'I thought that there might be a small chance of you waking up once your body started to burn but it's so hot in there even if you did momentarily regain consciousness, you'd be out again in a matter of seconds.'

'You mean . . . you mean you're going to burn me alive?'

'The plan was to lure you here, give you so much Xylazine

you'd never wake up again anyway and then yes, burn the evidence.'

Kitt felt her whole body tense at Sykes's words. For a moment she thought she was going to be sick but thankfully she managed to control herself. 'I'm not evidence. I'm a human being. Where's Ruby?'

'She's safe. Until midnight at least. After that, well, she'll pay the price for setting Justin Palmer on his path all those years ago.'

'Please . . . don't do this, Arnie . . . I mean Victor.' More than anything she wanted to scream at the man but that wasn't going to help her get out of this. Reasoning with him might not either but if she could keep him talking long enough Grace might be able to pick up her trail. Or the police might have tracked his vehicle to this spot via CCTV. Either way, there was still hope. The crematorium wasn't *that* far from the fairground.

Sykes's face darkened on hearing his real name. 'Victor Greenwood doesn't exist anymore.'

'I know what happened to your farm,' said Kitt, making eye contact and seeing a flicker of sadness in Sykes's eyes as she did so. 'I am so very sorry you went through that, but this, all this, what you've done, is not the answer.'

'What is then, eh?' Sykes snapped. 'You tell me that. Because after I lost everything I spent the six years it took for the bankruptcy to be removed from my credit history trying to figure out what the answer was to having everything crumble. All the hard work your father and his father have done, gone in one fell swoop. And there's nothing you can do about it.'

'You have suffered but there is help, even now there is help, and there is hope. If you don't take this any further, if you admit what you've done, accept the consequences, you can get real help.'

'I find it interesting that once you start picking people off, once you really get their attention, all of a sudden people are so keen to help you. Never mind before, when you're just a hard-working farmer who never did anything to hurt anyone and had everything taken away. People weren't remotely interested then. If you want to find out who your real friends are, I can recommend going bankrupt. You soon learn who will stand by you and who will stab you in the back. But now that I am a killer, now that I'm a threat, you're falling over yourself to help me, and you're not the only one. Every last one of the victims offered me something to try and save themselves but it is too little, too late.'

'Well, if you're really going to kill me,' said Kitt, thinking of yet more ways to bide time, 'at least grant me the satisfaction of knowing why you selected the victims you did. We know that your second victim was a police officer who worked in Sandersdale and likely, to your mind, didn't do enough to shut down the camp; and I know that Ruby was accidentally a guiding force in Justin Palmer's life, but why the other two? Is it because of their connection to Ayleen?'

'No, it is not. To be honest I didn't know those three people were connected. If anything, that was an unfortunate coincidence for me as I was trying to avoid any obvious patterns. I had to be careful when I was selecting the victims. Don't get me wrong, my plan was to go for them all, every last person involved with the Children of Silvanus, and their children on top of that. I wanted them all gone, no trace left, no lasting legacy of that vile man.

'But I had already taken a big risk in killing Palmer's son. Something like that, if it had been discovered sooner would have blown my whole plan.'

'When did you kill him?'

'Last December. I used his house for the rest of that month as a base and to plan the killings. It was easier with him out of the way, without worrying that he'd somehow tip someone off that something untoward was happening in that house.'

'Just before the killings we knew about started,' said Kitt. 'So that's why you didn't paint a V on his door? You didn't want anyone to find him because then the police would look back in his history and might discover he was Palmer's son?'

'That's right. After that, I couldn't just go for all the people at the top of the cult, not right away. I had to bury them beneath people who were not so obvious. Who were part responsible for what happened at that camp but in such a way that no one would guess they had any affiliation with them unless they dug a long way into that person's history.

Otherwise the police would have likely figured out the pattern and traced it back to me. Nobody knew me around here, so they just believed me when I said I used to work in insurance. But it wasn't a cover story that would hold up to police scrutiny.'

'So why kill Tucker in the first place?'

'I didn't intend to kill him quite when I did. I'd built up a . . . a friendship is a bit strong. Tucker didn't trust easily. But he thought I lived on one of the neighbouring farms. That's what I told him about four years ago when I explained to him that the post office said they had accidentally delivered some of my mail to him.'

Kitt frowned for a moment, and then realized the significance. 'Stella Hemsworth's replies to the letters you sent. Tucker handed them over thinking they'd been incorrectly delivered . . .'

'Aye. I stopped by now and then after that. You know, just to check nothing else had been falsely delivered. But I knew even then that one day I would kill him. I knew he had his father's journal. Unfortunately, he caught me snooping around for it during one of my visits when I thought he was in the kitchen making us a cuppa.'

'So you killed him for it?' said Kitt.

'Not right away. I held him hostage at his house for a good while before I did that. Six weeks or so. Benefit of him going off the grid. So long as his bills were paid nobody bothered us. Eventually, though, once I had got all of his passwords and banking information out of him, he had to die. I needed him out of the way so I could get on with bringing everyone else to justice. There were so many people involved in what happened in that place. So many people complicit. Some of them were already dead, but many of them are walking around in society without paying any price for what they've done. That's not justice, so I had to dish out some of my own.'

'But what connection did Anna and Alix have to the group?'

'Anna Hayes was another one of Palmer's offspring. Like most cult leaders he wasn't exactly into monogamy. She didn't know who her father was, but I did, thanks to his journal. I couldn't let all that evil pass down from one generation to the next. As for Alix, as well as publishing books online she was a journalist. She planned this big exposé on the cult right at the beginning of her career. She must have heard some rumours and started digging around. But Palmer intimidated her out of running the piece. The camp could have been shut down years before it was if she'd run that story. She decided not to. She decided to turn a blind eye. So myself and who knows how many other victims lost out.'

'Until you burned the place to the ground, killing Palmer.'

Sykes shrugged. 'Someone had to do something. The police weren't going to help. Nor the media. Who else was left to get rid of them?'

'There are other people onto you besides me, Arnie. Regardless of what happens next, you're not going to get away with this. So why make it worse on yourself by killing me? I'll be just another murder you get charged for.'

'Well . . . I am sort of thinking now that it's in for a penny, in for a pound. You see, you've got in the way of me ridding this country of some truly evil people. I had so many other people set-up to take the fall. Stoke Bramley, Demir, Armitage, Hemsworth. Nobody was ever going to look at me. If it wasn't for you, I could have just kept whittling them down until they were all gone, but now I will be going to jail, if I don't kill myself first. And if it's really over then the final thing I am going to do is find a way to torture the people who loved you. That's the penalty for getting in my way.'

'What do you mean by that?'

'You are going to burn like the interfering little witch you are. And then I'll sweep up anything recognizable as a body. By the time anyone knows I've been here the furnace will have cooled. Even if they do guess what happened to you, they won't be able to separate your ashes from any of the others. There won't be anything left of you, Kitt. What they will find, though, is a jar of your blood and that will be enough to leave your police inspector boyfriend wondering. Did you get away? If you didn't, where is your body?'

Kitt's eyes filled with tears. This was all just too much. If she didn't find a way out of this right now, she would be gone and Mal would be left never knowing the truth.

It seemed however that Sykes wasn't about to waste any more time in executing his plan. She watched Sykes pick up a needle and in her desperation, the only thing Kitt could think to do was scream.

THIRTY-ONE

'No, no, no!' Kit screamed. 'Not like this!'

With all her might she threw her weight against the side of the coffin. It was made of thin plywood and to her surprise it shunted towards the edge of whatever table she was lying on.

'Don't make this harder than it needs to be. You're not getting out of here,' said Sykes turning away to reach, Kitt presumed, for yet more Xylazine. If he drugged her again there was no way she would ever wake up. Once more, she rammed her whole body against the right side of the coffin and this time it was enough to shunt the box off the table. It rear-ended as it clattered to the floor and Kitt hit the hard stone. Not even waiting for the pain of that to register, she at once grabbed for a shard of wood and began working it against the duct tape around her wrists.

'What are you doing?!' Sykes spat as he kicked at Kitt's side and tried to roll her over to face him. Kitt resisted, keeping her hands hidden. She had to break free of the bonds if she was going to get out of this alive.

'The coffin was just a little flourish,' Sykes said. 'You're going in that furnace one way or another.' Kitt craned her neck to get a clearer view of Sykes. The needle in his grasp was filled with liquid; without a blink, he began moving it towards her neck but just before the needle met her skin she managed to free one of her hands and stop him, grabbing his wrist and squeezing it hard enough for him to know she wasn't going out without a fight. Sykes flinched and renewed his efforts to push down harder. Twisting around so she was facing him, Kitt brought her other hand up, fending him off while the needle danced just inches from its mark.

'You can't hold me off for ever,' Sykes said with a satisfied grin, and Kitt knew he was right. Her hands were already beginning to weaken. If she didn't think of something quickly, he would get the better of her and Halloran would be left to suffer. For the second time in his life the woman that he loved would have been taken by a serial killer. Given how he still bore the psychological scars from the first time it happened, Kitt didn't know if that was the kind of trauma Mal would ever recover from. She had to live. Not just for herself but for him.

For a few seconds this thought offered her renewed strength as she pushed back against Sykes's assault. There was no missing the fact, however, that he was stronger than her and within a few moments he had regained the advantage. Kitt felt the needle graze her neck. Tears of exasperation and dread were flowing freely now and she was just preparing herself for the worst when the unexpected happened.

Something long and hard crashed over Sykes's head, momentarily stunning him. Both he and Kitt turned to see Ruby standing next to them holding a pitchfork.

'How did you get free, witch?' he spat at Ruby. In response Ruby swung the pitchfork back and hit him again with the blunt side of it. This time, Sykes did go down and the needle dropped to the floor. Without even stopping to think, Kitt began tearing at the duct tape around her ankles.

'Run,' Kitt said to Ruby.

'Run? I know I've got a new set of knees but—'

'Just go!' Kitt said, at last freeing her legs from the tape and clambering to her feet. She paused just long enough to stamp on the needle a couple of times. Hard enough to shatter it.

She took just a moment to watch the Xylazine trickle away when Sykes grabbed her ankle. 'What have you done? You've ruined everything. Everything.' He moaned. He was trying to move but after two hard strikes from the pitchfork, Sykes couldn't find his balance. Kicking away his grip, Kitt ushered Ruby up the stairs to the room where funeral services were probably held. She closed the door on the crypt and bolted it shut, praying there was no other way out and that by the time the police arrived the Vampire Killer would still be down there waiting for justice to be served.

THIRTY-TWO

Kitt, Grace, Evie and Ruby sat on a bench on Whitby pier. It had not taken the police long to arrive at the scene and arrest Sykes. Kitt and Ruby had been given a quick medical check-up at the scene. She still felt woozy after being drugged but was otherwise unscathed. Halloran had been out of his mind with worry, but once he'd reassured himself of Kitt's safety, he'd gone straight down to the local nick to interrogate Sykes. That had been four hours ago now and Kitt had spent those hours wondering over so many elements of Sykes's plan that it hadn't occurred to her to ask Ruby some vital questions about what played out between them.

'Ruby,' Kitt said. 'How exactly did Sykes manage to kidnap you from the guest house in broad daylight?'

'He drove me off in 'is car,' said Ruby.

'Yes, but how did he manage to get you into the car?'

'I went willingly,' said Ruby.

'What?' Grace, Kitt and Evie all said at once.

Ruby chuckled. 'I don't mean I volunteered, I mean, when he broke in through the back door I knew there wasn't much point in putting up a fight.'

'Doesn't sound like the same Ruby who hit the killer over the head with a pitchfork,' said Evie with a little giggle. 'I don't think I'm ever quite going to get over that you did that.'

'Yeah, I can't believe I missed that,' said Grace before turning to Kitt. 'You could've taken a picture.'

'Oh, I'm so sorry,' said Kitt, her tone arid. 'I was rather consumed with fighting for my life.'

'And when Sykes broke in to the 'otel, I didn't have a pitchfork handy,' said Ruby. 'That belonged to the crematorium. I had the choice of a rake or a pitchfork but pitchfork seemed more fitting given what that bloke has been doing to people associated with the occult for the past few months. And besides, I knew that the killer might go after someone else if they couldn't take me. I didn't want anyone else to take my place. I was the one who read those tarot cards all them years ago. I was the one who had to face the consequences of that.'

'But you didn't do anything wrong,' said Grace. 'You tried to pull Palmer back from going down a dark path.'

'I know, but it was still my mess. And I 'ad a feeling that Kitt would come to the rescue.'

'I remember it being more the other way around,' said

Kitt. 'You rescued me. But one thing I don't understand, if Sykes tied you up how did you manage to get free?'

'He did tie me up with duct tape in the small kitchen area in the crematorium, but there was a sink in there. Took me a while, but I managed to shuffle my chair over and get me hands under the tap.'

Kitt smiled. 'You weakened the adhesive and broke free.'

'Aye.'

'Very smart thinking,' said Kitt. 'Do we want to know how you knew what to weaken it with?'

'You make it sound so sinister,' Ruby said, shaking her head. 'I know I don't look it, but I've been around a long time and if you keep your eyes and your mind open you never stop learning.'

'And if you hadn't done that I probably wouldn't be here,' said Kitt.

'Which I suppose puts me for ever in your debt, Ms Barnett,' said a deep, familiar voice.

Kitt smiled as soon as she heard it. It was Halloran's.

As they had a bit of an audience, Halloran kissed the top of Kitt's head and gave her a squeeze – she had no doubt she'd be getting a lot more than that later though.

'What happened in the interview, was it awful?' said Kitt.

'These things are never pleasant, but he's confessed to all the murders,' said Halloran. 'We've found Palmer's journal and there are some sections in it that have been highlighted so we'll be looking into those.'

'Did you find out what weapon he used to make the marks on the victims' necks?' asked Grace. 'Was it a needle?'

'Of sorts,' said Halloran. 'He'd modified a cooking syringe used to inject brandy and such into cakes and puddings.'

There was a moment's silence as Kitt, Evie and Grace took in this strange discovery.

'That, and I don't say this lightly, is possibly the weirdest thing about this case you've told me yet,' said Kitt, barely able to believe what she was hearing.

'I know,' said Halloran. 'You can buy them in shops for a couple of quid. We'd never have thought of looking at something like that.'

'But when he tried to set up Cyril, he left medical needles to frame him. Why not leave the real weapon to make it more convincing?' said Kitt with a frown.

'I imagine it was just another level of insurance. If he'd provided the real weapon we could have started looking into places that sold them. He didn't want to take the risk that his name would eventually crop up when we started asking questions.'

'I'm not sure I'm going to be able to eat Christmas pudding ever again without thinking about that,' Evie said.

'You and me both,' said Halloran. 'The good news is, Sykes has admitted to manipulating Cyril, so he's now safely back at Seaview Care Home with all charges dropped as we speak.'

'Is he all right?' said Grace. 'Stupid question, I know, but

I hate to think about the long-term effect something like this might have on him.'

'I don't know exactly what the impact of this case will be but I promised that I'd check in on him and suggested that you and Kitt might do too.'

'Definitely,' said Grace. 'We need to reassure him that we never meant him any harm.'

'How did Sykes manage to get Cyril believing he'd done all this?' asked Kitt. 'The story Cyril told you was so elaborate, did he really believe he'd done all those things, including throwing that rock at me?'

'It started just as you suggested: Sykes wrote those letters to Stella Hemsworth and planned to frame her for the killings. His back-up was to find a way to blame the Creed of Count Dracula, which is why he bought the gargoyles. We received the description from the local stone works and they described Alan Jenkins, aka Arnold Sykes in disguise. The first thing Banks found at Sykes's home was the wig and moustache he used for the part.'

'And nobody saw through that?' said Evie.

'These things can be quite realistic now and in fairness most people aren't expecting a person to be in disguise. They just take people as they come,' said Halloran. 'At any rate, Sykes had a stroke of luck, from his point of view, that he wasn't expecting. He kept close tabs on anyone who had performed in his play in case another scapegoat presented itself, alongside Ayleen Demir of course who he knew had been up to no good on the camp and might prove a useful patsy if the other scapegoats didn't stand up to police interrogation.'

'But then he learned that Cyril was being moved into a home because of his dementia,' said Kitt.

'He'd deliberately started the bookshop to make himself look like more of a target for the killer, so nobody would suspect him. And running a shop like that in a small town, he was privy to all the local gossip, so keeping track of a situation like that wasn't difficult. Before Cyril was moved into the home he contacted him via email professing to be a distant cousin and promised to visit him. Cyril, who was probably scared at the time and with no other family around him, accepted Sykes's claim at face value.'

'And it wasn't much of a risk to pose as a distant family member,' said Kitt. 'Even if he did get some detail wrong about the family, he could pretend to Cyril that it was him who was misremembering because of his dementia.'

'From the sound of things, that's pretty much how he worked it,' said Halloran. 'But he also started planting things in Cyril's mind about his upbringing. About his parents being deeply religious and opposed to any kind of occult practice. That was all sewn into Cyril's mind over the course of about three years, so it was no wonder he believed it by the time he talked to us about it. When the time came, Sykes used his visits with Cyril to plant evidence in his wardrobe when he wasn't looking. One day, Cyril noticed it there at the back and got scared. So he did what he always did when he got scared about something.'

'He asked his only remaining family member what he should do,' said Evie. 'God, this is heartbreaking. That poor man. It's not just the manipulation, it's the fact that he made Cyril believe he had family left in the world. Now, he not only has to live with the knowledge that he's been so horribly manipulated, but also that he doesn't have any family left after all.'

'Ooh,' said Grace, punching her palm with a clenched fist. 'I could swing for Sykes, I really could.'

'Get in line,' said Kitt. 'So Sykes then convinced Cyril that those things were in his closet because he was the murderer?'

'That's right,' said Halloran. 'Sykes, disguised as Jenkins, told Cyril that he hadn't wanted to tell him the truth because he knew the truth would upset him, but he had known for a while that Cyril was having lapses of memory and carrying out the vampire killings. By this point, Cyril trusted Sykes more than he trusted his own memory. Sykes even rang him the day Kitt was attacked and told him he'd gone out that morning and tried to kill her. Then, of course, he put the phone out of service knowing that you were going to visit and Cyril would no doubt confess.'

'Eeee, this is a twisted tale even by my standards,' said Ruby.

'And all because he was made bankrupt,' said Grace.

'Well, this was back in the early nineties, don't forget,' said Halloran. 'Going bankrupt at that time was more serious than it is now. It affected people in all kinds of ways and if a person is made bankrupt it is publicized in the papers. It can cause terrible reputational damage on top of the financial hardship. I'm not justifying what Sykes did, of course, nothing could. But he must have been pretty desperate to go to these lengths.'

Again the group fell into silence. It was impossible for Kitt to feel pity for Arnold Sykes after he had tried to kill her and had murdered so many others. But it was also sad to think about how his life could have turned out differently. If the Children of Silvanus had never bankrupted Sykes, he may have, even now, been out on the dales herding cattle. Just as his father had before him. Instead he'd spent years trying to come to terms with that soul-destroying event and when he hadn't been able to he'd begun plotting his revenge. Between the arson, the organising of various scapegoats and committing the vampire killings, almost twenty-five years of his life had been consumed by his obsession. It was difficult not to think about what a terrible waste it all was.

'Well, I think I'm ready to go home now,' said Ruby. 'Get back to my little house, and me pets.'

'Yes, come on,' Evie said, offering Ruby a hand up off the bench. 'We'd better get packed up.'

Grace followed them, giving Kitt and Halloran a moment alone. He wrapped his arms around her and squeezed her tight. 'I can't believe how close I came to losing you,' he said.

She held him just as tight but wasn't about to give him more fuel for his nightmares. 'Oh, I would have thought of something,' she said. 'I always find a way out of these situations. And, of course, I did technically also manage to solve the case before you did. And you know what that means?'

Halloran withdrew just far enough for her to see the sparkle in his eyes. 'Oh dear,' he said. 'I'm so sorry I lost. I suppose now I have to be true to my word and be your unquestioning servant for twenty-four hours.'

'That's right, time to get your vocal cords warmed up, Mal. Your first task is going to be reading my favourite passage of *Jane Eyre* to me.'

The smile on Halloran's lips faded. 'Oh, is that er, all we're going to be getting up to, like?'

Smiling, Kitt patted him on the arm and began to follow after the others.

'Kitt?'

'You'll have to wait and see,' she called back to him as they started their walk back to the Elysium Guest House.

THIRTY-THREE

Whilst putting on her coat at the end of her Saturday night shift at the Vale of York University Library, Kitt took just a moment to appreciate the smell of old books filling her lungs and the vibrant colours of the mosaic that adorned the ceiling. It depicted Prometheus giving the spark of fire to humanity. After almost being burned alive by a serial killer just shy of a week ago, Kitt wasn't sure she would ever look at that mosaic in quite the same way but she couldn't deny she was glad to be back in the comforting environs of her book stacks.

Remembering that she needed to collect the post from the agency offices, Kitt picked up her satchel and turned off the lights on the third floor of the library. She then made her way down the spiral staircase and out through the large double doors at the front. She hadn't gone ten paces towards Skeldergate Bridge, however, when she sensed someone walking behind her and not a moment later a hand grabbed her shoulder.

Kitt only just managed to keep herself from crying out as she turned round to see who it was. 'Ruby!' she said. 'What are you doing lurking around here at this time of night?'

'I knew you were working the late shift, like, and I just wanted to check in with you about the case, see if there've been any new findings in the last week that haven't made it onto the news.'

'Couldn't you have swung by a little earlier?' Kitt said.

'No, I were busy today with me meditation.'

'Sounds frantic,' Kitt muttered under her breath.

'What was that?'

'Um, fantastic to see you, Ruby. I'm just heading to the office briefly, do you want to walk and talk?'

'Aye, that'll work,' said Ruby, following Kitt up the steps to Skeldergate Bridge. 'I just wondered if there'd been any leads on that Penelope lass, you know, the one who disappeared?'

'Nothing concrete, although Banks did learn that the people who disappeared for disobedience at the camp were kept in solitary confinement and that some of those people did escape when the fire happened, so there is still hope that she's out there somewhere.'

'Good,' said Ruby. 'Hope is very important. If I have any visions that I think are relevant, I'll let you know. I must admit, I was very glad to be able to provide you with such strong leads in this case.'

Kitt took a deep breath, trying to temper her frustration at that sentence. 'Strong leads? What were those, exactly?'

'Well, you know, telling you it was a witch and all that.'

'But it wasn't a witch. It was a bloke who'd been made bankrupt.'

''E might have been the one doing the killing but the person who led you to him was a witch – Ayleen Demir. She was the one who told you about the Children of Silvanus, and she owned a tattoo shop. I told you about the butterfly tattoo in me vision as well. If it wasn't for that then you might never have found out about that cult and so might never have found the killer.'

Kitt opened her mouth to argue but thought better of it. Ruby had been through a lot in the past few weeks and it wasn't in Kitt to be cruel, no matter how exasperated she was. But also, the sheer amount of false logic in Ruby's statements made it difficult to know where to start even if she had wanted to argue with her.

'I've heard on the news, about them other fires Sykes started,' said Ruby, clearly astute enough to know it was best to move the conversation on.

'Yes, he's admitted to starting fires every few years using Justin Palmer's journal to select targets.'

'Some of those places would have had smoke alarms though. I still don't understand how he managed to burn them down without the alarms going off. Or how he started the fires without the fire brigade determining the cause of the fire.'

'In the cases where the fire was in a house, he found a way in a good month before he was due to set the fire and replaced the batteries in the alarms for dead ones. In the case of hard-wired alarms he'd disconnected the power unit and removed the back up battery. The people in the house had no idea what he'd done so when the fires happened they weren't alerted until it was far too late.'

'He really did 'is homework,' said Ruby shaking her head.

'Yes, and I'm afraid it doesn't stop there. He claims he picked the lock into the premises he targeted a second time to start the fires. He wrapped a rag around a piece of wood, set fire to it and used it to set fire to the curtains, to the carpet, anything that enabled the fire to spread while the victims were sleeping. Once he was satisfied the fire wouldn't go out he took his home-made torch with him and extinguished it.'

'Eee, it's the amount of calculation in this case that really scares me. He waited years for payback, and had made sure he'd thought of almost everything, except for your love of books, of course.'

'How do you mean?'

'Well, most people wouldn't start a murder investigation in a bookstore; there's only one person I know who would do something like that. And if you hadn't, you wouldn't have been able to piece together the motive.'

Kitt chuckled. 'I wonder if I can convince Halloran that I should never walk past another bookshop again just in case it later becomes an important clue in unravelling a mystery.'

'Worth a try,' said Ruby, as Kitt slowed. They were approaching their offices and she began rooting around in her satchel for her key. After finding it, she unlocked the door, switched the light on, picked up the post and threw it on the desk.

'As well as checking in about the case, I just wanted to say thank you again.'

'You've already thanked me plenty of times, Ruby,' said Kitt. 'There's really no need to say it again.'

'I think there is. Lots of people would have looked at me, a lonely old woman approaching her ninetieth birthday, and thought, well, she's had a good run. No point wasting my time trying to save her life. But you didn't think that.'

'Of course I didn't,' said Kitt, her eyes glazing with tears at the idea that Ruby could even imagine someone saying that about her. 'You're part of this world and someone was trying to take you out of it before your time. I wasn't going to stand for that.'

As she said these words, Kitt reflected on how true they were for her too. Between the rock-throwing incident and the showdown at the crematorium, Arnold Sykes had tried to cut Kitt's time short more than once. Both times, it had almost been the end of her. It was by luck more than anything else that she was still standing there, and for that she was very grateful. She didn't intend to squander the second chance she'd been given to make every day count.

'I know, but many people wouldn't have bothered to

save someone like me,' said Ruby, snapping Kitt out of her thoughts. 'And I know I was spot on about the tattoo in my vision but I didn't understand what the butterfly meant at the time. I thought it was literal, that we were looking for a killer with that kind of tattoo. But that wasn't it.'

'Oh, enlighten me?' said Kitt.

'It was just a symbol from the powers that be that everything was going to be all right in the end. That there wasn't any need to worry. You see, a butterfly can be in its chrysalis between five and twenty-one days. I was in the dark for eleven but at the end of it I was allowed to fly free again. The butterfly was a sign that the light would return.'

No sooner had Kitt smiled at Ruby's rather sweet explanation than the room around her descended into darkness.

'Oh dear,' said Kitt. 'Grace probably forgot to pay the electric bill. We were on our last warning.'

'Not to worry, not to worry, I've got just the thing,' Ruby said. Kitt heard the sound of a match being struck and then a flame began to burn in the darkness. 'Here you go,' Ruby said, handing the candle to Kitt.

Thanking her, Kitt stared into the orange glow of the candle flame and finally permitted herself to feel true relief that they had managed to save Ruby's life. It seemed that, even in complete darkness, light was never far away if you had a friend by your side.

ACKNOWLEDGEMENTS

I am always posting to social media explaining how grateful I am to my readers, who have followed Kitt and her friends through so many adventures in this series. I think it's important to also mention here however just how much it means to receive such a wonderful reception to the stories and characters I have created. It brings me true joy to know I have played a part in yours.

Enduring thanks to Hazel Nicholson who provides such valuable feedback on police procedure. Fiction is a bit like elastic – you can only stretch it so far – and I'm very grateful to Hazel for ensuring the elastic never quite snaps.

Heartfelt thanks to Dan Freedman who shared his medical expertise in order to bring the Vampire Killer to life.

A huge thank you to my agency Hardman and Swainson who have not only championed these books from the moment I submitted the first instalment but have also worked to have the first in the series translated in several languages. Much gratitude also goes to Quercus Books and to my editors Stef Bierwerth and Kat Burdon; their ongoing commitment to the Kitt Harley series and their support of me as an author is beyond heart-warming.

Many thanks also, as ever, to my family and friends who are very gracious about the fact that I disappear into the world of Kitt Hartley for months on end before finally coming up for air.